That Mona Lisa smile . . .

Meredith shook her head. "But what if this killer is a case of life imitating art?"

Wally nodded thoughtfully. "I had an instructor once at the academy who said that if you smell a rat, it means there's a rat."

"Hmm," said Meredith. "And how exactly does that apply here?"

Wally leaned back and crossed his arms. "Let me put it this way: the scent of rodent is strong in the air."

"But we'll know more when the DNA tests come in," Claire pointed out.

Wally shrugged. "Maybe. But they may not be able to draw any useful conclusions from them either—who knows?"

"The Mona Lisa smile," Meredith muttered as she picked up her cards. "Very mysterious and alluring. Someone fell for that smile big time—and then killed her for it."

Erika,
Merry Xmas!
Love,
Santa Claus
2003

Who Killed
Mona Lisa?

CAROLE BUGGÉ

BERKLEY PRIME CRIME, NEW YORK

This is a work of fiction. Names, characters, places, and incidents either are the product of the author's imagination or are used fictitiously, and any resemblance to actual persons, living or dead, business establishments, events, or locales is entirely coincidental.

WHO KILLED MONA LISA?

A Berkley Prime Crime Book / published by arrangement with the author

PRINTING HISTORY
Berkley Prime Crime edition / April 2001

The Penguin Putnam Inc. World Wide Web site address is
http://www.penguinputnam.com

ISBN: 0-425-17919-2

Berkley Prime Crime Books are published
by The Berkley Publishing Group,
a division of Penguin Putnam Inc.,
375 Hudson Street, New York, New York 10014.
The name BERKLEY PRIME CRIME and the
BERKLEY PRIME CRIME design
are trademarks belonging to Penguin Putnam Inc.

PRINTED IN THE UNITED STATES OF AMERICA

10 9 8 7 6 5 4 3 2 1

For Tony,
in memory of our great and glorious adventures

Acknowledgments

I would like to thank my editor, Christine Zika, for her invaluable help in shaping this book, and my agent, Susan Ginsburg, as well as her assistant, Annie Leunberger, for all their hard work. Thanks also to Jeff Gogan of the Sudbury police for giving abundantly of his time in answering my many questions, Marina Stajic of the New York City Medical Examiner's Office for her generous help on the subject of toxicology, and Louise and Nikola Kronja for their research assistance. Special thanks to Amanda George for her wisdom and guidance in my journey. And finally, to the owners and staff of Longfellow's Wayside Inn, for creating a wonderful place where I spent a truly magical weekend.

Chapter 1

"*Nam yo ho reynge kyo.*"
Meredith was chanting. She sat in the front seat next to Claire, her thin white fingers pressed together, her pale eyes closed, the blond eyelashes flickering as her lips moved.

Meredith had taken up Buddhism. Or, to put it more accurately, she was trying it on, as one might try on a hat, to see if it fit.

"*Nam yo ho reynge kyo.*" Her voice was a steady monotone, droning out each syllable at the same low pitch.

Claire Rawlings tightened her grip on the steering wheel and focused on the road curling and twisting before her, the pale sun flat on its surface.

"*Nam yo ho reynge kyo.*"

Meredith Lawrence and an Eastern religion based on patience and stillness were not a natural fit. Still, ever since Meredith read *The Tao of Physics,* the girl had become a devout Buddhist—or so she claimed. Claire wondered if Meredith was doing this partly to annoy her father, Ted Lawrence. Claire wasn't crazy about the chanting, with its monotonous repetition, but she hoped it would make

Meredith calmer. Anything that made the girl calmer was a blessing, whether it was Buddhism or voodoo.

Claire pressed on the accelerator, and her old rust-colored Mercedes sedan shuddered and protested in response. They were entering the foothills of the Berkshires now, and the ancient diesel had to be coaxed up the steeper grades. The car was like a cranky old woman, rusty in the joints and resentful of any demands Claire made upon it.

"Come on, Bessie," she muttered as the engine labored and moaned against the pull of gravity. Claire thought that Bessie was a silly name for a car, and she had never actually named any of her cars before. But the old brown Mercedes—plodding, implacable, and stolid as a cow—was, from the first time she drove it up West End Avenue, unquestionably Bessie.

Claire looked out at the darkening sky wrapped around the fading Massachusetts countryside. A weak November sun was struggling to pierce through the cloud cover; the sky looked backlit, like a movie set. A few of the trees still sported bright red and yellow leaves, but others were losing their foliage in clumps. The hillside resembled a thinning head of hair, a patchy autumn baldness.

> *A weekend in the country, the bees in their hives,*
> *The shallow worldly figures, the frivolous lives . . .*

The words to Sondheim's song from *A Little Night Music* popped into Claire's head. She had been listening to the CD all week, and the songs floated in and out of her head as she drove. She and Meredith were on their way to eastern Massachusetts to meet Wally Jackson for Thanksgiving weekend at Longfellow's Wayside Inn, in the town of South Sudbury. Peter Schwartz, Claire's chief editor at Ardor House, had come back from a weekend there raving about the place. Claire respected Peter's opinion on most things except theatre (he had a taste for hideous, obtuse avant-garde productions), so when Wally suggested they get away for a few days, she suggested the Wayside Inn.

"There's even a guy in eighteenth-century clothes who greets you at the front door," Peter had said in his enthusiastic way. "There are no phones in the rooms, and no television—but there are three or four *real* fireplaces!" Peter was full of enthusiasms, like a child. It was one of his most endearing traits. Claire counted herself lucky to be working with such a man; some of the chief editors at the big houses had all the charm of attack dogs. She knew the horror stories; she had heard them all from her colleagues— the tantrums, mood swings, the childish jealousies, and power games. Peter was eccentric, but he was kind, and did his best not to dump the pressures of his job on the editors working under him. And because of his courtly weakness for attractive women, he was especially fond of Claire Rawlings.

Suddenly aware that the chanting had stopped, Claire looked over at Meredith. The girl had fallen asleep, her head resting on the topaz-green scarf Claire had given her last Christmas. Claire sighed. As of two days ago, her "romantic weekend" in Massachusetts with Wally now included Meredith. When the girl called Claire in tears, claiming she couldn't stand another Thanksgiving in Connecticut with her "evil stepmother," as she called her father's second wife, Claire agreed to take Meredith along. Ted Lawrence offered to pay for Meredith's room at the inn, so at least when Wally arrived the following day he and Claire would have some privacy. For the first night, though, Claire and Meredith would share a room. Claire had brought along earplugs to drown out the girl's snoring.

The pale sun fell on Meredith's burnished copper curls, kinky and as unruly as Meredith herself. She had her hair cut short just last week, and the first thing she said when Claire picked her up at her father's house was, "See my hair? *Yuck*—I *hate* it!"

Meredith was not given to neutral statements. In spite

of her extraordinary intellect, her emotional life was still that of an adolescent girl—melodramatic, extreme, and mercurial. She *hated* this and she *loved* that; she *hated* Connecticut Republicans, and she *loved* Pepperidge Farm cookies.

Claire looked out the window at the brown earth, the grass short and stubbled like a man's beard. She thought about Wally, of his face in the morning, his whiskers scratchy on her skin when he kissed her. She loved the feel of those rough hairs on her cheeks, just as she loved the smoothness of his skin after he shaved and the faint bitter lime taste of aftershave. She marveled at the way a man's face could change so suddenly with the swipe of a razor; the transition from sharp masculine bristle to the soft vulnerability just after shaving always struck her as something of a wonder.

Equally amazing to Claire, something she never tired of wondering at, was the bizarre way Wally Jackson had entered her life. She never would have imagined she would be dating a policeman—much less a detective—and yet here they were, less than a year after Wally and Meredith saved her from Robert's attempt to strangle her.

Robert. So handsome, so smooth, so British. With that accent and upper-class manners and the public-school-boy charm, was it any wonder Claire had fallen for him? He had worn his mask so tightly that she hadn't seen the real face behind it until it was almost too late. If it hadn't been for the sudden arrival of Wally and Meredith . . . Claire shivered. Well, Robert was dead now, and she was doing her best to put that chapter of her life behind her. Still, it was hard to forget the feeling of his fingers upon her throat, pressing down, cutting off her air . . . she still awoke in the middle of the night, shaken by nightmares that clung to her subconscious like leeches, sucking her down into a pit of memory and desire.

Claire slipped a tape of *Nixon in China* into the cassette player and turned up the volume. Surrounded by John

Adams's swelling harmonies and pulsating syncopations, she leaned back and let her shoulders relax. She looked out at the landscape, suddenly transformed by the music; all at once it seemed mysterious and unknowable.

Now, as she looked out over the frost-streaked fields, she wondered what secrets were hidden behind that copse of oak trees, what mysteries lurked underneath that bright pile of fallen leaves? Another Sondheim quote popped into her head, this time from *Sunday in the Park with George:* *"Order out of chaos. Order to the whole."*

Yes, order indeed; the need to create form out of chaos, the eternal search for patterns, for meaning. And no one craved order, Claire thought, more than the girl sleeping on the seat next to her. Her life thrown into internal chaos after the death of her mother, Meredith had seized upon reason and logic with a fierce tenacity. It was, for her, a kind of salvation, a way of both denying and coming to grips with her mother's death.

"Are we there yet?"

Meredith's voice startled Claire out of her reverie. "No, not yet," she answered, ejecting the tape from the cassette player.

Meredith sat up in her seat, stretched, and wiped the drool from her chin. "Ee-yew," she said. "That's disgusting. How come people drool only when they nap but not at night?"

"I don't know."

"Have you noticed that?" Meredith said, rubbing her eyes. "That you only drool during the day?"

"Yeah, I guess you're right. I don't know why that is."

"It's *weird.*" That was Meredith's new word—everything that was different or unusual or strange was "weird."

"Oh, look—*cool!*" she said, pointing out the window at a farmhouse with a gigantic grinning pumpkin perched atop a straw-stuffed scarecrow, a lumpy figure in flannels and overalls leaning against a pitchfork.

"Is it me, or are pumpkins getting bigger?" asked Claire.

"I think they're getting bigger," said Meredith. "You should *see* this one by my dad's house; it's *gigantic!*"

Meredith still spoke of her home in Connecticut as "my dad's house" instead of "my house." Ever since the death of her mother—Claire's college friend Katherine Lawrence—two years ago, Meredith described herself to anyone who would listen as "an orphan." She knew this hurt her father, but Claire thought she did it to punish him for marrying Jean, or, as Meredith called her, the Wicked Witch of Greenwich.

Meredith shifted restlessly in her seat and switched on the radio. The smooth mid-Atlantic accent of a newscaster filled the car.

". . . and in spite of public opinion, he will begin experiments aimed toward cloning human beings."

"Oh, I heard about that guy last night." Claire shifted into low gear as they approached another hill. "He's a scientist out west somewhere."

"Well, I'm surprised it took this long," said Meredith. "After all, it was only a matter of time."

The newscaster then read various denunciations of the man, including those from some religious groups who compared him to the devil. The president himself was in on the action, criticizing the scientist for his decision.

"Good Lord, get *real!*" said Meredith. "Of *course* someone was going to try it, for Chrissake! I mean, like they discovered nuclear energy and no one built a bomb? Come *on!*" She rolled her eyes and rubbed her finger on the inside of the car window so that it made a squeaking sound. "You can't stop science, for Chrissakes," she muttered, drawing a circle in the mist that had gathered on the glass. "It's a goddamn Pandora's box."

"Watch your language," said Claire.

In response, Meredith heaved a noisy sigh of displeasure and turned to stare out the window.

Pandora's box. Despite warnings, Pandora's box would always be opened; people were far more motivated by curiosity than by caution, Claire thought. And no one was more driven by curiosity than Meredith Lawrence; with her, caution hardly entered into the equation.

"It's weird, though, this whole cloning thing, don't you think?" she said, pulling her feet up onto the seat. Her pout this time was short-lived, Claire noted with relief. Meredith curled her feet under her, and Claire was amazed that she could fit those long legs there. Watching the girl was like watching a camel move, awkward yet with a strange kind of grace.

"I mean, how would you like to have a younger version of yourself walking around? It's creepy, if you ask me."

"Yeah," said Claire. It *was* creepy. If cloning was possible, all kinds of assumptions about individuality and free will would be called into question.

"I mean, I'm even a little creeped out by *twins,* you know?" said Meredith, rummaging through the glove compartment.

"Right," said Claire. "What are you looking for?"

Meredith shrugged. "I dunno. Gum, candy—something." She pulled a tattered map out of the glove compartment. "How would you introduce someone like that at parties? This is my clone?" She opened up the map on her lap and bent over it, her neck long and pale in the dying sun.

"What are you looking for?" said Claire.

"Oh, just trying to see where we are."

"Just outside Worcester."

"Ah, then we're not far."

Meredith peered at the map, her face close to the paper. She was nearsighted but refused to wear glasses. "No matter what frame I wear, I look like Atom Ant," she once told Claire. She held up the map, her hair brushing the section of eastern Massachusetts.

Massachusetts. Birthplace of Samuel Adams, site of the

Boston Tea Party, cradle of the Revolution. Home to crusty, bloody-minded New England types. Claire liked the people she had met in Massachusetts. It was a much friendlier state than Connecticut, with its frosty, status-obsessed Republicans.

Meredith fished around in the glove compartment and extracted a guidebook. "Listen to this. Right across from the hotel is an eighteenth-century gristmill—and they still make flour there! And there's a chapel, too, but they say it's a reproduction."

"That's nice," said Claire.

"Cool!" said Meredith suddenly. "Look at that!"

Claire turned and looked out the passenger side of the car. There, on the lawn of a respectable-looking suburban home, was a unique Halloween display. In fact, it was so amazing that she pulled the car over to get a better look.

Seated at a picnic table were three full-sized dummies made from straw stuffed into clothing, each with a hideous, ghoulish papier-mâché face. On plates in front of them were piles of what looked like entrails, strips of rubber tubing painted bright red, as well as other gruesome tidbits. The ghouls sat there grinning wildly, forks poised in their gloved hands.

Even more extraordinary, though, was the rest of the display: next to the picnic table was a wooden cage filled with children, their little bodies plump with stuffed straw, their papier-mâché hands clutching the bars of the cage. Outside the cage a gleefully evil witch stood turning a homemade spit, upon which was impaled one of the children.

They sat looking at this for several minutes. "Wow," Claire said finally, "talk about venting your hostility toward your kids!"

"Oh, the kids probably helped build it," Meredith said. "I bet the kids *love* it! They're probably the coolest kids in the neighborhood."

"You think?" asked Claire.

"Sure! It's *way* cool! And if you want to get Freudian on me, it's also an expression of children's fear of grown-ups."

Claire looked at the grinning witch, her yellow eyes bright with malice. "I guess you're right." She laughed. "I wonder what that family is like," she said, easing the old car back onto the road.

"I'll bet they're totally fun parents," said Meredith. Then, in a softer voice, she added, "My mom would have done something like that."

Meredith rarely spoke of her mother. Claire was both relieved and a little intimidated whenever Katherine's name came up; she knew Meredith carried around a lot of grief that she had never expressed, and she was glad the girl felt comfortable enough with her to talk about her mother.

But now Meredith lapsed into silence, staring out the window at the dimming sunlight. Claire glanced at her watch. It was only three-thirty, but already it was getting dark. She knew that many people were depressed by the approach of fall, followed as it is inevitably by winter, but she had always felt there was something thrilling in the gradual dimming of daylight, the snap in the air that replaces the oppressive heat of summer. Her blood ran more briskly and her pulse quickened at the thought of crisp fall days, the sun-shot brilliance of leaves as they turned from green to rust, vermillion, cadmium.

As the car sliced through the cool air, Claire experienced the feeling that driving in the countryside always produced: freedom. She loved the sensation of hurtling forward through space, the exhilaration that rushed through her when she galloped her horse across a field, the motion of the horse under her combining with the forward momentum to produce a trancelike state of ecstasy she otherwise experienced only during . . .

As if reading her thoughts, Meredith broke into her reverie. "When's Wally coming?"

"Tomorrow evening, after work."

Meredith nodded and looked out the window. "Do you love him?" she said after a minute.

Claire's fingers tightened on the steering wheel. "I don't know," she replied carefully.

Meredith turned to look at her. "You do—you love him. And he loves you," she added with a sigh.

"You think?"

"Oh yeah."

The temperature outside was dropping rapidly now, and tiny frost crystals were gathering on the windows. Meredith sketched a pattern of hearts on the frosted car window with her finger. "It's really quite nauseating to watch, you know," she remarked.

Claire laughed. "Well, I'm sorry to put you through such pain and suffering."

Meredith stopped drawing and looked at her. "What's so funny?"

"You are," said Claire. "You're what's so funny."

Chapter 2

By the time they pulled into South Sudbury it was almost five o'clock, and the sun was sinking behind the nearby hills. Claire stopped at a quickie mart in town to ask for directions to the Wayside Inn. The words were hardly out of her mouth when the short blond woman behind the counter nodded; it was clear this was a question she was used to answering.

"Just continue along east on Route Twenty and you'll see the turnoff to your right. There's a sign that points you to the inn." The woman's accent was very New England; she pronounced "there" as "theyah," stretching her vowels out as if reluctant to let go of them.

"Thank you." Claire was thrilled by the sound of her accent, shaped by what she imagined to be the woman's seafaring ancestors. South Sudbury was only about forty miles west of Boston, and though it was securely landlocked, Claire thought she could hear the New England seaside drawl in the voices of the people coming in and out of the quickie mart.

"Well?" said Meredith when Claire returned to the car. "Did she know where it was?"

Meredith was irritated because Claire had made her stay in the car. Meredith was a compulsive browser, and when in a store she often had to examine every aisle before she was willing to leave. Usually Claire was patient about this—a friend of hers who was a child psychologist told her that children often outgrow such behavior—but now she was tired and hungry, and anxious to get to the inn as quickly as possible.

"We're almost there," she said, backing the old car out into the side street before turning back onto Route 20. After less than a mile she saw a white sign with an arrow pointing off to the right: WAYSIDE INN. She turned down the road, and after passing a small stone cottage on the left, she saw the inn ahead.

"Look." Meredith pointed to a tall, square stone building across from the hotel. "That must be the gristmill I read about."

"And there's the chapel," said Claire, indicating another stone building just beyond the inn.

The Wayside Inn was built of wood, old-fashioned clapboard painted red. Smoke drifted out of a pair of thick stone chimneys, and Claire smelled the sweet, tangy aroma of burning pine. A broad circular drive swept up to the front door, and there was a parking lot behind the building for guests.

Claire pulled around the drive and parked next to a long black Cadillac. She and Meredith got out and hurried over the hard frozen ground, their breath coming in frosty little gusts. They were greeted at the front door by a good-looking ruddy-faced man dressed in eighteenth-century garb, complete with yellow breeches and maroon waistcoat.

"Good evening," he said, swinging open the heavy oak door, ushering them into the warmth of the front hallway. "Two for dinner?"

"Yes, please," said Meredith, and he led them down the long, narrow hallway. Claire noticed the dining areas off to either side as they approached the hotel's main desk, which was snuggled under the eaves at the end of the hallway, next to the gift shop. The aroma of broiled scrod in lemon butter mixed with the tangy smell of grilled lamb and rosemary. Claire suddenly felt light-headed. She was ravenous, having eaten nothing all day but a fried egg sandwich for breakfast.

The ruddy-faced gentleman in period dress stood at the front desk, which seemed to serve both as check-in for the hotel and cash register for the restaurant. The place was quite busy; waiters and waitresses scurried by with trays of food and drinks. They, too, were dressed in period costumes, the women in white ruffled low-cut blouses and bodices, the men in vests and breeches.

"Someone will be right with you," said their host. "If you'll excuse me, I have to return to my post. Have a pleasant stay," he added, tipping his three-cornered hat. As he retreated down the hall, Claire couldn't help noticing how well formed his calves were in the tight-fitting silk stockings. She liked a shapely leg on a man; she thought of Wally Jackson's nicely rounded calves and a little shot of warmth traveled through her body.

Claire and Meredith stood off to one side, out of the way of all the commotion, and looked around. Off to the left of the front desk was a narrow staircase that Claire supposed led up to the guest rooms. Just then, a stocky, authoritative-looking man emerged from the gift shop, a ledger book in his hand. When he saw Claire and Meredith he smiled. "Two for dinner?"

"Yes, please," Meredith replied.

"We're also staying the night," Claire added.

The man consulted his ledger book. "Oh, are you—"

"Claire Rawlings," said Meredith, trying to peer over his shoulder at the book.

"Ah . . . welcome!" he said, smiling broadly. "I'm Frank Wilson."

Frank Wilson was not a big man, but he was muscular and hearty, with a friendly Irish face. "And this is my wife,

Paula," he said as a thin woman emerged from the gift shop. She was a rail of a thing, slim as a whippet, with frightened eyes. She might have been pretty except for a hardness around the mouth; the muscles of her face were tensed, as if poised for battle. She smiled wanly at them, whispered something to her husband, and slipped quietly back into the gift shop.

If Frank Wilson thought his wife's behavior peculiar, he gave no sign of it. Claire thought they were an odd match. She knew that sometimes opposites attract, but even so, they struck her as a strange couple.

"You will be having dinner with us tonight, then?" Frank Wilson said as Claire signed the guest book.

"Yes—that is, if you have room," she replied. "We didn't make a reservation, and it looks like you're pretty busy."

Frank Wilson smiled, showing his big, even teeth. "Oh, this is nothing; wait until you see the Sunday-morning rush. Now, *that's* busy!" He led them through the hall to a large dining room. "This is our largest dining room," he said. "I see a seat there by the fire. Would you like that?"

"Yes, please!" Meredith chirped, bouncing up and down on her toes. She *loved* fireplaces.

"That would be wonderful," Claire said.

"We'll get you settled in your room later," he added, pulling the chair out so that Claire could sit. "Just come up to the front desk when you're ready. It's room number six."

"Cool!" said Meredith. "Six is my lucky number."

"Thank you," said Claire.

"Thank *you*!" Meredith added.

Frank Wilson gave them another of his big broad smiles and withdrew.

"Great guy," said Meredith, unfolding her napkin. "Wonder what he's doing with that straight-backed chair of a woman?"

"What?" Claire was immersed in the menu, which featured such eighteenth-century fare as bay scallops in cream sauce and Indian pudding.

"If she were a piece of furniture, she would be a straight-backed chair," Meredith explained, "with no seat cushion."

"Oh, I get it." Claire wanted a glass of wine very much, something red and dusky, with an aftertaste of blackberries. She wanted to drink until she was filled with a feeling of peace and goodwill. She settled back in her chair, a reproduction of an eighteenth-century chair, complete with armrests, and looked around the room. The fireplace was made of chunky gray river stone, and the ceiling low and cream-colored, with heavy dark wooden beams that hung over the room. Reminders of the past were everywhere, from the pewter pitcher on the windowsill to the brass candlesticks over the fireplace mantel. The smell of burning pine logs mingled with the faint odor of vanilla and sage. To step inside this place, Claire thought, was to leave the present outside and enter the past of a country that was still deciding how to interpret its own history.

Claire loved old buildings. They gave her a sense of being part of a continuum of human affairs. Places with a past excited her in ways she didn't fully understand, spoke to a deeply ingrained romanticism. She felt a kind of kinship with those who had gone before, felt their presence in the halls, the rooms, even in the woods. When she rode her horse up in Garrison, tracing the paths used by British and American soldiers during the Revolution, she felt the power of those turbulent days, and shivered a little every time she passed the site of the Anderson House, Benedict Arnold's headquarters during his treasonous sojourn at West Point.

"Look, there she is," said Meredith.

"Who?"

"Mrs. Wilson—there!" Meredith whispered.

Claire looked out into the hallway and saw Paula Wilson talking to a small boy of about ten. The boy was thin and pale, with nervous eyes. She held him by the arm, and was bending over whispering something in his ear, but whatever it was the boy evidently didn't want to hear it, because he kept trying to wrest himself from her grasp. Finally he wrenched free and took a few steps, but instead of continuing to walk away, he stopped. The boy and the woman both stood there, looking at each other, and in that moment Claire knew they were mother and son. Something about the way their bodies sculpted the space separating them expressed the link that bound them, willing or not, to each other.

The boy looked at his mother sulkily for another moment and then turned and walked away. Paula Wilson's thin shoulders drooped as she watched him go; her right hand twitched as if she wanted to call him back but was too proud. It was a brief moment, an aborted gesture, but Claire understood it all clearly. She looked at Meredith to see if she was watching the little drama, but the girl was studying her menu.

"Look," she said, "it says here they have Indian pudding. That's so *cool*! Can we get some? Can we?"

"For dessert, maybe, if we still have room," Claire answered.

Meredith put the menu down decisively. "Oh, I'll have *room* all right! No need to worry about that!"

Claire laughed. Meredith could get on anyone's nerves; with her intensity, her certainty, and her restless energy, she could be a lot to take, but usually Claire found her amusing.

"Okay," she said, "I believe you. We'll get the Indian pudding."

"What's so funny?" said Meredith.

"You are."

Meredith scrunched up her long thin nose. "Why am I so funny all of a sudden?"

Claire shrugged. "Oh, I don't know. Just take it as a compliment."

They did have Indian pudding, after the duckling with orange sauce and roasted potatoes. Claire was starving; she had spent the morning packing, making phone calls, and dropping her cat, Ralph, off with her friend Sarah, and was too busy to stop for lunch. There always seemed to be so many errands to do before leaving town, even only for a few days, and she was anxious to get on the road before it was too late. Usually she would have brought a tote bag full of manuscripts to read, but this time Wally had talked her out of it.

Now, sitting in the dining room of the Wayside Inn, basking in the glow of the firelight, filled with roast duckling and a rather insouciant Merlot, Claire felt her shoulders relaxing, the tension of the week dissolving. She looked across the table at Meredith, who was busy scooping out the last bit of Indian pudding from her dessert cup. Meredith mistrusted most cuisines, but she loved dessert, and would try anything sweet.

"Well, that was just great!" she said, leaning back in her chair, a yellow spot of pudding clinging to her chin. Claire was about to say something about it when the sound of voices in the hallway caught her attention. She looked over to see their waitress arguing with one of the waiters, a striking young man with curly black hair and a long Gallic jaw. Though the girl had her back to them, Claire recognized her light brown hair, pulled into a bun at the back of her neck. She was long and lean, maybe even a little taller than he was. Though they were speaking softly, Claire could hear them clearly. She had inherited her mother's sensitive ears, and often heard things other people missed.

"No, Philippe, I won't!" the girl was saying.

"But Mona, we talked about this and you said—"

The young man's tone was pleading. He attempted to put a hand on her shoulder, but she pulled away.

"I don't want to talk about this right now, Philippe," she whispered fiercely, looking around. Claire pretended to study the menu, and even Meredith knew enough to look away when Mona's glance fell on them. Her deep-set eyes glowered, and her pretty face was flushed.

But the young man would not be deterred. "When, then? When are we going to talk about it?"

"I need time to think about it—I just need some time!" she answered, but just then their conversation was interrupted as Frank Wilson strode up to them and clamped a big hand on Mona's shoulder.

"Okay, kids, we got tables waiting," he said in a friendly voice, giving no hint that he had heard them arguing.

Without as so much acknowledging the innkeeper's presence, Philippe turned and stalked off into one of the smaller dining rooms. Frank Wilson watched him go, then turned to Mona, who stood with her head lowered. There was something defiant in her pose, as though she were deliberately avoiding eye contact with her employer. Frank said something in a voice too soft for Claire to make out, then turned and went back in the direction of the front desk. Mona stood for a moment looking after him, then, jamming her hands into her apron pocket, strode off in the opposite direction.

"Wow," Meredith exclaimed softly when they had all gone. "What was *that* all about?"

"I don't know," said Claire, "but something's going on."

"*I'll* say," Meredith replied. "I'll say something's going on. But what, I'd like to know?"

Claire's curiosity was slowly being replaced by drowsiness, and as interesting as she found the little drama they had just witnessed, she was beginning to find the idea of bed even more appealing.

"I'm getting sleepy," she said. "Let's go upstairs."

As the two of them climbed the staircase to the second floor, Claire thought about the centuries of footsteps that had come and gone on these same stairs: not only Longfellow, but others before him, and more to follow. Artists and writers and bankers and—the thought came to her unexpectedly, unbidden—maybe even murderers.

At the top of the stairs was a little drawing room, furnished with antiques and, Claire supposed, a few reproductions. To fill a place this size with antiques would be prohibitively expensive, she thought, as well as hazardous; even though the place allowed no pets, there were always small children capable of destroying a priceless heirloom with a single swipe of a plastic laser blaster.

She followed Meredith to room number six, which turned out to be about halfway down the back hallway. Frank Wilson had sent their bags up earlier, and as Claire turned the big brass key in the old-fashioned lock, the smell of bayberry potpourri drifted out from the room.

The room was even better than she had imagined. The bed was brass, covered by a handmade quilt coverlet, with squares of rich burgundy and deep blues. On the polished wood floor was a round hooked rug, the kind Claire remembered seeing in her grandmother's living room as a child. The scent of bayberry mixed with the fresh smell of eucalyptus, which was in a brass pitcher on the windowsill. A handsome oak dresser complete with brass handles and a beveled mirror stood against the wall opposite the bed. Just as Peter had promised, there was no phone and no television in the room. The room was still and quiet and peaceful, and Claire felt like sinking onto the quilted bedspread right then and there.

Meredith, however, had other plans. Evidently refreshed by her nap in the car, she started poking around the room. She began by opening the closet and sniffing the interior.

"Cedar," she said, wiping her nose, which, like a dog's, always seemed to be wet in cold weather. She went into the bathroom and emerged a few moments later holding a small wicker basket of toiletries.

"Not bad," she said, pawing through the little plastic bottles of shampoo and hand lotion. "They even give you aloe vera gel . . . and a little sewing kit. Pretty good. Not as good as the Drake Hotel, of course, but pretty good."

"When did you stay at the Drake?" Claire asked as she unpacked her suitcase.

Meredith flopped down on the bed and put her hands behind her head. "Oh, I've been around . . . I stayed there once with my mom when she was in Chicago."

Claire folded her underwear into the bayberry-scented dresser drawers. She was sorry she had asked; she felt the pang of jealousy she always felt when her dead friend's name came up, and was angry at herself for feeling it.

Meredith rolled over onto her side and leaned up on one elbow. "Cool room. All this stuff looks like antiques—you think?"

"Probably some things are reproductions," Claire replied, closing her suitcase and sliding it onto the top shelf in the closet. She always liked to unpack right away, even if she were only going to be in a hotel a day or two. It made her feel more at home.

"Yeah," Meredith said, opening the drawer in the oak bedside table. "Hey, look at this!"

Claire turned to see Meredith holding up a stack of letters. "Where did you get that?"

Meredith pointed to the open drawer. "Here—they were in here."

Claire went over to the table for a look. The drawer was filled with letters—a thick pile of them, all different shapes and sizes. She pulled out a handful and looked through them. Some were on Wayside Inn stationery, some on cheap notebook paper ripped from a loose-leaf notebook; there were even a couple written on the backs of paper place mats from roadside diners. The handwriting on each was different, and some were dated while others were not. Many were signed and some were not, but all of them contained the same salutation: *Dear Secret Drawer Society.*

Claire looked at Meredith. "What *is* this?"

Meredith shook her head. "Beats me. I never saw anything like it before."

"I've done a lot of traveling, and I never even heard of a Secret Drawer Society."

"I guess people write letters and leave them in drawers for other people to read. I think that is way cool!"

Claire looked at the stack of letters in her hand. "Yeah, I guess so . . ." She imagined all the people who had stayed in this room, writing their hearts out to people they would never meet, unfolding innermost secrets that they then tucked into a drawer for strangers to read. She sat on the edge of the bed, the letters in her hand, torn between curiosity and her desire to respect other people's privacy.

Meredith had no such compunctions. She lay on her back reading greedily, chewing on her cuticles as she read, her pale blue eyes squinting in the dim light.

"Why don't you turn on the other lamp?" said Claire.

"Mmm," Meredith murmured, not really listening.

Claire got up and went to the other side of the bed to turn on the lamp, and as she did a letter fell from the pile she held. She picked it up and looked at it. The letter was on Wayside hotel stationery and was undated. The writing was firm but girlish, the handwriting of a young woman, she thought. She was about to put it back in the pile when the first sentence caught her eye.

Again and again I ask myself why I am doing this, and I arrive at the conclusion that I seem to be powerless to resist . . . why this is I don't know; there is a dark pull in the man which keeps me coming back, like a hopelessly charmed rabbit frozen in front of the swaying snake who is about to devour it.

Meredith rolled over and looked at Claire. "What are you reading?"

Claire handed her the letter.

Meredith read the first couple of sentences and shrugged. "Mundane metaphor . . . the whole snake thing's been done to death. It is an interesting sexual subtext, though," she said, brightening a little. "Looks like a case for Dr. Freud."

Claire looked at the letter in her hand. "I wonder who she is."

"Look! Here's another one—same handwriting!" Meredith pulled another letter out of the drawer. She read it aloud to Claire. " 'What would he do if I broke it off with him? What would he do? I don't know, and that frightens me. Do you ever really know someone, know what they are capable of when they feel they have run out of options?' "

Claire shook her head. She could sympathize with the emotions expressed in the letter. After all, how well had she known Robert, known what he was capable of? She had not listened to that inner voice warning her . . . and here was a young woman listening to that voice—and what she heard frightened her.

There was a knock at the door. Claire quickly stuffed the letter back into the drawer and headed toward the door, but Meredith beat her to it.

"Who's there?" she said.

"It's Frank Wilson."

Meredith flung the door open. In the hallway stood the innkeeper, his big face ruddy.

"Ms. Rawlings?" he said. "You have a phone call at the front desk."

"Oh," said Claire, surprised. "Thank you."

"Who is it?" asked Meredith.

Claire turned to her. "Why don't you stay here. I'll be right back."

Meredith sighed and flopped down on the bed. "*Okay!* But don't be too long. Bet it's Lover Boy," she added as Claire closed the door behind her.

"Here, you can take the back staircase—right this way," Frank Wilson said, turning left down the hall. At the end of the hall was a crooked, winding staircase, and Claire followed him down, the ancient stairs creaking under her feet.

When they reached the front desk, he handed her a telephone.

"Sorry it's so noisy here, but it's the only phone we've got," he said as Claire picked up the receiver.

"Hello?" she said, and heard Wally Jackson's familiar baritone on the other end of the line.

"Oh, hi. It's me."

"Hi. Where are you?"

"I'm in New York. I'm calling to say that I'm going to be held up a day longer than I expected. There's some breaking information on a murder investigation, and I—well, I hope to get there by Thanksgiving Day."

There was a pause and then he spoke again. "You're not mad, are you?"

"No, of course I'm not mad. I'm just disappointed."

"Me, too. But I'll see you soon as I can. What's it like there? Is it nice?"

"Yes, it's really nice," she answered. She almost mentioned the Secret Drawer Society, but decided to wait until Wally arrived and she could show him the letters.

After she hung up the phone, Claire looked around for Frank Wilson, but he was nowhere to be seen. She started up the staircase, but just as her foot touched the first step she turned and looked back. She heard no particular sound, but she had a feeling someone was standing behind her. Peering out of the gift shop, which was closed now, was the boy she had seen earlier with Mrs. Wilson. His thin, pale face was serious and unsmiling, and he stared at Claire as though he wanted to speak to her but was too shy. She smiled at him, and he withdrew back into the darkened store. Claire hesitated and then turned and went up the stairs.

Back in the room, Meredith was sprawled out on a cot reading, a stack of letters next to her.

"Where did you get that?" Claire pointed to the cot.

Meredith rolled over onto one elbow. "Oh, I asked for it to be sent up. I'm a restless sleeper, you know."

Claire sat down on the bed and began unlacing her shoes. "Yes, I know. You also snore, but there's nothing we can do about that."

Meredith rolled her eyes. "Well, you don't have to rub it in."

Claire laughed. "Sorry. But you do."

"I *know*. It's my adenoids . . . I'm an adenoidal breather, at least that's what the Connecticut quack doctor says."

Claire took her shoes over to the closet, the hardwood floor cold under her bare feet. "I used to think only fat old men snored, but I was wrong."

Meredith rolled over onto her back again. "Yeah, and marathon runners can have heart attacks—big woo."

Claire pulled off her turtleneck sweater, the air crackling with little white bursts of static electricity.

"Cool—static!" Meredith said as Claire folded the sweater and put it in the dresser drawer. "You should get a load of these letters; they're really wild," she added, holding up a fistful of them. "There's all *kinds* of weird stuff here! Some of it's not even PG reading. Man, if my dad only knew!"

"Oh yeah?" said Claire, pulling on the red-and-gray-striped flannel pajamas Wally had given her for Christmas. She had mentioned once that when she was a kid she loved her red flannel pajamas, and Wally had gone out and found her some the next day. "Can I see?" she asked, settling down under the covers. She still had to brush and floss, but first she wanted to feel the sheets on her bare feet. "Mmm . . . this is nice," she murmured, leaning back on the fluffy goose-down pillow. "I could get used to this."

"Here's another letter from that same girl we read earlier." Meredith flung a letter across the bed. Claire picked it up and recognized the same handwriting: *At first I was caught up in the thrill of it, even though I knew it was wrong—or maybe* because *I knew it was wrong—but even when I got more scared I was unable to stop . . . I'm afraid to talk to him about it, and I can't talk to anyone else. What am I going to do?*

"Pretty weird, huh?" said Meredith. "I wonder who she is—who they are?"

"Yeah," said Claire. "So do I. But now it's time for all weary travelers to get some sleep."

"Oh, *man.* I was just getting settled in. And look at all these unread letters." Meredith sighed, pointing to the pile next to her.

"There will be time for more reading tomorrow. It's lights-out time."

"*Okay,*" said Meredith, putting the letters back in the drawer.

Claire went into the bathroom to brush and floss, and by the time she returned to the bedroom Meredith was asleep, lying on her back, mouth wide open, snoring gently. Mere-dith was like that: she could drop off to sleep instantly, like a cat. Claire envied her this; she always took much longer, and tended to lie in bed replaying the events of the day before finally succumbing to sleep.

She turned off the bedside lamp and lay in the dark inhaling the scent of bayberry mixed with eucalyptus. She turned her head to look out the window, where there was a large maple tree just outside. It looked so brave and lonely in the stark November night sky. Stripped of leaves, the branches shook and dipped in the wind. Claire lay awake a long time listening to the wind. It reminded her of childhood winters out on the lake, where she had the same feeling of isolation, of being at the end of the world. Here, tucked away in the corner of Massachusetts, surrounded by woods, the nearest village was only a mile away, but tonight that mile could have been ten or twenty. Claire felt cut off from life outside the Wayside Inn, isolated by the wind that wrapped itself around its weathered eaves.

As she drifted off to sleep, once again the words to the song from *A Little Night Music* drifted into her head:

Every day a little sting, in the heart and in the head,
And you hardly feel a thing—brings a perfect little
death.

Chapter 3

The next morning Claire looked out the window at the maple tree, its outline black against the bleak November sky. In the middle of the trunk was a huge, gnarled knot. Claire gazed at its whorls and swirls, which reminded her of a face—the eyes, nose and mouth of some ancient and wise creature, old as the Massachusetts landscape—perhaps a woodland gnome whose spirit was trapped in the old tree by a witch's curse.

The sun had slipped below a low grey cloud cover, but higher up the sky was a clear pale blue, the sun's light reflected off sparse, wispy clouds. The effect was surreal, like a Magritte painting.

Why, Claire wondered as she dressed, did she love this change of season, this slow dimming into winter's darkness? She had learned to thrive on a sense of oddness, as Meredith had; sometimes Claire thought the girl accentuated her eccentricities on purpose, just to prove she didn't mind being different.

" 'Oh, oh, oh, what's love got to do, got to do, got to do, got to do with it? What's love but a secondhand emotion?' "

Meredith was singing to herself while she dressed. Since she had taken up chanting, something had opened up in her, loosening a flood of vocalizations. She sang and hummed to herself all the time now; Claire caught bits of popular songs, snatches of themes from Beethoven symphonies, advertising jingles. It reminded her of her father, who often walked through rooms snapping his fingers while humming to himself.

" 'What's love but a secondhand emotion?' " Meredith stood on the round braided rug in the center of the room, clad only in a long white man's shirt and socks. Lately she had taken to wearing men's shirts several sizes too large for her. Claire wondered if she had pilfered them from her father's closet. If so, maybe it wasn't such a bad thing. Still, she worried about the girl's breezy contempt for her father. Ted Lawrence loved his daughter, but he was perplexed by her—as were a lot of other people.

"Where are my pants?" Meredith said, arms crossed over her thin chest.

"Right there," Claire answered. "You're standing on them."

"Oops. So I am." Meredith bent down and picked up her pants, sliding them over her thin white legs.

"Come on," said Claire, "or we'll miss breakfast."

"Okay, o*kay!*" Meredith replied in her Alvin the Chipmunk voice.

Max von Schlegel was a bear of a man. With his bullet head, thick neck, and pale blue eyes, Claire thought he looked exactly like a movie Nazi. He was the chef at the Wayside Inn, and now he stood presiding over breakfast like a king watching over his subjects. He was making the rounds of the breakfast room, chatting with customers, doing a part of his job he clearly enjoyed. So far the only other guests in the breakfast room besides Claire and Meredith were two men, one middle-aged, with sandy blond hair, the other young and dark. They sat at the other end of the room and spoke in hushed tones.

Max von Schlegel approached Claire and Meredith's table, smiling broadly. "So, you are liking the eggs Sardou?"

"Yes, everything is very good," Claire replied.

Max nodded. "Good. The recipe is from my Viennese grandmother." A trace of his Austrian heritage clung faintly to his consonants, thickening them ever so slightly, like the hint of cornstarch in a sauce. Max's bluff, friendly manner belied his intimidating physical appearance. Here was a man who enjoyed his food—his girth was evidence of that—without embarrassment. He stood over their table, a spotless white apron covering his impressive stomach like a drop cloth thrown casually over a sleeping leviathan.

He closed his eyes and rocked back on his heels, an expression of bliss on his smooth pink face. "Ah, what a cook she was; she could coax the flavor out of any food! A genius with fish, a virtuoso with veal." He opened his eyes and smiled modestly. "I like to think I have inherited a little of her talent, perhaps."

"Oh, definitely," said Meredith, lifting a blueberry muffin from the breadbasket on the table. "That duck last night was kick-ass!"

Max frowned. " 'Kickass'? What is 'kickass'?"

"It means really good," Claire said quickly.

Max smiled dubiously. "Oh. The duck is a secret recipe; nobody alive knows it but me."

Just then Frank Wilson walked up to their table. "Good morning, ladies. Did you sleep well?"

"Like the dead," Meredith replied.

"Good, good; I always say a good night's sleep leads to a healthy appetite. Right, Max?" he said, with a glance at his chef.

Max nodded—a little stiffly, Claire thought. It was hard to read how the chef felt about his employer, but Claire thought she sensed some tension between them.

The big Austrian turned a broad smile toward Claire and Meredith. "Ja, I like customers who like to eat—otherwise I am out of business!" He chuckled a little at his own comment, then wiped his hands on his pristine white apron. His fingers were short and thick as sausages. "Well, I get back to the kitchen now. God only knows what goes wrong when I am not there." He gave a little bow, turned, and walked regally from the room.

After he was gone, Frank Wilson laughed gently. "Max is a real character, as they say, but I'm lucky to have him. He really is a first-class chef . . ." He seemed to be about to say something else, but stopped himself.

"Drinking problem?" said Meredith.

The innkeeper turned to her, surprise on his face. "What?"

"Does he have a drinking problem?" Meredith repeated.

"Meredith!" Claire said sharply, loud enough that the two men at the other table looked up from their conversation.

"What?" Meredith asked defensively.

"That's rude, and you ought to know it."

Frank Wilson smiled and shook his head. "It's all right—as Art Linkletter once said, kids say the darnedest things."

"I'm not a k—" Meredith began, but Claire cut her off.

"As long as you say foolish things like that, you are."

Meredith shrugged and poked at the basket of muffins with her fork. "A lot of adults say stupid things."

"Maybe, but that's no excuse," Claire replied. "I'm sorry," she said to their host.

"Don't think twice about it," he answered. "As a matter of fact—"

"Oh, hey!" Meredith said suddenly. "We have a question to ask you."

Frank Wilson looked down at her with a benevolent smile. "Yes?"

"What is it with those letters upstairs—that Secret Drawer Society? What's that all about?"

"Oh, you found your secret drawer?"

"Yes, we did," said Claire. "I wonder why I've never heard of it before."

"Well, it's a tradition going back centuries, mostly in old inns . . . I'm not sure when it started exactly, but we've had it here at the Wayside since before I became innkeeper. Someone told me the whole thing is a New England phenomenon. I did a Web search once, but didn't come up with much. It's amazing what people will write about—the most intimate details of their lives."

"Well," Claire remarked, "people have the need to get things off their chest, I guess, and the anonymity of the letters offers a safe outlet."

Frank Wilson cocked his head to one side. "That's true, but you'd be surprised how many people actually sign their letters."

"Like what kind of intimate details do they write about?" said Meredith.

"Well, there's a lot about illicit love affairs, as you can imagine."

"Yeah, I know," Meredith agreed. "Do you know we were reading one this woman had written, and she seemed really upset."

"Did she sign her name?"

Meredith shook her head. "Nope. But the man sounds kinda creepy, if you ask me."

"Well," said the innkeeper, "I inherited more letters from my predecessor, and they're carefully preserved in the basement, if you ever care to read them."

Meredith shrugged. "Maybe, if it gets dull around here."

Frank Wilson laughed—a big, hearty bark of a laugh—and slapped the girl on the shoulder. "Okay. You just let me know." He moved off toward the hallway, passing their waitress as he did. "I think they could use some muffins at table six, Mona," he said, pointing toward Claire and Meredith. As he spoke he touched the girl's elbow ever so briefly, and Claire thought she saw her flinch and pull away. She was the same waitress they had seen last night arguing with the young waiter, who was apparently not on duty this morning.

Without a word, Mona approached their table, picked up the empty breadbasket, and went off in the direction of the kitchen. As she passed the table where the two men sat, the younger, dark-haired one stopped her and said something Claire couldn't make out. She shook her head and continued on her way, and the older, blond man frowned at his companion.

"Really, Jeffrey, that young woman has enough trouble, don't you think?" His voice was cultivated, smooth, urbane.

The younger man shrugged and leaned back in his chair. "Don't be such a stiff, Richard. I was only kidding. She needed cheering up a little." His accent was rougher, with a working-class edge to it—perhaps Brooklyn, Claire thought.

"Well, that was rude. Her sex life is none of your business."

"Oh, but that's where you're wrong. It *is* my business."

As Claire was wondering what he meant by that, Meredith shook her head. "I don't quite believe Mr. Wilson's 'jolly innkeeper' act."

"What do you mean?" Claire poured herself more coffee from the silver-plated coffeepot.

Meredith took a big bite of blueberry muffin. "I don't know. There's just something not quite believable about him . . . I can't quite put my finger on it. I feel like he's hiding something."

The two men at the corner table looked up as Meredith spoke—Claire couldn't tell whether they had heard her or not—then returned to their conversation, heads low. It looked as though they were having a serious discussion, but they had lowered their voices so that Claire couldn't make out their words. Richard, the older one, was doing most of the talking, and Jeffrey kept shaking his head in response. His shoulders had the world-weary attitude of a bored teenager, though Claire put him in his early thirties.

Meredith saw Claire watching them and leaned over her plate of muffins. "Boyfriends, if you ask me," she whispered.

"No one's asking you," Claire whispered back.

Just then Claire heard the creak of floorboards and looked up to see two other men enter the room. Both were tall, rangy, and wiry looking, with deep-set brown eyes and a long nose—obviously father and son. The son held his father by the elbow to steady him. The older man looked to be in his seventies, and walked with the uncertain, halting gait of a stroke victim, putting his feet down carefully, as if the ground might give way under him at any moment.

"Right here, Papa," the younger man said, guiding his father to a table by the window. "Good morning," he said, catching Claire's eye.

"Hello," Claire replied, watching as the son settled his father slowly into his chair. The old man moved with the deliberateness of the old and infirm, and once seated, he ran a hand over the few wisps of white hair that still clung to his head. The son unfolded his napkin, tucked it into his father's shirt, then sat opposite him. The old man regarded the napkin with curiosity, as though it were a strange white bird that had suddenly landed on him, then turned to stare blankly out the window.

"You staying here, too?" Meredith said.

"Yes, we're in room eight," the son answered. Broad-shouldered and athletic looking, with salt-and-pepper hair and beard, he looked to be about fifty or so. His accent sounded to Claire like a northeastern drawl, and she guessed him to be a New Englander. At the base of his neck a little silver cross lay nestled among his chest hairs.

"We're in room six," Meredith said.

"Chris Callahan," he replied, extending a tanned, strong-looking hand.

Meredith shook it solemnly; his hand was so big it totally enveloped hers. "Meredith Lawrence. This is my friend Claire Rawlings."

"Pleased to meet you, Claire," he said, taking her hand. Claire could feel calluses on his palms, the pleasantly rough, weathered skin of a man who was used to outdoor life.

"This is my father, Jack." He indicated the older man, who looked as though he were beginning to doze off. "Say hello, Papa."

Jack's head jerked a little and he made an effort at a smile. "Hello," he said to no one in particular.

"Alzheimer's?" Meredith whispered to Chris, who nodded. The girl shook her head. "That's too bad. What brings you here?"

"We're here visiting my sister, who works here—ah, there she is," Chris said as their waitress reentered the room.

"She's your sister?" said Meredith as Mona approached their table.

"Well, actually my half sister; we have different mothers," he replied. "Her mother was Italian. Called her Mona Lisa Marie, a name for a good Catholic girl. Dad looks pretty alert this morning, don't you think?" he asked as she placed a pot of coffee on their table.

"I guess," she answered with a little shrug. She folded her tray underneath her arm and put a hand on her father's shoulder. "Good morning, Papa."

The old man swiveled his head toward her and studied her face as if he had never seen it before. "Mona Lisa Marie," he murmured with a vague little smile.

Mona returned his smile. "That's right, Papa, it's me."

At that moment a dog came bounding into the room. It trotted over to Chris and Jack's table and sat in front of

Jack, looking up at him expectantly, its pink tongue hanging out of the side of its mouth.

The dog looked as though it had been assembled from miscellaneous spare parts. Its ungainly body was low and long, set on stubby legs, so that when it walked quickly it put one in mind of a centipede, the little legs moving quickly to keep up with each other. Its tail was absurdly long, and jutted out at a forty-five-degree angle from its back side, reminding Claire of a weather vane. The dog had the face of a terrier and the ears of a beagle, the brisk muzzle of an Airedale and the big black nose of a basset hound. Its coat was a mottled black and white like an English setter and its fur curly in some places and straight in others.

It was as though Nature, tired of the responsibility of creation, had, in a frivolous mood, decided to throw together leftover bits and pieces from other animals to make this dog. It was, all in all, the ugliest, most mismatched creature Claire had ever seen.

"Whose dog?" said Meredith.

"Oh, he's Mrs. Wilson's dog," Mona replied as she poured coffee for her brother.

"What's his name?"

Mona placed a basket of rolls on the table. "Shatzy."

"He's a nice dog, isn't he, Papa?" said Chris.

Jack gazed at the dog. "Yes, he does pretty well," he said after a moment, then added, "He has to study to move his little legs."

"Really?" said Meredith.

Jack leaned forward, encouraged. "He gets all his knowledge from the little books he reads."

Meredith nodded politely, but Claire wasn't sure whether she should promote this train of thought.

"Poor Papa," said Mona, stroking his cheek. "His mind isn't really there anymore—is it, Papa?"

Jack thought for a moment. "I think you might try look-

ing in the kitchen," he said. "Maybe I just misplaced it
somewhere."

Mona turned to her brother. "Have you talked to the
people at the home about him yet?" she said softly.

"You know how I feel about that," he replied tightly. "I
promised Mama—"

"You promised her that you would look after Dad. That
didn't mean dragging him around with you wherever you
go."

"I told her on her deathbed—"

Mona snorted. "Oh, don't dredge up that deathbed guilt
thing; it won't work on me!"

"He has a better life with me than he could ever have in
a home!"

"You don't know that—but it certainly gives you control of his money, doesn't it?"

Chris glanced over at Claire's table and his sister
blushed, as if suddenly realizing that their conversation
had been overheard. Claire and Meredith were, at this
point, the only other diners, the two men at the corner table
having slipped out of the room so quietly Claire hardly noticed them leave.

Chris laid a hand on his sister's arm. "Look, Mona, let's
try not to argue, okay? We came here to have a nice time
with you."

Mona sighed and nodded. "Okay. I'm sorry. It's just
that . . ." Instead of finishing her thought, she sighed and
turned away.

"What?" said Chris. "What's wrong?"

Mona shook her head. "Nothing. I'm just tired, that's
all. I've got work to do. I'll see you later." She turned and
left the room, followed by the little dog, its toenails clicking on the hardwood floor.

Meredith shook her head as she watched it go. "Man,
that's one ugly dog. I wonder how many breeds they
crossed to get that thing?"

Jack stared at her, his eyes cloudy. "They crossed when the light was green."

Meredith looked at Chris. "What did your father mean just then?"

Chris shook his head. "See, my father randomly responds to words, and not necessarily to the sense in which they're being used. He understands that it's a question, but beyond that he's just confabulating."

"Confabulating?" said Meredith.

"Yes, that's when the demented person is inventing what he thinks is an appropriate response—or making up things to mask his dementia. It's like they're following the forms of social intercourse, but the context is gone."

Claire thought of her own mother and father.

"If we ever get like that, just shoot us—please," her mother had once said after a visit to Aunt Ellen, Claire's great-aunt, who had gradually lost her mind through a series of small strokes. There had been no such gradual decline for Claire's parents, however—a drunk driver had seen to that.

Mona entered the room again and walked over to their table. "Can I get you anything else?" she said politely to Claire.

"More muff—" Meredith began, but Claire shook her head.

"No, thanks; this ought to hold us until lunchtime."

"Why can't I have more muffins?" Meredith said when Mona had gone.

"Because you only ate half of your eggs. You can't live on cake, Meredith."

"But it isn't cake, it's muffins."

"Cake, muffins, cookies—they're all full of sugar, and too much of it is bad for you."

Meredith sighed and tossed her napkin on the table. "All *right,* I get it already!" She looked over at Chris and Jack. "See what I have to live with?"

Chris shook his head. "It's tough being a kid."

After breakfast Claire suggested a walk to look at the old gristmill and church. Both were closed up for the winter, but she and Meredith wandered around the buildings, stepping on the frozen hard-stubbled grass, peering in the windows. The gristmill sat over a stream, which flowed swift and cold over the rocks below, and through the dusty window Claire could make out the shaft of the huge wheel inside where the grain was ground up. There was a faint smell of cornmeal in the air. The place looked spooky, silent, and deserted, but Claire found it easy to imagine it two hundred years ago, filled with people working the mill, carting sacks of flour and cornmeal off to the inn to be used for baking bread and Indian pudding. Though there were no hands to work the mill inside, the huge wheel turned slowly and inexorably, pushed along by the water flowing and bubbling beneath it.

The church across the road, too, was empty and locked up. As she and Meredith stood on the steps in front of its thick wooden door, Claire thought what a nice place it would be to get married. The guidebook had mentioned that it was a popular spot for weddings, and Claire imagined coming out of the church to a big reception at the inn. There could be no more festive place for a party.

Meredith stomped her feet and hopped up and down. "Gettin' cold. Let's go have some cocoa or something."

The wind had picked up and was blowing strongly from the north. As they walked back to the hotel Claire noticed for the first time another house just down the road from the inn, nestled behind a copse of beech trees. It was a rambling wood-frame house, of the type built in the late Victorian era. A single light burned from a third-floor bedroom; other than that, the house was dark and quiet.

That afternoon, the snow began to fall. At first it fell so lightly that Claire, sitting by the window, felt she could trace the path of each flake as it fluttered slowly to the ground. But even as she sat watching, she could see the sheet of white advancing steadily from the north.

Soon the individual flakes thickened into a mass, then a swarm, and finally an army. By dinnertime the sky was a blur of white that blocked out the outline of trees, cars, and people, until even the maple tree outside their bedroom window was swallowed up in the advancing blanket of white.

After dinner Claire and Meredith retired to their room to watch the falling snow.

"Ooo, are we going to be *snowed in*?" Meredith said, bouncing up and down on the bed.

Claire turned away from the window. "I don't know. It sure is coming down hard."

"*I'll* say!" Meredith yelped, bouncing harder.

"Okay, that's enough of that," said Claire. "Time to give the bedsprings a rest."

"Oh, all *right*." Meredith flopped down onto her stomach and shoved her forefinger in her mouth. "Can we go downstairs and get the weather report?"

"Okay," Claire said. She, too, was curious about the approaching storm. "Put your shoes on."

Meredith complied, and together they crept down the creaky staircase to the bar, which was a cozy room just off the main entrance. The broad, dark floorboards were splattered with candle wax and stained from the splashing of a century of Scotch and sodas. The room was almost empty except for a young couple in the far corner, hunched over their beers, apparently oblivious to anyone else. Meredith stood shaking her right leg impatiently, humming to herself. She was standing at the bar, her nose close to a pot of mulled cider. Claire could smell the round, juicy aroma of the apples simmering in cinnamon and cloves.

"Want some of that?" said the bartender. He was young, in his twenties, with pink skin and a faint hairlip.

"Mmm . . . I guess," Meredith replied, shrugging, her shoulders thin under her thick green wool sweater, a birthday present from her father.

"What'll it be for you?" the bartender asked Claire. She

thought she detected a slight Irish twist to his consonants, a faint Celtic cadence to the vowels.

"Oh . . . I guess I'll have the same," she replied. "It smells so good."

"Apples from the orchards out back," he said, stirring the pot with a wooden ladle. "Been apple trees there ever since Longfellow's time, they say."

Claire noticed that in New England people had a tendency to leave off the beginnings of sentences, as though there wasn't time enough to say all the words.

"Have you heard the weather report?" Meredith asked as the boy poured out two steaming mugs of cider. He put a fresh cinnamon stick in each one.

"Oh, haven't you heard? Biggest nor'easter to hit New England since the blizzard of 'eighty-nine." He placed the mugs on the bar counter. "Charge it to your room?"

"Uh—yes, please," said Claire. "Room six."

"How did you know we were staying overnight?" said Meredith, tapping her foot against the bottom of the bar.

The young man shrugged. Claire noticed that his shoulders were broad and thick, like a football player's. She could see the round outline of muscle under his white shirt.

"Everyone who isn't an overnight guest has left by now, with the storm coming and all. Besides, I saw you check in."

"Oh?" said Meredith. "You're pretty observant."

The boy smiled. "That's pretty hard not to notice," he said, pointing to Meredith's bright sweep of orange hair.

Meredith scrunched up her nose. "Very funny, Einstein. So why aren't you headed home?"

"I am in another half hour," he replied, wiping the counter down with a rag. "Soon as the honeymooners over there go up to their room and I can close up the bar." He indicated the young couple in the corner. If they heard his remark, they made no sign of it. They appeared completely wrapped up in each other; one of the woman's legs dangled on top of the man's, and their foreheads were touching.

Her face was obscured by her long dark hair, which hung straight and smooth, like a curtain. His hair was dark blond and curly as a spaniel's.

"If they were any closer to each other they'd be sharing DNA," Meredith muttered. Meredith had once told Claire she thought that "necking and stuff is *yucky*." Claire had actually been relieved to hear it. Although she hoped sooner or later Meredith would break out of her geeky phase and date boys, Claire saw the girl's nerdiness as a way of protecting herself from the pressures of incipient adolescent sexuality.

Claire took a sip of cider. It was hot and spicy and tasted so much like fresh apples that it was startling. The insides of her cheeks contracted sharply.

"This is great," she said to the bartender. "The apples are from here?"

"Yup—orchard's on the property, right out back."

"You live in the village?" Meredith asked, sipping her cider.

"Nope, next town over."

"I'm Meredith Lawrence, and this is Claire Rawlings," she declared. "What's your name?"

"Otis Knox," he replied, wiping his hand on his apron and offering it to Meredith. The hand was broad, with yellow calluses along the finger pads.

The door behind the bar opened and Mona Callahan entered. "Hello," she said, seeing Meredith and Claire.

"Hello," Claire responded. Meredith was occupied fishing the cinnamon stick from her mug.

"Hello, Otis," Mona said, putting her tray down on the bar.

"Hey, Mona." His tone was casual, but Claire thought there was something forced about it. A flush worked its way up his muscular neck, spreading over his face until his cheeks shone. Mona brushed past him, and his color intensified. Claire had not at first thought that the waitress was especially attractive, but now, following Otis's gaze, she saw, through his eyes, the soft line of Mona's hair, the delicate eyebrows, upturned nose, the full lips.

Mona Lisa Marie Callahan was an attractive young woman, Claire thought, if not exactly beautiful. What set her apart from other pretty girls Claire had seen, though, was her smile. It was a secret smile, as though she knew something very interesting she wasn't telling. Claire had seldom seen so expressive a smile, though when she separated it into its various components it was not immediately obvious why the smile should seem to portend as much. Was it the way Mona's mouth turned up at one corner slightly more than the other? Or maybe the secret was in her eyes: deep green, almond-shaped, with their thick dark lashes, they were her most striking feature. When she smiled, her eyelids half closed, like a cat's, creating an aura of mystery. At that moment Mona Lisa Marie, the waitress, became Cleopatra, Mata Hari, Salome, Helen of Troy—a woman men would lose their heads over, daring destruction for the sake of a single kiss. Her smile held a subtle promise, an invitation to pleasure to come, of sun-baked seaside landscapes, swaying palm trees, perfumed summer nights—in short, whatever the lucky recipient of that smile might envision as absolute bliss.

Claire watched as Mona turned her smile upon Otis Knox. She watched the red flush shoot up his neck and the way he averted his eyes, as if the strength of that gaze was too much to bear for long.

"Do you have ice?" Mona said. "We're all out."

"Help yourself. You still got customers?"

"One table. They've just finished dessert."

Otis wiped his strong hands on a white linen napkin. "They're gonna have a helluva time getting home."

"Oh, they've got one of those four-wheel-drives."

"Yeah?"

"Yeah, I heard them talking about it," Mona replied, fishing around in the ice bin.

"I gotta get one of those. You can go anywhere in those things."

Mona pushed a wisp of hair from her face. "Where is it you want to go, Otis?"

"Oh, I dunno. Anywhere." He turned away so that she couldn't see the color creeping back into his face, but Claire saw it.

Mona shook her head. "Otis Knox, if you aren't just the big adventurer."

The boy shrugged and turned an even deeper shade of pink. "All I'm saying is that it'd be nice to know you could have that kind of freedom, is all."

"Well, you'll never earn enough to get one working here, that's for sure," she said, flicking the same strand of hair from her face.

Otis sighed. "I know it—that's for certain."

When the girl had left, Meredith leaned toward Claire and whispered, "He likes her."

"Shh," Claire whispered back, with a glance at Otis, but he didn't appear to have heard Meredith's remark.

Claire sighed; it was evident the young bartender did like the waitress, but probably because of his harelip he hadn't approached her. To Claire it was a minor imperfection in an otherwise extremely attractive young man, but she could understand his self-consciousness . . . She thought of Wally Jackson and his beautifully shaped mouth. No imperfections there; she loved his face and could look at it for hours on end, she thought, without tiring of it.

Just then the door to the bar opened and in walked the man who had greeted them upon their arrival the night before. Tonight he wore a maroon vest over a billowy ivory-colored shirt, black knee-high boots, and amber breeches. The young couple in the corner looked up at him briefly, then returned to their intimate conversation.

"Hiya, James," said the bartender as the man strode over to the bar, his leather soles making a scuffing sound on the wooden floor. Once again Claire couldn't help looking at his legs, his thighs thick and strong under the linen breeches.

" 'Lo, Otis," he replied, tipping his tricornered hat to Claire and Meredith as he passed.

"Slow night tonight," the bartender commented as he poured a draft beer from one of the taps at the bar.

"Weather's keeping people away in droves," James replied. He settled himself at a table next to Claire and Meredith and raised his glass. "Cheers."

Meredith raised her cider. "Cheers."

"We weren't properly introduced yesterday. I'm James Pewter."

"James is the inn historian," said Otis, leaning forward with his elbows upon the bar.

"Oh, you're a historian?" Claire asked.

James hung his hat on the back of his chair and shook his head. "Unofficial. It's a hobby of mine. I greet people at the door and answer questions about the place."

"Cool," said Meredith. "Tell us something about it. Are there any ghosts here?"

He took a sip of beer. The firelight reflected in the amber liquid in his glass, and Claire felt mesmerized by the warmth of the room, the hour, and the sweet smell of burning pine.

"Kind of night Laura's likely to be out in," Otis said as he stood behind the bar polishing glasses. "Why don't you tell them about her?"

"Who's Laura?" said Meredith. "Is she a ghost?"

James Pewter leaned back in his chair and crossed his legs. "Well, some people would say so," he answered, running a hand through his soft brown hair. "The legend goes back to the eighteenth century, when the place was owned by a fellow named Ezekiel Howe. His daughter Laura was married to a local businessman, but when the war came along she fell in love with a dashing British soldier who was wounded at Concord."

"That's not far from here, you know," Otis interjected. "In fact, every April we have a march—"

"What happened to Laura?" Meredith interrupted, her face eager and shiny in the firelight.

"Well, Laura nursed the man back to health, and then she was so in love with him that she couldn't bear to live without him. The story goes that she threw herself into the millstream, and was chewed up by the mill wheel . . . kind of a horrible death, really."

"Wow," Meredith said softly. "We just saw it today— the gristmill, I mean."

Claire imagined what it would be like to fall underneath that slowly turning wheel . . . she shivered and rubbed her arms to warm herself. She looked over at the young couple in the corner, who were also listening to Pewter's story.

"They say that ever since then she's been seen roaming the halls of the building in a long white dress, in search of her lover."

"Wow," Meredith said softly. "That is way spooky."

Pewter leaned forward in his chair, the firelight warm on his honey-brown hair. "Her body is reputed to be buried on the grounds somewhere. Since she killed herself, the church refused to bury her in hallowed ground, so her father dug a grave in the woods somewhere around here."

"I wonder if we'll see her?" Meredith said to Claire.

"Her ghost even returned after the fire," James added.

"Fire? What fire?" said Claire.

"There was a fire two years ago that demolished a lot of the original structure of the building. It was only after extensive rebuilding that the inn was able to open again. Fortunately, most of the original timber survived the fire.

"By the way, this room is the oldest one in the building, this and the museum. You haven't seen the museum yet, have you?"

"No," Claire replied. "Where is it?"

"It's that room right across the hall. It's been closed for

some cleaning and restoration work, but should be open tomorrow. You should go take a look. It's very interesting."

"Wow. What was the cause of the fire?" said Meredith.

James shook his head. "Never determined. Arson was suspected, but nothing was ever proven."

"Arson, huh?" Meredith replied. "That can be hard to trace. Arsonists are sneaky. I once saw a thing on *60 Minutes* about this firefighter who—"

"How about another round?" Otis said suddenly, coming out from behind the bar to collect glasses. As if on cue, the young couple in the corner rose from their table and silently left the room.

"Who are they, anyway?" said Meredith.

"Lyle and Sally. He's a poet—they arrived here two nights ago," Otis replied.

James leaned back in his chair. "Otis here is a direct descendant of Henry Knox, George Washington's chief engineer and gunner during the Revolution."

"Really?" said Claire. "That's very interesting."

Otis laughed. "He was quite a character. Big fat man, a real eccentric. He adored Washington, and left his job as a bookseller to join the Continental army."

"Yeah, I remember reading about him at school," said Meredith.

Otis shrugged and went back behind the bar to wash glasses. "Everyone's got a history," he said, plunging beer mugs into a basin of soapy water and rinsing them off under the tap. "Who knows? I'm sure on the other side of the family I must have ancestors who were bank robbers."

"Really?" said Meredith. "Bank robbers?"

"I'm just saying it's possible."

"Hmm . . . I wonder what *my* ancestors were."

"Probably horse thieves," James Pewter remarked.

Meredith turned to him. "Really? You think so?"

Claire laughed. "I think he's just having fun with you."

"Oh. Well, I think you're wrong anyway," she replied. "I don't even *like* horses."

"No?"

"Nope. They're sweaty and smelly, and they're not very bright."

"Oh, I don't know," the historian replied. "There are all kinds of intelligence." He rose from his chair and stretched himself. "Well, I guess I'd better get on home before the snow gets much deeper."

"Where do you live?" Meredith asked.

"Just down the street. It's the only other house on the road besides the Wilsons'."

Claire remembered passing a little stone house after turning off of Route 20. "Oh, we saw it when we came in," she said. "That's your house?"

"Yup," he said. "Also dates back to the eighteenth century. Frank and Paula's house is more modern—about 1890, I believe."

"Oh, is that their house—the big wood-frame across the street?" said Claire.

James nodded. "It is. Lived in it ever since Henry was born."

"Is that their son?" said Meredith, and James nodded again.

"I think we saw him last night," Claire said. "Thin and pale, with dark hair?"

"That sounds like Henry. Well, I'm off." James handed some money to Otis. "This one's on me," he said to Claire.

"Oh, you don't have to—" Claire began, recognizing the phrase her father had used so often.

"I know I don't have to," James replied as he pocketed his change. "I want to, that's all." He leaned toward Claire and the tips of his fingers brushed her shoulder. She felt her skin heat up through her clothes at his touch. He stood and tipped his hat. "Enjoy your stay." He opened the door to the bar, letting in a rush of cold air from the hallway, and then was gone.

Claire felt a pang of disappointment at his departure; she had to admit she found James Pewter very attractive.

Later, back in the room, she was afraid Meredith was going to comment on it; sometimes the girl had an uncanny ability to know what Claire was thinking. Instead, though, Meredith sat on the cot taking off her shoes and tossing them into the corner.

"Did you see Otis around Mona? He thinks she's awesome."

"He does seem to like her," Claire agreed.

Meredith flopped onto her bed. "*Like* her? He's *nuts* about her." She rolled over onto her back and pulled off her socks, flinging them vaguely in the direction of her shoes.

"She has an interesting smile, don't you think?" Claire observed.

"Yeah, I guess so," Meredith answered, picking at her toes.

"It reminds me of something," said Claire, "but I can't think what it is."

"Hmm . . . let's see." Meredith bent over her feet, her thick red curls hanging over her face like a veil. "I know!" she cried suddenly. "It's like the *Mona Lisa*—the painting."

"Yeah, maybe that's it. It has that same mysterious quality, you know?"

"Yeah, like she's keeping a secret or something."

"Right," Meredith agreed. "And the secret the *Mona Lisa* was keeping was that she was pregnant?"

"Right. Except didn't they discover that da Vinci used his own face as a model or something?"

"Yeah, I think they found some early sketches or something."

"That explains why she's not so foxy. I mean, who'd want to look like some old Italian guy? Ugh."

Claire laughed. "I wouldn't mind, if it meant I was worth twenty million dollars."

Meredith shrugged. "Whatever. Still, it's weird, if you ask me."

Claire looked out the window at the knot in the trunk of

the maple tree. For some reason, William Blake's poem
The Tyger popped into her head.

> *Tyger! Tyger! burning bright*
> *In the forests of the night,*
> *What immortal hand or eye*
> *Could frame thy fearful symmetry?*

"There's something going on here," Meredith mused.

"What do you mean?"

Meredith shrugged. "I'm not sure. But don't you get the
feeling these people know more than they're telling?"

Claire sat on the bed across from her. "I guess so. But
we're just visitors. Why should they tell us everything?"

"That whole fire thing's suspicious, for example. I
mean, James brought it up but then he didn't want to talk
about it. He changed the subject right afterward . . . I don't
know, it's just a feeling I get, that's all."

"Where's my mohair scarf?" Claire said, noticing it was
gone from the peg in the closet.

Meredith lay back on her bed, the blankets pulled up to
her chin. "You had it on in the bar, I think."

"Oh, right. Then the room got warmer and I remember
taking it off. I'll bet I left it on the back of the chair. Don't
go anywhere—I'll be right back," she said, throwing on a
robe.

Meredith scrunched up her face. "Now, where would I
go at this hour?"

Claire went down the main staircase and through the
front hall to the bar. Sure enough, she found her scarf dangling from the chair where she had been sitting. She
scooped it up and crept up the back stairs to the second
floor.

Chris and Jack Callahan occupied the first room at the
top of the main staircase. It was, Frank Wilson had told
Claire, one of the two remaining rooms from the original
building; the rest had been added on some years later. As

Claire was making her way back up the stairs, she heard
voices coming from inside the room.

"Well, why did you come here, then, if you don't want
to talk about it?" It was a woman's voice, and Claire
thought it sounded like Mona.

"Oh, for God's sake, Mona, can't we just have a good
time for once?" Claire recognized Chris Callahan's dis-
tinctive voice, and he sounded angry.

"He's my father, too, you know," Mona replied, and
then she said something Claire couldn't make out. Claire
crept down the hall to her own room, closing the door quietly behind her.

Later, as Meredith lay snoring gently in her cot, Claire
gazed out at the snow falling on the fields and woods behind the inn. She thought of the young woman in white
whose body lay buried not far from here, a tragic victim of
love.

She forced her mind away from Robert, away from her
own narrow escape from death at his hands, and thought
instead of Wally. She imagined him lying in the bed beside
her, warm and solid and as comforting as the blanket of
snow that fell softly upon the frozen landscape outside,
burying sadness and grief in white silence.

Claire heard the creak of a floorboard out in the hall
and, being wide awake, decided to investigate. Creeping to
the door, she opened it quietly and peered out. There, at the
other end of the hall, she saw the white-clad figure of a
woman. For a moment, Claire froze where she stood, an
icy chill in her veins. In the dim light, the woman looked
insubstantial, diaphanous, backlit as she was, and her white
nightgown seeming almost to glow from within. But then
Claire realized she was looking at Mona Callahan, who
was just coming out of her brother's room.

She stood in the hall outside the room for a few moments, and as the hall light caught her face, Claire thought
that she looked disturbed. She was so preoccupied with her
thoughts that Claire didn't think Mona saw her, because

the girl turned and disappeared around the corner without a word.

Claire stepped back inside her room and closed the door, but she couldn't help wondering what it was that had upset Mona. It wasn't unusual for the decline of an aging parent to cause dissension among siblings. She had seen it in her friends' families: disagreement as to treatment, estate questions, control of the parent and their money—all of this could cause rifts in the closest of families. And by the look of it, she thought, Jack Callahan had made some money in his time. His son had the smell of prosperity about him.

In the middle of the night, Claire awoke from scattered dreams to the sound of a dog howling. It was a mournful, hollow sound, as if the animal was lonely and was calling out for company. The sound rose to a high, plaintive note, then died down to a low, sad moan before dissipating into the silence of the night. Claire sat up and looked over at Meredith to see if the howling had awakened her, but the girl lay sprawled on her back, the covers twisted around her thin body. Claire lay back down again and pulled her own blankets up to her chin. She had an impulse to untangle Meredith from her bedclothes, but she knew from experience that even if she did this, the girl would still awaken in the morning in the same twisted tangle of blankets.

That night Claire dreamed of floating above the woods in a long white dress, over fields and streams—floating, flying, hovering like a cloud over the stark chaste landscape of a Massachusetts winter.

Chapter 4

The snow fell all through the night and was still falling when Claire awoke shortly after dawn. She looked out at the thick cloud of white, the maple tree outside her window a dark, blurry outline, like an Impressionist painting. She looked over at Meredith, asleep on her cot, her blankets in such disarray that it seemed as though she had fought a wrestling match with them.

Claire tried to remember what summer days were like, the kind of sweltering August afternoon in New York when people wandered out into the street and headed straight for any patch of shade. She tried to imagine that feeling, but her memory failed her, and she couldn't think of anything other than the snow falling so insistently outside her window.

Claire got out of bed and slipped on her navy-blue cotton sweater. The sweater was old and tattered, with rips in the shoulder, but that only made her love it more. It was one of the last things her mother gave her before the car crash that claimed her life.

She tiptoed downstairs to the dining room, in hopes of finding coffee. No one else in the building was stirring, and the creak of the ancient floorboards under her feet sounded preternaturally loud.

The main dining room was deserted, and there were no sounds coming from anywhere else in the inn. The coffee station stood gleaming in the corner, its polished stainless steel surface reflecting the falling flakes. Claire opened the drawer of the cabinet beneath the coffeemaker and found a box of Maxwell House coffee. She extracted a shiny blue packet, poured the contents into the top of the coffeemaker, added water, and sat down to wait. The machine hissed and sputtered, and the smell of brewing coffee filled the room as Claire sat watching the snow fall inexorably all around, burying the building in a thick shroud of white.

The floorboards creaked and she looked up to see Chris and Jack Callahan standing at the dining-room door. "Hello," she said.

"Hello," Chris answered in his deep, sleepy baritone. Jack gave her a vague little smile. "Look, Papa, it's Claire," Chris said, propelling his father in the direction of her table. For a moment Claire thought they were going to sit with her, but they passed her and settled at the table behind her.

"I thought we were the first ones up," said Chris. "What brings you down here so early?"

"Oh, I don't know. I just couldn't sleep anymore."

"I know what you mean. Sometimes I just have to get up—right, Papa?" Jack nodded obediently, smiling his wan little smile.

"I made some coffee, if you'd like some," Claire said.

"Great, thanks." Chris arranged his father's chair so he could look out the window. "Pretty amazing, huh?" he said, indicating the falling snow.

"Yes, it really is."

"I heard some of the staff ended up having to spend the night," he commented as Claire poured them both coffee. "Do you want some coffee, Papa?"

The old man looked at his son and nodded. "Good to the last drop," he mumbled.

"It's interesting you should say that, Jack," said Claire, setting a cup in front of him. "It just so happens this is Maxwell House coffee."

"Jingles seem to stick in his mind," Chris remarked as he placed the cup between his father's stiffened fingers. "It's funny, but it's as though there's another person living in my father's body . . . like the old Jack is gone, you know, but a new one has come to take his place." He sighed and wiped a drop of coffee from his father's chin.

"It must be hard," said Claire.

"Have you—have you been through something like this with a parent?"

Claire shook her head. "No, I haven't." After her parents' car accident, she couldn't imagine a tragedy more horrible, but now, looking at Jack sitting there staring blankly at his son, she knew that seeing either of her parents like that would be worse. They had both been so energetic and active—though like Claire herself, her father also had a more contemplative side.

"Why didn't you *tell* me you were getting up?"

Claire looked up to see Meredith standing in the doorway, her thin arms folded in front of her chest. Her left pajama leg was pulled up over her knee, exposing a skinny white shin, dotted with bruises. Meredith bruised like a banana, and her body was a road map of her encounters with inanimate objects.

"I thought I'd let you sleep," Claire replied as Meredith walked over to her table and plopped down on a chair across from her. "I woke up and couldn't go back to sleep, so I came down here."

"But you *know* I don't want to miss anything," the girl replied plaintively, running her fingers along the edge of the tablecloth, where the cloth met the wood at the table's edge. "Hi," she said to Chris.

"Good morning."

"What are you doing with no slippers on?" Claire indicated the girl's bare feet.

Meredith heaved a deep sigh and rolled her eyes. "What do you *think*? I don't have any."

"Well, we'll have to get you some. It's cold outside."

"I *hate* slippers."

"Then at least put on some socks. We don't want you to get sick."

Another sigh. Meredith picked up a spoon and tapped the tabletop. "For your infor*m*ation, people don't get sick from cold feet; they get sick from *viruses*."

"That may be, but go back upstairs right now and put on some socks."

"O*kay!*" Meredith swung herself down from the chair and sauntered out of the room, expressing disdain in the swing of her shoulders.

When she was gone, Chris laughed softly, a sound curiously like the low nicker of a horse. "You handled that like an expert."

Claire smiled and shook her head. "Well, thanks, but . . . sometimes I wonder."

"What is she, twelve?"

"Thirteen—going on thirty-five."

Chris laughed again. "Do you have any of your own?"

Claire shook her head. "You?"

"Four boys."

"Yikes."

"You said it. At least she's a girl."

"Sometimes I wonder if she's *human*." This was perfectly true: Meredith was such an odd child that she seemed outside not only the realm of gender but of humanity itself.

"Hey," Chris said, "have you looked in the drawers of your bedside table yet?"

"Oh, you mean the letters?"

"Yeah—what's that all about? Mona didn't mention it to me."

"I've never seen it before either. Pretty interesting, isn't it?"

"Yeah. I stayed up half the night reading them. There was

this one that mentioned something about a fire in the hotel some years ago."

"Oh, we heard about that last night. What did it say?"

Chris leaned his elbows on his knees and lowered his voice, though no one else was around to overhear him. "Well, it's funny. The letter is unsigned, but whoever wrote it seemed to imply they knew something about who started the fire."

"Wow, *that's* interesting. I'd like to see it."

"Sure, no problem," Chris answered, standing up. "In the meantime, would you be willing to keep an eye on my father while I go to the bathroom?"

"Sure, go ahead."

"Thanks." He loped off, with the long-legged, loose-jointed stride of a cowboy.

Jack Callahan watched his son go, then turned to look out the window. Claire followed his gaze and saw the furiously falling flakes outside. What struck her most was how quiet everything was; insulated by the snow, the only sounds she could hear were those within the inn itself: the occasional clank of a heating pipe, or the creak of a floorboard. But outdoors all was stillness. Claire felt as though she could stare at those flakes forever, mesmerized. She looked at her watch: it was six-thirty. Though the sun was obscured by the snow and grey cloud cover, a gradual brightening of the sky told her that it was well after dawn. Across the street, through a blur of snowflakes, she thought she saw a light go on in the Wilson house. When she looked again, it had gone off.

"Well, I hope you're *satisfied*." Meredith was back, a heavy pair of grey woolen socks on her feet.

Claire glanced at her, determined not to make too much of this incident. "Yes, I am. Thank you."

Meredith sat back down in her chair with a grunt. "Where's Chris?"

"Gone to the bathroom."

"Oh."

"Where'd he go?" Jack said sleepily. His voice was brittle and cracked, dry as kindling.

"He went to the bathroom," Claire answered, a little louder this time.

Jack nodded, his eyelids drooping. "I know him," he said in a confidential tone of voice.

"Yes, I'm sure you do," Claire replied.

"He's not what you'd think."

"Really? In what way?"

Jack leaned in toward her, and she could smell his breath, sour like old shoe leather. His lips had a bluish tinge; they matched the liver spots on the backs of his hands. "He's a spy," he said softly, a little waddle of spit forming on his lower lip.

"Really?"

"Oh, yes. There's a lot people don't know about him."

"Who are you talking about, Papa?"

Claire turned to see Chris standing in the doorway. Jack turned away as though he hadn't heard his son.

"Papa? What were you saying to Claire?"

They were interrupted at that moment by the sound of heavy footsteps descending the front stairs. This was immediately followed by the appearance of Max von Schlegel, his large body filling the doorway.

"Good morning," he said cheerfully, his plump cheeks pink with good health.

"Hello," said Meredith. Claire wasn't sure if the girl liked the big chef or not; her voice was neutral, but she was smiling.

"You're up early," he remarked, directing his words to Claire.

"She couldn't sleep," Meredith said.

"Ah, yes—insomnia." He nodded his big bullet-shaped head. "You know, I have some herbs I can give you for that."

"That's very kind of you," said Claire, "but I really don't—"

"Oh, it's no trouble at all. You'd be surprised what herbs

can be used for. People in this country are just beginning to realize—"

Just then Jack broke in with a loud sort of bleating sound, like a sheep in distress.

Chris took his father's hand. "What is it, Papa?"

Jack stared at him. "They try, but they can't do it," he said ominously.

"What's he mean by that?" Meredith asked.

Chris shook his head. "Who knows? Sometimes what he says seems to refer to a subject people around him are discussing, but really he's thinking about something else entirely. Sometimes there's no way to tell what."

Meredith swung her legs back and forth under her chair. "Ooo, did you see that *Star Trek* episode where Captain Picard goes down to this planet to meet with an alien captain and the alien talks only in metaphors and Picard has to figure out what he means?"

The words came tumbling out, rushing over each other in the girl's eagerness to get them all out, and Claire had to smile.

"No, I missed that one," Chris replied seriously.

"Well, maybe it's like that with your dad," Meredith continued. "I mean, maybe there's a code, if only you could read it."

Jack grunted. "Wouldn't it be pretty to think so?" he muttered.

Claire recognized the quote from *The Sun Also Rises*. It figured that Jack would be a Hemingway sort of man, she thought—he and Chris had the rugged, weather-beaten looks of a Hemingway hero.

"Well, I'd better be getting into the kitchen," Max said, rubbing his plump hands together. He indicated the falling snow outside. "Do you know several of us had to stay here last night?"

Meredith leaned her elbows on the back of her chair. "Really?" She tipped the front legs of the chair off the ground.

"We couldn't dig our cars out from under the drifts," said Max.

Meredith turned around and sat down again. "Wow," she said, looking out at the snow. "It's a good thing there were enough rooms for you!"

Max nodded. "It's odd; normally the inn would be booked this weekend."

"Maybe the threat of snow kept people from traveling," Chris suggested.

Claire thought about Wally, stuck in New York. She wondered when he would be able to get through the snow and make it out here.

Max sighed and ran a hand over his smooth pate. "I guess I'll go down to the wine cellar and choose a few bottles for tonight."

He turned and left the room, the old floorboards shaking under his heavy tread. Claire heard the creak of rusty hinges, then the thud of Max's footsteps going downstairs.

Meredith went to the coffeemaker and made herself a cup of tea. "These things are so cool," she said, pushing down the red handle of the hot water spout on the side of the machine. "It'd be neat to own one."

"Yeah," Claire replied, "if you had about fifty people over for dinner every day."

"Well, *I'd* like to have one," Meredith said, but as she spoke they heard Max coming back up the basement stairs. What made them all stop to listen was the tempo of the footsteps. Max was running, not walking, up the stairs.

A moment later he appeared in the doorway, red-faced and out of breath. His blue eyes were wide with horror.

Claire rose from her chair. "What is it? What's happened?"

Max wiped the sweat dripping from his forehead and swallowed hard. "Somebody c-call the police," he stammered. "There's been a murder."

Chapter 5

For a couple of seconds, nobody moved. It was as though the air had suddenly thickened; his words seemed to take longer than normal to travel through it. Then everybody spoke at once. Chris and Meredith both said the same thing, the thing people so often say when they are presented with such an incredible statement:

"What?"

Claire, however, just said softly, "Oh, my God." She was disturbed to realize that the news, while upsetting, did not come to her entirely as a shock. Was it possible that she had dreamed this scene somehow, or was she finally becoming psychic, like her grandmother was reputed to have been?

Meredith was halfway across the room before Claire could stop her. "Meredith, don't—"

"I won't touch anything," the girl replied. "I just want to *see!*"

"Who is it?" Chris asked. At that moment Max's legs failed him and he sank into the nearest chair. Even though the dining room was cold and drafty, sweat continued to gather on his forehead.

"It's your sister," he replied in a low voice.

Chris Callahan gasped, a rush of air followed by what sounded like a stifled sob. "Mona? Are you sure?"

Max nodded, averting his eyes.

"Are you sure she's—"

The big Austrian wrung his hands. "I have seen bodies before, Mr. Callahan. I know what death looks like."

"Well, I'm going to call the police, if nobody else will!" Meredith declared, heading for the front desk.

"I think Max should call," said Claire.

"All *right*," said Meredith, plunking herself down in the nearest chair.

Chris Callahan sat stone-faced, as though he were trying to comprehend something unfathomable. Jack stared into space, his long grizzled face blank. If he understood Max's words, he gave no sign of it. Claire looked at Max, who was still sweating and wringing his hands.

"Are you all right to call?" she said.

He nodded. "I can do it. I just—I don't understand who—why someone would . . . it doesn't make sense." He tottered unsteadily into the hall, only to return a moment later. "The phone line is dead," he said blankly.

"Must be the snowstorm," Meredith observed calmly. At times like this, Claire did have to wonder if the girl was entirely human; she could be so matter-of-fact in the face of tragedy.

"Now what?" said Max.

"Well, I guess we wake the others," Claire replied.

They sat there for a moment contemplating the idea, none of them wanting to move. Then Jack broke the silence, his voice as rusty and dry as the hinges on the basement door.

"It seems we can't always know who is who."

Chris Callahan laid a hand on his father's gnarled hand. "It's all right, Papa. Never mind, everything's going to be all right."

Claire thought it was a strange thing to say just after

hearing that your sister has been murdered, but she said nothing.

Meredith wanted to help awaken the others, so they split up the task among her and Claire and Max, while Chris remained with his father. It turned out that besides Max and Mona, Philippe the waiter and Otis Knox had also spent the night at the inn, sharing a room at the far end of the hall by Claire's room.

Meredith volunteered to go across the road to the Wilsons' house, but Max shook his head. "No, it is better that I do it. Frank Wilson has been a good friend to me, and I will get him."

Claire watched as Max set out across the desert of white, his thick legs pumping as he plowed through the powdery drifts, which were already piling waist high.

They agreed to wait until everyone was assembled before breaking the news to them, and then do it all at once. It was after eight by the time everyone was assembled in the main dining room, waiting for the Wilsons to arrive. Otis and Philippe, Claire noticed, did not sit together but were at opposite ends of the room; both of them wore expressions that could either be construed as curiosity or guilt, depending upon how you looked at it. None of the hotel guests looked especially keen or well rested; Richard and Jeffrey sat at their usual table in the corner, Richard crisp in chinos and a blue Brooks Brothers shirt, Jeffrey surly in jeans and a white T-shirt. He tapped an unlit cigarette on the table; there was no smoking anywhere in the building, but Jeffrey managed to make even an unlit cigarette look vaguely like a threat.

The young couple from the bar the night before, Lyle and Sally, looked as though they hadn't had four hours of sleep between them. Sally's face in the pallid morning light was ghastly: dark circles surrounded her eyes and her skin had a yellow tint. In the morning light Claire was able to get a good look at her, and her thin hands shook as she tugged absently at a strand of hair. She wore a fluffy blue

bathrobe over a white flannel nightgown, and there was
something pathetic about the way her eyes darted around
as she pulled at her lank, unwashed hair. Claire didn't have
much experience with junkies, but in Sally the signs were
unmistakable. Her long thin fingers were darkened with
what looked like tobacco stains. Lyle sat next to her, hands
folded in his lap. Though his face was outwardly calm,
Claire noticed his jaw was tightly set and his fingers
twitched. With his curly blond hair and full lips, he was attractive in spite of his unkempt appearance.

She heard the sound of the front door being flung open
and the stomping of feet on the floor, then Frank Wilson
emerged from the front hall, followed by Max.

"What is this?" the innkeeper demanded, looking
around, a frown on his big Irish face.

"If you would have a seat, we'll tell you," Max said
gently.

"I don't want a seat," Wilson replied gruffly. "What's
going on here?"

"Where's Mrs. Wilson?" said Philippe. "I thought we
were waiting for everyone."

"My wife will be here shortly," Frank replied curtly.
"She's getting herself and Henry dressed."

Otis looked around the dining room. "Where's Mona?"

Max cleared his throat and stepped to the center of the
room. He hung his head as though he were responsible for
the horror in the basement.

"I regret to inform you," he said, as though he were an-
nouncing staff cutbacks or something, "that a crime has
been committed here."

There was a murmuring among the others, and Frank
Wilson stepped forward. "What? What sort of crime?"

Max took a deep breath, and Claire realized she had
been holding hers. Why doesn't he just get it out all at
once? she thought, and suddenly she had an image of her
father standing in the shallow end of their swimming pool,
splashing water on his arms to "get used to it" before going

in. She remembered equally well her mother's approach, diving cleanly into the deep end, slicing through the water like a knife . . .

"A murder."

Max's pronouncement fell like a blade on the tense silence, and a collective gasp went up from the others. Frank Wilson sprang forward, his stocky body more agile than Claire would have guessed.

"*What?* Who? Who was murdered?"

To Claire's surprise, Otis Knox began to cry. "It's Mona, isn't it?" he said. "Mona's dead."

Everyone looked at him, and then back at Max, who nodded sadly. "Yes, I'm afraid so. It is Mona."

Another gasp arose from the group, and Claire had a horrible, perverse impulse to laugh. It wasn't that she found the situation funny; it was just the combination of fatigue, tension, and suspense made her giddy, and there was something darkly comic about the reaction of the others, as though they were badly rehearsed movie extras overacting their parts. Real people's reactions to actual events, Claire found, often exemplified every behavioral cliché one is presumably taught to avoid in acting school. This was no exception: everyone stared wide-eyed at Max; even Frank Wilson appeared chastened by the news.

Then he said the thing people say when confronted with bad news: "Are you sure?"

"You mean sure it's her or sure she's dead?" Jeffrey interjected, a smirk on his handsome face. The others glared at him, and Claire thought he wouldn't be winning any popularity contests soon.

"Both, I'm afraid," the big chef replied.

"Oh, my God," Lyle said softly. "What happened?"

Max studied his immaculate fingernails. "She was stabbed."

A little gasp came from Sally. "Oh, my God," she murmured softly.

Lyle stroked her hair and looked up at the chef. "Are you sure?"

Max nodded. "I'm afraid so."

Suddenly Philippe, who had been sitting as if he were made of stone, rose from his chair and emitted a loud, high-pitched wail.

"*Nooooo!* It can't be!" The words shot from his body in a rush, and then he continued his wailing. The sound was eerie, like the howl of an animal.

Just then there was the sound of the front door opening.

"Someone's here," Meredith whispered to Claire. "Maybe it's the police." She sprang from her chair and dashed into the front hall. She returned moments later, followed by Paula Wilson and her son Henry. The boy's face was pale and he clung to his mother's thin arm as the two of them entered. When Philippe saw them, he abruptly stopped his wailing and, sitting down heavily, buried his face in his hands.

"What is it, Frank?" Mrs. Wilson said. "What's happened?"

"It's Mona," he replied in a low voice.

"What about her?" Paula Wilson cocked her head to one side. With her spindly neck, she reminded Claire of a goose.

Her husband avoided looking at her as he spoke. "She's dead."

The words fell like a deadweight upon the assembled crowd. Even Jeffrey averted his eyes as Paula Wilson looked wildly around the room.

"Dead? What do you mean she's dead?" she said, pulling her son closer to her.

By way of replying, Otis Knox pulled a chair over for Mrs. Wilson to sit on. She sat heavily and stared at her husband.

"How can that be? I just saw her last night." Henry Wilson remained standing next to his mother, and gazed at the others with frightened eyes.

"I'm afraid she was murdered," Frank Wilson replied. "Isn't that what you said?" he said to Max, as though accusing him. "That she was murdered?"

Max nodded his big head slowly. "It looked that way to me."

"Have you called the police?" Richard asked, but Max shook his head.

"The phones are out."

Once again Claire heard the front door opening, and moments later James Pewter appeared at the dining-room entrance. He wore knee-high rubber boots and a thick blue parka with a fur-lined hood. Snowflakes clung to the fur on his hood, and his cheeks were ruddy from the cold.

"My phone's out," he said, seeing Frank Wilson and Max standing in the center of the room, but then his eyes fell upon the silent group gathered all around. "What's going on here?"

"There's been an accident," Wilson replied, but Meredith cut in loudly.

"It's no accident—it's murder!"

The historian's face registered disbelief. "Is this some kind of joke?"

"No, James, it's no joke," the innkeeper replied.

"Who's been—who is it?"

This time Max answered him. "Mona Callahan. I found her this morning in the basement," he said softly. "By the looks of it, she'd been stabbed."

"Oh, my God," said Pewter, and once again Claire was struck by the unoriginality of people's reactions to tragedy. "Do you know—" he said, turning to Wilson, who shook his head.

"We don't know anything yet, James."

"Well, we have to get the police—"

"Yes, but we can't!" Philippe broke in suddenly. "The phones are down and nobody can get through in this blizzard anyway."

Jeffrey stood up from his table and stretched himself.

Claire noticed how the white T-shirt emphasized his knotty, hardened muscles.

"Well, I'm going out for a smoke," he said in response to Richard's inquiring look. The older man shrugged and looked away as Jeffrey sauntered out of the room.

Otis Knox rose from his chair and glared at Frank Wilson. "Well, what are we going to do?" he demanded angrily.

The innkeeper studied his hands. "I don't see what we can do until the phone is working."

"Does anyone have a cell phone?" Meredith interjected.

Chris Callahan shook his head. "I have one but the battery is dead."

Richard sighed. "I have one, too, but I purposely left it at home on this trip. I didn't want anyone at the office to be able to reach me," he added apologetically. Claire hated cell phones and had resisted getting one, but now she regretted it.

Lyle laughed softly. Up until now, he and Sally had been sitting quietly in the far corner.

"Wizards of technology, slowly becoming widows in the storm," he said, then lapsed back into silence.

Sally looked at the others through her dark-ringed eyes. "It's from one of his poems," she explained.

"There must be some way to alert *someone*," Otis declared, gripping the back of his chair until his knuckles stood out.

James Pewter glanced out at the gathering blizzard. "I could try to walk into town."

Frank Wilson shook his head. "It's coming down really hard. Even if you made it, it would take them a long time to plow through this."

Otis Knox began to pace the room. "Well, we can't just *sit* here and do nothing!"

Frank Wilson sighed. "We can and we will. One thing we can do is maintain the integrity of the crime scene. I don't want anyone going into that basement."

Meredith groaned. "Oh, *man*! I wanted to check out the crime scene," she whispered to Claire.

Claire shook her head. "You heard what he said."

"But I won't touch anything—I promise!" she whined.

Once again they heard the front door opening, and Jeffrey appeared in the doorway.

"What did I miss?" he asked, a little smirk on his face. Looking at his bloodshot eyes, Claire wondered if it was tobacco he had been smoking. She wasn't sure, but she thought she saw a glance pass between Jeffrey and Lyle as he walked by. He sat down again, ignoring Richard's disapproving look. Philippe began drumming his fingers on the table. For a few moments it was the only sound in the room, until the silence was broken by a stifled sob coming from Otis Knox. He buried his face in his hands, his broad shoulders shaking.

Frank Wilson went over to him and laid a hand on the boy's shoulder. "Look," he said, "we all feel the loss. I wish . . . I wish there were something I could do."

Chris Callahan shook his head and stared out the window. "I really can't believe it," he murmured almost to himself. "It doesn't seem possible."

"Murder seldom does," Meredith remarked solemnly, and again Claire had to bite her lip to keep from laughing. She suddenly felt giddy from fatigue and tension, and since childhood she had an unfortunate habit of laughing at the worst possible moment. The whole scene took on a surreal aspect. Sitting in the dining room as they were, sealed in by the swiftly falling snow, they might have been waiting for brunch instead of the police. It seemed impossible to her that there was a body in the basement, and it even occurred to her that this was some kind of prank, a joke dreamed up by Max, but one look at his face and she knew it was no joke.

"Well, if nobody has any objections, I'm going up to my room," Jeffrey said with a look at Richard.

"I—I think we should all remain on the hotel grounds until the police are contacted," said Frank Wilson.

Jeffrey laughed, a harsh, hard sound, like the scraping of metal on metal. "Where would we go?"

"All the same . . . I think we should all be here when the police arrive."

"Whenever *that* is," Otis Knox muttered.

Max shook his head. "I don't think you have to worry much about that."

Claire looked at the others, and wondered if they were all thinking what she was: that, in all likelihood, someone in this room was a murderer.

Chapter 6

After sitting around in stunned silence, most of the hotel residents finally retired to their rooms, some bearing hastily assembled sandwiches Max threw together in the kitchen. Everyone appeared genuinely dazed and upset by the sudden tragedy; only Jeffrey had the sangfroid to return to the dining room and devour a full brunch. Richard, Claire noticed, did not accompany him, but retired to his room like everyone else. Frank Wilson closed and bolted the door to the basement, much to Meredith's dismay, and declared the area off-limits; so Meredith had no alternative but to retire with Claire to their room.

The snow continued to fall throughout the afternoon and into the evening, burying them all beneath its soft whiteness, smothering all sound outside the building. It was as if life outside the inn had entered a state of suspended animation.

Claire lay on her bed thinking about the inn and its inhabitants as trapped within one of those winter scenes in the little glass containers that you shake to make the snowflakes fall; it was as if some unseen hand were continuously shaking it so that the snow would continue to fall.

Meredith lay on her cot playing with a piece of string. Tying the ends together, she looped it between her fingers to form a cat's cradle, all the while chewing heavily on a piece of bubble gum. Meredith always had to be doing something, preferably several things at once.

Meredith blew a large pink bubble and popped it loudly. "Well, I'll tell you one thing: this girl was killed by someone who knew her."

Claire rolled over onto her right side and propped her head on her hand. "I was thinking the same thing."

"Yup," Meredith continued. "You know how I always say there are two kinds of murders?"

"Cold-blooded and hot-blooded."

"Well, this is a crime of passion or I'll eat my hat."

"You don't wear hats."

"All right, then I'll eat your hat." Meredith rolled over onto her stomach. "Wonder when the phone lines will go back on."

"I don't know. They say it's the biggest storm in New England since—"

"Since the Blizzard of '89," Meredith interrupted. "I know. I just wish someone would *do* something." She sighed. "If Wally were here, *he'd* do something."

Claire felt the sigh echo in her own throat. "Well, we'll just have to think of something to do until he arrives."

Meredith sat up on the bed. "Really? Like what?" The promise of activity always brightened her mood.

"Well . . . let's see."

"We could talk about who might have done it."

"All right . . . well, Max discovered the body."

Meredith flopped back down onto her back and resumed fiddling with her piece of string. "Means nothing. Lots of killers are the ones who 'discover' the body. They either think that will deliver them from suspicion—if they're good enough actors—or they revel in displaying their crime before others."

"Sort of like a cat who drags a dead mouse to your bed in the morning."

"Exactly."

"Well, of course everyone's going to suspect Jeffrey, because he's so rude," Meredith observed. "What the hell does Richard see in him? I wonder."

"Youth," Claire replied. "He sees youth in him."

Meredith shrugged and looped the string over one of her bare toes. "Well, he looks like rough trade to me."

Claire watched as Meredith tried to create her cat's cradle using only her toes. "Rough trade? Where did you learn that expression?"

Meredith shrugged. "I dunno. Some English novel I was reading."

Rough trade. It did seem to fit Jeffrey perfectly; he was the prototype of a young thuggish character out of a novel. There was something melodramatic, Dickensian even, in his surly attitude. Richard was something else altogether, however. Claire had seen plenty of May–December relationships among both gay and straight people, but usually, she thought, there was a better match of cultural values and personality. It was true that Jeffrey was young and good-looking, but she had yet to see why someone as refined as Richard would choose this young vagabond; he appeared to be a dangerous choice. But maybe that was it, she thought; the danger itself could be part of the lure. Without knowing Richard, it was impossible to say. Maybe . . .

"Maybe he's got something on Richard." Meredith's words broke the silence, echoing Claire's own train of thought.

"Funny you should say that. I was just thinking—"

"Of course you were. Great minds, and all that. He could be blackmailing Richard or something, don't you think?"

"It's possible. But what connection would that have with Mona's death?"

"Maybe none."

There was a knock on the door and Meredith, catapulting herself from her cot, lunged to open it. "I'll get it!"

She opened the door, and Claire saw James Pewter standing in the hall outside.

"Hiya," said Meredith.

"Hi. I just thought I'd see if there's anything you need," he said as Claire approached the door.

Meredith stepped to one side to let Claire stand in front of her, but as she did so she pinched Claire's arm.

"Ow," Claire said.

"Are you all right?" James asked.

"What? Oh, fine—we're fine—right, Meredith?"

"Whatever you say." Meredith was back on her cot, the string dangling over her head.

"We're fine."

"Okay." He leaned on one arm against the door frame, and lightly brushed his other hand across Claire's hair. "Just thought I'd check." The gesture was so casual and yet so full of implication that she caught her breath.

He cocked his head to one side. "If you need anything, I'm right across the road."

"Thanks," Claire said. Her brain seemed to be working in slow motion, and she felt confused. Her body, though, was responding; she felt her face flush, and warmth crept up her neck. She met his eyes, and at that moment she could see that he knew she responded to him. He raised his hand again, and she hoped, feared, that he would touch her face. He stopped just short of it, though, and she exhaled in relief.

He smiled. "All right, then, good night." His voice was low and rich, and the hall light glinted off his honey-colored hair.

"Good night."

"Wow," Meredith said as Claire closed the door. "He's *hot*."

Claire looked at her, simultaneously resentful and relieved that she was there. Her presence made it impossible for anything to happen.

"Time for bed," Claire said automatically, but she was thinking about the light reflecting off James Pewter's hair.

Chapter 7

Claire awoke from crowded dreams to the sound of engines grinding. Disoriented, at first she had the impression she was on a jet about to land, but then she opened her eyes. The flowered burgundy border of the wallpaper reminded her where she was, and she rubbed her eyes, trying to recapture her dream as she drifted back into consciousness, but the sound of engines increased in volume, rendering her efforts futile. Lying there, she had the feeling that something about the quality of light in the room was different, and then she realized what it was: pure yellow sunlight streamed through the curtains, which meant it was no longer snowing. Almost at the same instant she knew also what had awakened her: the loud noise outside her window was the sound of snowplows.

Throwing off the covers, Claire reached for her robe, and saw that Meredith's cot was empty. The clock on the bureau said that it was just after eleven; was it possible that she had slept that long? She wondered what Meredith was up to, and was about to throw on some clothes to go look for her, when the door opened and there she stood.

"Good morning, sleepyhead," Meredith said, a term she

had picked up from Claire. Claire smiled—Meredith was obviously enjoying her chance to play the adult for once. Claire had never seen anyone in such a hurry to grow up. If only the girl could slow down and appreciate childhood while it lasted, she thought, but that wasn't in Meredith's nature. She wanted to be everywhere and do everything all at once, and patience was not her long suit.

Meredith flopped down onto her stomach on the cot, resting her chin in her hands. "Do you hear the plows outside? They're digging us out!"

"So I see. When did you get up?"

Meredith shrugged. "Oh, about an hour ago, I guess."

"What have you been up to?"

"Nothing much."

Claire knew from her tone that Meredith was hiding something. The girl was a lousy liar—thank god, Claire thought.

"All right, what did you do?"

Meredith rolled over onto her back. "Promise you won't be angry?"

"I can't promise how I'll feel," Claire replied carefully, "but I want you to tell the truth, so I promise I won't yell at you. How's that?"

"Okay."

"So—what did you do?"

"I went down and saw the body."

"Meredith!"

Meredith shoved her pillow over her face. "You promised you wouldn't yell at me!"

"But you know it was off-limits. Why did you do that?"

"I was *curious*." She said this as though the answer was obvious even to an idiot.

Claire sighed. "All right. Did anybody see you?"

Meredith lifted the pillow from her face and shook her head. "Negative. They were all out talking with the snowplow guys, so that's when I saw my chance and took it." She propped herself up on her elbows, resting her chin on the pillow. "Do you know she was stabbed in the *stomach*?"

Claire was intrigued in spite of herself. It was never possible to be annoyed at Meredith for very long, she had found; try as she might to sustain her anger, it usually withered and dried up within minutes. "Really? In the stomach?"

"Oh yeah. Very sexual, if you ask me. Shades of *Carmen* and all that."

Claire shook her head. What Meredith knew about sex she certainly had not learned firsthand, that was for sure; her intellect so far outstripped her social skills that the girl was hardly a boy magnet—fortunately. Claire prayed that she would not be forced into an early maturity like so many young people these days.

"I don't think this murder was carefully planned," Meredith added.

"Oh?"

Meredith nodded and popped a lemon vitamin-C drop into her mouth. "Disorganized and poorly planned, that's what I'd call this murder," she said as Claire made her bed. With the snow so high, there was no telling when the hotel maid would make it out there—certainly not for a day or two, Claire thought.

"Disorganized? How so?" Claire said, tucking in the sheets and smoothing over the quilt.

"Oh, from the look of the crime scene, I'd say this was a last-minute decision, a spur-of-the-moment killing, probably set off by some incident that caused the killer to snap."

"I see."

"And the stabbing, though effective, was clumsily done. I don't think this is an experienced criminal; quite the contrary."

"Hmm . . . I guess that leaves just about everybody as a possible suspect."

"Yup. It also means the least likely person could be the killer."

Claire stopped to think about the residents of the inn. With the possible exception of poor, demented Jack Callahan, she had little trouble imagining any of them as a murderer. Perhaps her imagination was taking a morbid turn, but it seemed to her that any of them, sufficiently provoked, was capable of murder, even Richard, cultivated and refined as he was; she could imagine him hiding a well of passion beneath that elegant exterior. As for Chris Callahan, his laconic speech and lazy manner could hide just about anything; who knew what resentment toward his sister might be simmering beneath his sleepy surface? There was simply no way of telling . . . not yet, at any rate.

There was a knock on the door. Claire opened it, and standing there in the hallway, a pile of towels in his arms, was Henry Wilson.

"Would you like some fresh towels?" he said. The words sounded carefully rehearsed, and his voice shook a little as he spoke, a thin adolescent tremolo. Claire immediately felt sorry for him—he looked so frail standing there, his arms piled up with towels—and she had an impulse to hug him. The boy had his father's eyes, large and round and rimmed with dark lashes, almost as though he were wearing eyeliner, but he had his mother's tight little mouth, thin-lipped, dour, turned down at the corners. Claire didn't think she had seen the boy smile once since they arrived. She wondered what was going on in that serious little head of his; she thought it was sad for a boy of his age to be so contained within his own lonely world.

"Why, thank you," she said, taking two towels off the top of the pile. He nodded nervously, a few strands of brown hair falling over his forehead. He began to move off down the hall, but Claire, wanting to engage him in conversation, called after him.

"So I see your parents have put you to work."

He turned back to look at her, twisting around awkwardly, and nodded. His movements were jerky, even clumsy, though whether from nervousness or lack of coordination Claire couldn't tell. It was as though the different parts of his body had their own agendas and were only reluctantly giving up control to his brain.

"There's no maid b-because of the snow," he said, "so they asked me to g-go around with towels. I've d-done it before," he added, hanging his head and staring at his feet. "It's not so bad."

Meredith appeared at the door of her room, sucking loudly on a vitamin-C drop. Seeing her, Henry's pale face whitened even more, his eyes dropped lower, and his stammer increased.

"I g-g-gotta go f-finish. S-s-see you later."

He turned and stumbled on down the hall.

"Wow," Meredith said, shaking her head. "That's one messed-up kid."

"I think he likes you," Claire observed.

"Oh, *please*!"

"No, really. He gets even more tongue-tied when you're around."

"Well, I'm no shrink, but that's one screwy kid, if you ask me."

Claire had to agree; the boy radiated emotional distress, and evoked in her a strong instinct to look after him. She thought of his mother, Paula, whose nervous mannerisms he reflected. The boy was so unlike his father, big, hearty Frank Wilson, with his bluff and outgoing manner.

"Weird kids don't just get that way on their own, you know," Meredith remarked as she closed the door behind her. "There's usually a reason . . . makes you wonder about his family, doesn't it?"

"Yeah . . . poor kid."

"Yeah, well, there's a lot of them out there," Meredith replied, plopping down onto her back on her cot, her kinky orange hair spreading out on the pillow, springy as tree moss. Claire knew Meredith's family life was not easy, but she didn't want to press the girl into talking about it. There was a fiercely private side to Meredith, and she had to respect that.

"Well," said Meredith, "are you ready to go downstairs?"

"Just about," Claire replied, pulling on a cream-colored cable-knit sweater.

They arrived downstairs just in time to see the entrance of the police on the scene.

The tall police detective stamped his feet loudly on the mat as he entered the hotel. Claire thought the action was deliberate, his way of taking control of the situation, letting everyone know that he was in charge. She was beginning to understand the ways of New Englanders; they were not as direct as the New Yorkers she was used to, who were always in a hurry and had neither the time nor the temperament to dissemble. But here in New England it was different: people could talk around a subject for hours, homing in on it gradually, like a hunter stalking a deer; sooner or later they would go in for the kill, but until then there was time to enjoy the process.

The detective removed his hat and looked around. He was tall and lanky, with the profile of a hawk: sharp, clean features with a long, thin patrician nose that dropped like a hook at the end, the tip of it shading his upper lip. It was impossible to guess his age: he might have been forty or sixty. His skin, though weathered, was stretched tightly over his high cheekbones; he reminded Claire of Jack Palance, his face as rugged and timeless as a canyon. What made his face really unusual, though, was the merest wisp of a beard on the very end of his chin, a white patch of hair so small that it looked as though it had been left behind inadvertently by a lazy swipe of the razor. At first Claire thought it was a piece of tape or a white Band-Aid stuck on to cover a shaving accident, but then she realized it was hair.

"I'm Claire Rawlings," she said, shaking his hand.

" 'Lo," he replied in a classic New England accent. "I'm Detective Hornblower. Clyde Owens said you sent for me? 'Lo, Frank," he said as the innkeeper entered the hall.

"Thanks for coming so quickly, Rufus," Wilson replied, shaking his hand. The two men stood talking quietly, their voices lowered, heads close together. If Frank Wilson's face was typically Irish, Detective Hornblower's was a map of Scotland: craggy, jagged, and as intimidating as the hills of the Highlands.

"Who's Clyde Owens?" Meredith asked.

"Drives one of the town plows that dug you out," said the detective. "He radioed me to come on over."

"Cool," said Meredith.

"All right, Rufus, I'll help round everyone up," Frank Wilson said, running a hand through his hair, which looked uncombed.

"You want me to help get everyone together?" Meredith asked. "I'm Meredith Lawrence, by the way," she added, extending a hand.

"Rufus Hornblower, at your service." Here was a man who liked children, Claire thought as she watched him shake Meredith's hand.

"Cool name!" Meredith said.

The sherriff smiled. "I wouldn't have agreed when I was your age."

Meredith nodded and sighed. "They made fun of you, huh? Well, kids make fun of everyone . . . teenagers pretty much suck, if you ask me."

He laughed, a dry, thin sound like the cracking of a log being split by an ax. "Are you including yourself in that description?"

Meredith removed the lollipop she had in her mouth with a loud sucking sound. "Well, I'm actually thirteen, so I'm just barely a teenager."

"I see. You're very tall for your age."

Meredith sighed. "I'm very tall for *any* age. I'm five

seven and three-quarters—way bigger than most the boys in my class. And if you don't think *that* doesn't suck—"

"Meredith, the detective has work to do," Claire interrupted. "Sorry," she said to him, "she does get going sometimes."

"But only when I like someone," Meredith interjected, smiling almost flirtatiously.

Claire and Meredith followed Detective Hornblower into the dining room, where Max was serving brunch to the hotel guests. Claire and Meredith seated themselves, but the sound of the front door opening again brought Meredith running back into the front hall. A moment later she came back into the dining room.

"There's something you'd better see," she said to Claire.

Claire went out into the foyer. There, standing in the front hall, was Wally Jackson.

Seeing him was always a surprise; Claire was never quite prepared for the little jolt of electricity that shot through her when she saw his curly grey hair, always a little shaggy at the edges, and his heavy-lidded eyes. He stood there on the threshold in a forest-green parka, his cheeks ruddy from the cold, his breath coming in little white puffs. When he saw her he smiled, and Claire wanted to run up and fold her body into his and just stay like that. But there were other people around, so she resisted the impulse and stepped up to kiss him on the cheek. He startled her by drawing her close to him and kissing her fervently. To her surprise, his hands were trembling.

"Thank God you're all right," he said, holding her close. "I saw the cars outside and didn't know what to think."

"Oh, you mean the police cars."

"Yes. What's going on? Where's Meredith?"

"Here I am," she answered, appearing in the doorway to the main dining room.

"What's been going on?" Wally asked.

"There's been a murder," Meredith replied, swinging back and forth on the handle of the door.

Wally looked at Claire. "Is that true?"

"I'm afraid it is. That's why all the police cars are outside."

Just then Detective Hornblower entered the front hall. "Hello," he said, his gaunt face expressing neither surprise nor interest. "I'm Detective Hornblower."

"Detective Wallace Jackson, Ninth Precinct, Manhattan," Wally said, extending a hand.

"Pleased to meet you, Detective Jackson," he replied cordially, shaking Wally's hand. "You're a friend of Ms. Rawlings?"

"That's right. Is it true you're here—"

"Investigating a probable homicide, yes."

"Can I be of any help?"

"I don't see why not. I always say two heads are better than one."

"What about three?" Meredith chirped from where she stood, still hanging on to the doorknob.

Hornblower regarded her curiously. "Well, there's also the saying that too many cooks spoil the broth."

"I won't spoil anything, I promise!" She let go of the door and approached the men. "I've already made one or two interesting observations, you know."

"Oh?"

"Yup. For instance, I noticed that the killer was—"

"Meredith, if the detective needs any help, I'm sure he'll let you know," Claire intervened.

"Tell him about the murders I've already helped solve!"

"Really?" Hornblower said to Wally, who nodded.

"It's true, actually; she—"

But they were interrupted by the sound of shouting coming from the kitchen.

"Sounds like a fight!" Meredith cried, darting past them toward the direction of the shouts.

Wally, Claire, and Detective Hornblower hurried after

her, arriving in the kitchen just in time to see Otis and
Philippe scuffling, their arms locked like wrestlers. They
grunted and strained, pushing against each other, and
Claire was reminded of two rams in a field, locking horns
over a ewe. Otis was the bigger of the two; he had about
twenty pounds as well as a couple of inches over Philippe,
who was wiry but slighter of build.

Pots and pans shook on their metals hooks, a metallic
rattling like the ripple of a snare drum. Before anyone
could say anything, Max stormed into the kitchen, grabbed
each of them by the shoulder, and pulled them off each
other easily, as though they were children. Bulky as he
was, Claire hadn't realized the full extent of Max's
strength until then.

"Stop it right now!" the chef bellowed, addressing both
of the young men, who stood glowering at each other as
Max held them apart. "I will not tolerate this kind of thing
in my kitchen, do you understand?"

They did not respond, but continued to glare at each
other, until Max shook them as you might shake out a dust
rag.

"Answer me when I speak to you!" he roared. "Do you
understand?"

"Yeah," Otis muttered, and Philippe looked away and
nodded.

Max brought his big pink face close to the waiter's. "Do
you understand?"

"All right," Philippe muttered.

"Good, I'm glad we cleared that up," Max remarked,
releasing his hold on them.

"Wow," Meredith muttered under her breath, and Claire
had to agree that Max's display of strength was impressive.
She couldn't help thinking how easily such a man could
slide a knife into a woman's body.

Chapter 8

After the medical examiner's officers had removed poor Mona's body, Detective Hornblower gathered everyone in the main dining room and announced that he would begin questioning as soon as someone from the state DA's office arrived from Boston.

"Wow," Meredith whispered to Claire. "This must be a big deal."

As everyone cleared out of the room, Detective Hornblower turned to Wally. "You're homicide at the Ninth Precinct?"

"Yes."

"That's downtown, isn't it? East Side?"

"That's right. You know the city?"

Detective Hornblower stretched his long back and pulled at his odd little beard. "I spent some time there," he replied. There was something enigmatic about him, Claire thought, as though he were reluctant to release more information than necessary. Even his movements were guarded, calculated, devoid of excess. Here was a real Yankee, she thought, his profile reflecting the craggy New England coastline.

The assistant from the DA's office arrived in about an hour. She was a young black woman, conservatively (and expensively, Claire thought) dressed in a three-piece wool suit, warm honey brown in color, several shades lighter than her skin, which was the color of dark chocolate. Her clothes were tailored with the kind of style that is always in vogue. Her small, elegant head was set atop an impossibly long neck; she had the classic beauty of African sculptures Claire had seen in art stores on the Upper West Side. Her close-cropped hair accentuated the graceful lines of her neck and the size of her large, luxuriant eyes.

"Rebecca White," she said, extending a hand. Her handshake was firm and lean, an expression of her determination, and did not last a second longer than necessary. When Claire saw the quiet intensity of her gaze, it was clear that here was an ambitious, focused young woman who lacked nothing in the way of self-confidence.

Ms. White sat in as Detective Hornblower questioned Claire, every once in a while interrupting with a question of her own: did Claire hear anything unusual during the night Mona was killed; was anyone at the hotel behaving strangely?

Claire wanted to answer that, in her opinion, everyone at the hotel was a little strange, but she supposed this was a subjective judgment.

If Detective Hornblower minded having Ms. White present during his questioning, he gave no sign of it. He was always gracious, standing politely when Claire entered the room and again as she left it. He was, she decided, of the "old school" of manners, like her father. In spite of her official position as a feminist, Claire enjoyed the courtly deference of such men; at a time when everyone seemed to be rushing to get ahead of everyone else, it made the world feel more civilized.

"What did they want to know?" Meredith asked excitedly after Claire returned from the questioning.

"It was all pretty obvious stuff: did I know the victim;

did I know of anyone who would want to kill her—you know, the usual."

"Yeah, me, too."

The front door to the inn opened and a uniformed policeman entered, stomping the snow off his shiny black knee-length boots. "Detective Murphy, Massachusetts State Police," he said. He was very young, with blond eyebrows.

"Wow," Meredith remarked, "they even called in the state troopers! This must be a big deal."

"They usually do in cases like this," said Ms. White, emerging from the interrogation room. Her voice was as crisp as a fall apple.

"Like what?" Meredith asked.

"Murder cases," replied the trooper. "In a small town like Sudbury there aren't too many killings, you know." He had a classic Massachusetts accent: flat *r*s, languid vowels; he pronounced "aren't" as "ahnt."

"So when there's a murder they always call in the state cops?"

"Yup."

"What, they're afraid the locals can't handle it?"

"Between you and me, after the Ramsey case in Colorado, everyone's a little spooked," Trooper Murphy remarked.

"Oh . . . yeah." Meredith nodded slowly. "I still can't believe they've never even charged anyone in that case."

"Well, nobody wants that to happen in their town, so everyone's being real careful. And we've got resources the local cops don't always have."

"The state crime lab's right over in Sudbury," Ms. White commented.

"Cool," said Meredith.

"Well, we should let the officers get on with their work," said Claire. "Why don't we go up to the room?"

"Aw," said Meredith.

"I brought Trivial Pursuit," said Wally, emerging from the direction of the kitchen.

Meredith brightened. "Okay." She loved Trivial Pursuit.

By the time they had played one game, the pale evening sun was setting over the frozen landscape. Claire went downstairs to get them all some tea. On the way upstairs, balancing the tea tray carefully as she climbed the smooth wooden steps, Claire heard music coming from one of the rooms, and she paused in front of the door. She recognized the taut, compact singing voice of Edith Piaf.

> *Non, rien de rien,*
> *Non, je ne regrette rien.*

As she stood listening, Claire remembered the first time she heard Piaf sing. She was at a party in college, and someone put on a recording of "La Vie en Rose." Suddenly Claire's attention was pulled from the conversation she was having and fastened upon that voice. She had never heard anything like it—not pretty, exactly, but so full of pain and experience and passion. Here was a woman who knew who she was, and who could communicate that directly to an audience, without frills or tricks or even pretty sounds.

The sound of the door opening startled Claire, and suddenly she stood facing Richard. His blond hair was immaculately combed, his blue-and-white pinstripe shirt perfectly crisp and ironed.

"Can I help you?" he said, holding the door open only far enough so that Claire could see part of the bed. To her surprise, Sally sat on the edge of the bed. When she saw Claire, she smiled and gave a little wave.

"I—I was just listening to your Piaf recording," Claire answered, feeling the blood rush to her face.

Richard's face softened. "You like Piaf?"

"Yes—yes, I do."

"Sally does, too." He nodded toward her. "I don't want

to disturb the other guests, but I don't like to travel without my tapes."

"Well, it won't disturb me at all. I was just eavesdropping."

Richard sighed. "With all that's been going on, I'm especially glad I brought my tapes. It's soothing to have something familiar around at a time like this. Do you want to come in and join us?"

"No, thanks," Claire replied, peering over his shoulder to see a tape recorder on the bedside table.

"If you're looking for Jeffrey, he's not here," Richard remarked dryly.

"No, I was just—"

"He disappeared about an hour ago and I haven't seen him since. Said he was going outside for a smoke, but then he never came back."

"Oh, I'm sure he's around somewhere."

Richard looked at her. "My dear, don't concern yourself. Jeffrey has been known to disappear for days at a time. Don't worry; he'll come back when he needs money."

"But where would he go?"

Richard shrugged. "Who knows? Can't be much action in South Sudbury, though if there's a bar scene, you can count on Jeffrey to ferret it out."

Claire felt uncomfortable, as though she were hearing more than she wanted to.

"I'm sorry." Richard sighed. "This can't possibly be of interest to you."

Claire could just hear what Meredith would say in response to this: *Actually, everything is of interest to me.* But she just smiled and shook her head. "No problem—really."

What she really wanted to say was, *Do you think Jeffrey is capable of killing?* But she kept that question to herself.

"Hey," Richard said. "Do you have letters in your bedside table?"

"Oh, the Secret Drawer? Yes, we do. Meredith is enthralled by them."

"I can see why. There are some pretty interesting ones. We found one by someone who claimed to have seen this so-called Woman in White."

"Really? Can I see it?"

"Sure—just a minute." Richard disappeared into his room and came out a moment later holding a letter on hotel stationery. "There's no date, but it looks to be fairly recent."

Claire took the letter, which was written in flowery script in blue ink. "Do you think I could show Meredith? She'd be really interested in this."

"Sure, go ahead, take it. I think they're interesting, too, but Jeffrey finds the whole thing silly—or so he says."

"Thanks," Claire said. She didn't want to get into the middle of Richard and Jeffrey's relationship. "Well, I'll see you later." She started down the hall.

"Let me know if you want to borrow my tapes," Richard called after her.

"Thanks, I will."

When she arrived in the room and found Meredith and Wally absorbed in another game of Trivial Pursuit, Claire took her tea down to the bar. She also took along the letter Richard had given her. As she turned the corner at the bottom of the stairs, she saw Lyle and Jeffrey at the other end of the hall, next to the kitchen. They were engaged in conversation, their heads bent toward each other in a way that looked surprisingly intimate to Claire. They didn't notice her, and she took advantage of this to linger by the front desk.

"No, I'm sure," Lyle was saying.

"But can you believe her?" asked Jeffrey.

"I can't worry about that anymore," Lyle replied with a shrug, then sighed and looked away, in Claire's direction. He caught Claire's eye, so she gave a quick little smile and hurried down the hall. She hoped they hadn't realized she was eavesdropping. She wasn't sure what they were talking about, but she had an idea that it involved drugs.

She pushed open the thick oak door to the bar and took a seat in front of the fire. The room was empty; there were no other customers, and no sign of a bartender.

Claire watched the steam rising from the hot tea, its warmth quickly dissipating into the cold, thin air. She stared into the yellow firelight and felt the mesmerizing effect of the dancing flames, so like a living thing. The hiss and crackle of the fire was a soothing background as she read over the letter.

Can it be possible? Am I going mad, or did I really see her last night? Of course, the fire has us all rattled, but even now my blood turns cold when I think about that thin white figure at the end of the hall, her dress flowing about her like a shroud, even her skin translucent! I can't tell anyone else of this—he would think I am truly mad, of course . . . at any rate, he would use it against me in some way. I know him too well by now, too well . . . if it was Laura I saw, then perhaps it was because we are kindred spirits after all, and both know what it is to have a broken heart.

I can't help feeling that in seeing her, I am also seeing myself, for I, too, sometimes feel I am just a ghost, a wraith wandering these halls, with no future and no past. I wasn't even afraid of her, not really, and found myself wishing she would talk to me, feeling that she would understand me, but she just looked at me with those great haunted eyes . . . poor spirit, caught between two worlds, as am I . . .

The writing trailed off, as if the author had simply lost heart. Claire put the letter back into her pocket. The poor woman—and she was certain it was a woman—seemed so lost, so lonely. Her identification with the ghost was so pathetic. Claire didn't believe in ghosts, not really, but even so she pulled her cardigan closer around her shoulders.

Surrounded by swirling snow and ice, her skin felt so dry, as if it might crack, no matter how much lotion she slathered on it. She stared into the glowing fire.

There were aspects of the letter writer Claire identified with—except that she herself had chosen the solitude in her life. She wondered if her parents' death had caused her to fear becoming too deeply involved with other people. She tended to shrink away from the messier side of human interaction. People could be so clingy, so unpredictable. And now Wally and Meredith mattered so much to her . . . more than she would have wanted, perhaps, but there was no going back. It was as though, after standing on a river-bank for a long time, she had finally dived into the water, and could do nothing but swim with the current. Still, she couldn't help looking back at the receding shoreline from time to time, remembering the security of feeling her feet upon solid ground.

The door to the bar opened and Meredith entered, clutching a letter in her hand. "Look what we found," she said. "It's dated during the big fire two years ago."

Claire took the letter from her, and immediately recognized the handwriting. She read it over quickly.

Dear Secret Drawer,

You are the only one I can write to about this. Such fear and dread fill my heart that I am afraid it will burst. What have I done to deserve this? I feel as though I've been caught up in a whirlpool and am being slowly dragged down to the depths . . . I have been betrayed by those closest to me, and yet how can I think of betraying them? I have been put in an impossible situation, with no one to talk to, and I'm afraid I'll go mad.

"Pretty wild, huh?" Meredith said when Claire finished.

"Yes," Claire answered. "Wait just a second." She fished the other letter from her pocket, and sure enough, the handwriting on the two letters matched.

"Wow," said Meredith when Claire showed her. "Bingo!"

Claire handed the letter back to her. "Yeah. But there's really no way of knowing who wrote them."

Meredith plopped down into the nearest chair. "Sure there is."

"Really? How?"

"Oh, I have my methods, Watson; I have my methods."

Just then Detective Hornblower ambled into the bar. He sat down in one of the unoccupied chairs and ran his hand over his close-cropped grey hair, then tugged at his beard stubble.

"How's it going?" said Meredith. "Any clues yet?"

He shifted his lanky body and shook his head. "I can't really discuss the case, I'm afraid."

"That's too bad," said Meredith, "because I could really be of some help."

"I'll tell you what," he suggested, "if I need some help, you'll be the first one to know."

He sighed and looked around. "Is there anyone around who can get me something to drink?" he said, shifting his weight again. Even at rest, there was a tension in his limbs, a coiled readiness for action.

"I'll go get someone!" Meredith chirped, launching herself from her chair, but just then Philippe came into the room.

"Hiya, folks," he said. "Can I get you something?"

"Any chance of getting some coffee?" the detective asked.

"I think there's a fresh pot on in the kitchen," Philippe replied. "I'll be right back."

"Where's Wally?" said Claire.

Meredith sat down again. "Taking a bath."

"Oh, there's one thing I forgot to mention," Claire said to Detective Hornblower. "I don't know if it's important or not, but the night before last I heard a dog howling."

Detective Hornblower nodded slowly, his big face serious. "When was that?"

"In the middle of the night sometime. I didn't look at my clock."

"I see. Was it nearby, do you think?"

"Yes," said Claire, "it was."

"The Wilsons have a dog," Meredith offered.

The detective swiveled his large head toward Claire. "Could it have been their dog, do you think?"

"Yes, I think so. Was I the only one it woke up?"

"No one else has mentioned it, but they may not have considered it important."

"Even the most seemingly irrelevant detail is potentially important," Meredith declared.

"I agree with you there," the detective replied.

Just then, as if on cue, the Wilsons' dog trotted into the bar, right behind Philippe, who entered carrying a steaming mug of coffee on a tray.

"Here you go," he said, setting it on the table next to Detective Hornblower. The dog stood watching and then lay down at the detective's feet.

"Is this the dog?" he said.

"Yup," said Meredith. "Ugly, isn't it?"

For all its homeliness, the dog was appealing in its own way: its large, dark-ringed eyes were soulful, and it carried itself with a solemn dignity, as if it were unaware of its jumbled potpourri of a body.

"Hey there, Shatzy." Meredith leaned down to pet him. Detective Hornblower reached a long arm over the side of his chair and absentmindedly scratched his ears.

" 'Shatzy' is German, isn't it?" he said.

"Yes," Claire replied. "It means 'sweetheart' or 'beloved.' "

He nodded and took a sip of coffee. "Are the Wilsons German?"

Claire shook her head. "I don't know . . . maybe Paula is. I thought he looked Irish."

Just then Wally entered the bar. His hair was wet and his face had a pink, scrubbed look; he looked much more rested than he had when he arrived.

"Speaking of sweethearts," Meredith murmured, with a little poke in Claire's side.

"Hi there," said Claire. "You look better."

Wally sat down. "I feel better." His glance fell on Shatzy, who had rolled over onto his back. "Is that a dog?"

"Yup," said Meredith. "Ugly, huh?"

"Poor Shatzy," said Claire. "People can be so rude, can't they?"

The dog lifted one floppy ear and let it fall again, closing his eyes with a sigh of contentment. It was clear that he was utterly indifferent to whatever was being said about his appearance. He had all the things that mattered to a dog: plenty of food, a warm fireplace to loll in front of, and an endless stream of people to scratch his ears. All in all, it was not a bad life if you were a dog, Claire thought.

"Well," said Detective Hornblower, "I'd better be going."

"What about that lady who was here?" said Meredith.

"You mean Ms. White, from the DA's office? She left a while ago."

"What was she doing here?"

"Standard procedure in a murder investigation. Well, I'll see you folks later." He stood up. "Thanks for the coffee," he said to Philippe, who was at the bar washing glasses.

"Anytime," the young man replied.

Wally offered to walk him as far as the front door, and Claire could hear the sound of their voices as they stood in the hall talking, presumably about the case.

Philippe wiped off the bar and then brought a mug of hot cider over to Claire and Meredith's table.

"So, do you have a boyfriend?" he said to Meredith.

She looked at him with disgust. "Yeah—*right*," she muttered.

"No?" he said.

"I'm not really interested in boys my own age all that much."

"You like older men, then?" Philippe said as he placed a cinnamon stick in the mug, wiping the sides clean with a linen napkin.

"Yeah, but like *much* older," Meredith replied disdainfully, with a toss of her head in case he didn't get the message.

"Like Detective Hornblower?" Claire offered.

Meredith's face reddened. "Maybe. Someone like him—I like that type."

"Oh, I see." The waiter nodded, exchanging a glance with Claire.

"Were you Mona's boyfriend?" Meredith suddenly asked Philippe.

"Meredith—" Claire began, but the waiter shook his head.

"It's all right," he said softly. "I was for a while, then something happened. I'm not sure what, but something came between us. I always thought it was someone else, but Mona would never talk about it."

"Did you love her?" asked Meredith.

"Look, Meredith," said Claire, but Philippe just smiled sadly.

"Yes," he said after a moment. "Yes, I think I did. The problem was—"

But at that moment Otis came into the bar, and Philippe stopped midsentence and turned away.

"What?" said Meredith, but Claire pinched her elbow and nodded toward Otis.

"Oh," Meredith said.

"Do you have any lemons in here?" Otis said to Philippe in a flat voice, but Claire could hear the buried rage beneath it. "Max needs some in the kitchen."

"Yeah, there are some in the fridge," Philippe replied without looking at Otis, instead busying himself wiping off the tables.

Otis bent down to look in the small bar refrigerator, and Meredith exchanged a glance with Claire. The animosity between the two men filled the room, thicker than the smoke rising from the fireplace.

Otis found what he was looking for and left without a word, and Philippe returned to his post behind the bar. Meredith looked as if she was dying to say something, but Claire cautioned her with a stern look, and she remained silent.

Philippe came out from behind the bar and approached their table. "Want to see something?"

"Sure," said Meredith.

He reached behind his ear, and when he withdrew his hand there was a quarter in it. He let the coin fall into Meredith's outstretched hand.

"Hey," she said, examining the quarter. "Where'd you learn to do that?"

Philippe shrugged. "From my father. He was a circus clown and a magician."

"Wow." Meredith twirled the quarter on the tablecloth. "That must have been so cool when you were a kid. My father's a *lawyer,*" she added with disgust.

Philippe sighed. "We traveled a lot, so I never got to keep one set of friends. It's kind of hard when you're a kid."

"I'll bet," said Claire. Philippe was good-looking and intelligent, but there was something solemn about him—solemn and almost sad.

"What other tricks can you do?" Meredith asked. "Can you juggle?"

"Some. I'm a little out of practice. My dad could juggle

six balls at once, though—and the most anyone's ever done is seven."

"Wow," said Meredith. "Awesome."

Suddenly the lights in the room flickered once and then went out, leaving them in darkness except for the still-glowing embers in the fireplace.

"All *right*!" Meredith cried. "Blackout!"

"Shit," Philippe muttered, then added, "Sorry."

"No problemo," Meredith replied. "I've heard much worse. My evil stepmother—"

But Philippe wasn't listening; he was rummaging around behind the bar. "Now where does Otis keep those damn candles?" he muttered. Claire heard the sound of cupboards being opened and closed again, of cluttered drawers being rifled through. She could see the outline of Philippe's body as he ducked behind the counter to search the cupboards there.

"Ah, here we go," he said at last, and she heard the scraping of a match. There was a flare of blue light under Philippe's face, which looked ghoulish lit from below, like a monster in a cheap horror film. She heard the sound of heavy footsteps in the hallways outside, then the door to the bar opened.

A moment later Max's hulking figure appeared in the doorway, silhouetted against a thin blue slice of moonlight, his bald head shiny in the pale light.

"Who's in here?" he called. "Is everyone all right?"

"Yes—I've found some candles," Philippe replied.

A second figure appeared in the doorway next to Max, and Claire recognized the outline of Wally's broad, sloping shoulders. His head looked almost square next to Max's bullet-shaped pate.

"Looks like we have a blackout," he observed, walking carefully into the room.

"Probably the snow on the power lines," Max remarked. "That's my guess, anyway—that they collapsed under the weight of all that snow."

"Did Detective Hornblower leave?" Meredith inquired.

"Yes, he went home," Wally replied. "Can I give you a hand with those?" he asked Philippe, who was rummaging around behind the bar for more candles.

"Sure, thanks."

"Me, too!" Meredith chirped. "Let me help!"

"So you're all under control in here, it looks like," said Max.

"Yeah, we're fine," Philippe replied as he dug through drawers for some more supplies.

With a grunt, the big chef lumbered off down the hall. Claire could hear the sound of doors opening and closing throughout the building, the patter of hurried footsteps, and the murmur of voices as people attempted to cope with the blackout.

Suddenly she felt something cold and wet being shoved into the palm of her right hand. She jerked her hand away instinctively, but realized at the same instant that the cold, wet object was in fact Shatzy's nose. With a laugh, she felt for the dog's head and stroked his ears. He responded by pressing his warm body against her leg. Meanwhile, Philippe had managed to find a dozen or so candles, and Wally and Meredith were hunting around the room for more candlesticks.

"We have some emergency lanterns in the basement," Philippe remarked, "but I'm not going down there."

Just then Frank Wilson appeared at the back entrance to the bar, carrying a kerosene lantern, which he held aloft as he opened the Dutch door separating the bar from the dining room.

"Everyone okay?" he asked, handing the lantern to Philippe.

"Fine, thanks," Wally replied.

"I guess *he* didn't mind going into the basement," Meredith whispered to Claire. "Isn't that illegal? I mean, isn't it roped off?"

"I won't tell if you won't," Claire whispered back.

The room glowed from the light of half a dozen candles, and now, with the addition of the kerosene lamp, it was quite cozy. Claire got up and put another log on the fire, which had died down to glowing embers. The fire sputtered and sparks shot out from behind the log.

"What can I do to help?" said Wally, lighting another candle.

"I think we're okay for now," the innkeeper answered. "I'm sending a lantern around to each room. Otis is bringing some more up from the basement right now. I'll give you one for your room."

Claire was a little surprised that Otis was willing to go down into that dark place of death, especially given the way he felt about Mona, but she said nothing.

"How long do you think the power will be off?" Wally asked.

"Don't know—depends on how widespread it is, and how bad the damage is," Wilson replied. "And Boston Edison will have to drag people away from their Thanksgiving dinner to fix the problem. That won't be any fun."

Thanksgiving. Claire realized for the first time that it was Thanksgiving—out in the world, at least, but here at the inn, where time seemed to have stopped, it could have been any day at all.

Chapter 9

"**D**o I *have* to?" Meredith lay on her back on the bed, shoes unlaced, pulling at the loose laces.

Claire put down her book, *In Search of Schrödinger's Cat;* Meredith's recent interest in quantum physics had rubbed off on her. "It's Thanksgiving. Don't you think your father will be hurt if you don't call?"

Meredith sighed and rolled onto her stomach. "I guess."

"Then why don't you want to call?"

"Well, it's just that I never know when *she'll* answer the phone."

"Meredith, your stepmother can't hurt you up here."

The girl rolled her eyes. "I know. I just can't stand her. Oh, well"—she heaved herself up from the bed—"better get it over with."

When Meredith was gone the room was very quiet, and Claire buried herself in her book until the girl returned— which wasn't long. Meredith threw herself on the bed without a word, but with a big sigh that expressed her dissatisfaction.

"There," Claire said cheerfully. "Don't you feel better?"

"Yeah, I guess." There was silence while she tied the

two laces together, then looped them over her fingers to form a cat's cradle. Then, rolling onto her stomach once again, she sighed again.

"Yes?" said Claire.

"I didn't say anything."

"You didn't have to. What is it?"

"Nothing."

"Okay." Another silence.

Claire put her book down once again. "Okay, Meredith, what's on your mind?"

"I don't know . . . did you, I mean, could you—well, talk to your parents about . . . stuff?"

Claire thought a moment before answering. "Yes. Yes, I could. I could usually talk to my mother. My father didn't always listen, but I could talk to him sometimes, too."

Another sigh. "My dad . . . I don't know. I feel like he just wants everything to be okay all the time, but it just isn't. And then if there's a problem, he doesn't want to talk about it—like he thinks if he ignores stuff it'll just go away, you know?"

Claire nodded. "Yeah. Yeah, I do know. I had some of that in my family, too."

Meredith's face brightened. "Really?"

"Really."

"What happened?"

"I moved to New York and found a good therapist."

Meredith laughed, and the sound made Claire feel better; it cleared the air, like a sudden shower.

"Wow," she said. "I can't imagine how my dad would flip if I went to a therapist. It would be like—like he'd failed as a parent or something."

"That's too bad. Therapy still has so much shame attached to it in this country. No one feels ashamed of having heart disease or diabetes, but—well, I think there would be a lot fewer heart attacks if everyone had a good therapist."

Meredith's eyes widened. "Really?"

"Oh, that can't be news to you. Even the AMA is recognizing the mind-body connection."

"Yeah, but my dad . . . he even feels guilty about getting a cold."

"Really?"

"Yeah."

"Wow. You know, I once had a cardiologist boyfriend who told me—"

"When was that?" Meredith put her chin on her elbows.

"Before I met you. Anyway, he used to say—"

"A cardiologist. That's so cool!"

"Can I finish?"

"Sorry."

"He used to say that even heart attacks were often literally the result of broken hearts."

"Wow . . . you mean, because people were sad and stuff?"

"Right."

"Jilted lovers, things like that?"

"Sometimes, yes."

"That's amazing. It's sad, too, if you think about it." Meredith's face was solemn, her blue eyes darker than usual.

"Yes, it is."

They were interrupted by the arrival of Wally, who had been downstairs helping Frank Wilson shovel snow from the eaves.

"Hiya," he said, closing the door behind him. His cheeks were ruddy and a light dusting of snow lay on his red-checkered wool cap.

"Do you know Claire used to date a cardiologist?" Meredith answered

"No, I didn't. But then, there's a lot about her I don't know."

"Well"—Claire felt her face reddening—"a little mystery is a good thing."

"A little, yes," he agreed, sitting next to her, "but not too much."

"I'm *starving*," Meredith proclaimed suddenly. "When's dinner?"

"I think Max is working on something now," Wally said, removing his coat. "Shall we go down?"

Meredith hopped off the bed. "Sure! Let's go."

Even though there was no electricity, the stove in the kitchen used natural gas, so Max was able to heat up a pot of soup for everyone's dinner. Meredith insisted on helping, and soon the aroma of beef barley soup floated up through the halls of the inn.

It was a strange and motley group that gathered for a rather pathetic Thanksgiving dinner—soup instead of roast turkey, bread and butter instead of mashed potatoes and gravy. No one really felt much like eating; the mood was anything but festive, and the little group gathered in the big dining room with the central fireplace was rather glum. Even Meredith was subdued, eating her soup quietly, folding her napkin carefully when she was through.

Claire had been looking forward to a few days of not having to answer to people, of getting away from the work of being around people, and now, ironically, here she was stuck with a group of strangers, all in the same boat, all having to deal unwillingly with each other. To counter the tension of the occasion, she ordered a bottle of wine with dinner.

Claire remembered how much her parents had enjoyed drinking, their lives so intertwined with alcohol, remembered cheerful parties full of hard-drinking friends, knocking back glass after glass of Scotch or gin or (for the more delicate) vodka and orange juice. She remembered her father, normally shy and distracted, full of bonhomie and good cheer, making his way through the crowd of people gathered in the living room, "freshening drinks." She could still hear his party mantra: "Can I freshen your drink?" No one in those days, among her parents' friends at least, considered drinking a "problem." Even though AA had been around for decades at that point, no one she knew of was "in recovery."

Well, something was gained, but then again . . . her parents never lived long enough to join "the program" or any other self-analyzing, self-examining movement. Claire tried to imagine her proud, reserved mother standing up in a room full of strangers saying, "My name is Elizabeth and I'm an alcoholic," but such a scene was beyond her. She had heard her father dismiss psychiatrists as "professional navel gazers," and her mother had turned denial into an art form; if she did drink too much, it was always, always controlled; with Claire's mother, control was second nature, as effortless and natural as swimming is to an otter. She ducked and dove through the waves of reality, letting them wash over her like so much flotsam and jetsam. Claire had to admire her. She always had an admiration for people who thumbed their noses, even at reality itself; Claire had to tip her hat to such boldness.

A quote from Goethe came to her:

> *In boldness there is genius.*
> *What you can do, or think you can, begin it.*

She looked across the table at Wally, who sat quietly staring into the fire. What was it she was about to begin? Claire wondered; what was she beginning with Wally, or with Meredith? Together, the three of them formed a kind of surrogate family, even as the people in the hotel formed a surrogate family of sorts—albeit a sad little family, eating soup instead of roast turkey and cranberry sauce. Now that the roads were finally open, both Philippe and Otis had gone home, so Max was serving the soup, with the help of Frank Wilson's son Henry.

Chris and Jack Callahan sat at the corner table; Jack seemed unaware that anything out of the ordinary had happened and was his usual placid self, a white linen napkin

tucked under his chin, staring blankly into space, a little
half smile on his lined face. His son showed no obvious
signs of grief, though Claire thought he was moving even
more slowly than usual.

Lyle and Sally arrived after all the others had already
been served. Maybe it was the candlelight, always kinder
than artificial lighting, but Claire thought the circles under
Sally's eyes looked a little less pronounced; she looked as
though maybe she had a nap before dinner. She wore a
loosely fitting black dress, and Claire thought that there
was a touch of lipstick on her lips, a little rouge on her
cheeks. Lyle wore a thick dark turtleneck, which served to
accentuate the blond sheen of his hair. Sally's thin, nervous
hands shook a little as she reached for her napkin, but she
looked calmer than she had before. That struck Claire as a
little odd, since everyone else was understandably jumpier
than usual.

Lyle and Sally sat very quietly, though, as Max brought
them a basket of fresh scones. There had been no bread de-
livery because of the storm, so Max had whipped up a
batch of scones that afternoon.

The fire crackled warmly, and the candles on each table
cast their flickering shadows on the whitewashed ceiling
of the dining room. It if weren't for the circumstances,
Claire thought, this would be a cozy, relaxed way to dine,
just as people did in the eighteenth century when the inn
was built—without the aid of artificial light, but by candlelight. The soft glow of the candles accentuated the
heavy dark beams above them, sending ghostly patterns
flickering and wavering over the walls. What dark and ancient secrets did these walls hold within them? Claire wondered. And now there was a new secret.

Richard and Jeffrey sat at the table nearest the entrance,
Richard cool and crisp in freshly pressed chinos and a
Brooks Brothers shirt, Jeffrey in a black button-down shirt
and jeans. He sprawled restlessly in his chair, his eyes
searching the room for something to occupy his interest. In

his left hand he held an unlit cigarette, which he tapped impatiently on the table.

"If you want to smoke so badly, why don't you go out and do it?" Richard said in a low voice. Sound in the room carried so, however, that Claire could hear every word they said.

"What if I just smoked it here?" Jeffrey replied with a sneer. "What could they do to me—kick me out?" He laughed and stuck the cigarette in the side of his mouth.

Richard sighed. "Don't you think it's high time you started acting your age?"

Jeffrey removed the cigarette from his mouth and regarded Richard with mock surprise. "Oh, but I *am* acting my age. It's you I'm worried about, Richard. You're beginning to *look* your age, and that's distressing."

Richard's eyes narrowed. "You little shit. I should have . . ."

Jeffrey laughed. "Should have what? Left me on the street where you found me? Oh, please—spare me the melodramatics! It's a little late for that, don't you think?"

Richard shook his head. "Don't you care about anything?"

Jeffrey threw his handsome head back. "Yes, Richard, I do. I care about *moi*. Survival, baby, that's what it's all about. If I don't look after me, no one else will."

"I've had just about enough of you," Richard said, leaning forward; even in the dim light Claire could see his face redden.

"Oh, you have?" Jeffrey replied smoothly. "Why don't you just get rid of me, then? That should be easy enough."

Instead of replying, Richard rose from the table and stalked out of the room. The other guests' heads turned to look, and Jeffrey snorted softly.

"Glad we could provide you with some evening's entertainment." With that he got up and strolled out of the room. Claire heard the sound of the front door opening and closing; she guessed Jeffrey had gone outside to have his cigarette after all.

"Thank you, Max," Claire said as the chef lumbered over to their table with a fresh basket of scones. She passed the basket to Wally, who took one and gave them to Meredith.

Meredith took one and made a face. "E-yew—*raisins.*" She plucked a raisin from her scone, placing it carefully next to her teacup.

"You don't like raisins?" Wally said with a smile.

Meredith scrunched up her nose. "They look like mouse turds."

Claire had heard that one before; Meredith once made the remark within hearing of her stepmother, whose thin body had stiffened immediately at the child's deliberate vulgarity.

Claire thought about Jean Lawrence and her sad eyes . . . it seemed the more she tried to forget about certain people, the more their faces lingered in her mind. It was odd that Ted Lawrence had married a woman like that. Meredith's mother, Katherine, had been the kind of person who made people feel secure and happy just to be around her. She was, Claire always thought, devastatingly competent, but with little hint of superiority; she just didn't seem to see obstacles quite the way other people did. In college, Claire had always marveled at the way honors seemed to fall on Katherine like rain, her star rising brightly in the scholastic zodiac of the English department. Claire didn't mind playing second banana to her brilliant friend; she was comfortable with the role. But now her friend was dead and this strange elfin daughter, an only child who had inherited her mother's brilliance, had somehow been cast up at Claire's feet.

There was someone else who gave her a similar feeling, who had a similar sad, lonely personality, Claire thought, but she couldn't remember who. At that moment Paula Wilson entered the room, and Claire realized that she was the one who reminded her of Jean Lawrence. She had the same haunted look in her eyes; even her body was similar: lean and stringy, as though years of worry had melted all excess fat from her bones. The taut, ropy muscles of her long thin neck stood out when she moved her head; her every gesture was tight and carefully controlled.

She walked up to her son, who was putting another log on the fire. "Henry," she said sharply, and the boy turned abruptly, as if he had been struck.

"Yes?" he replied, his eyes downcast.

"Did you see that all the guests received clean towels this morning?"

"Yes," he answered, still not looking at her.

"Very well, then, why don't you go see if Max needs any help in the kitchen?"

The boy glanced at Meredith, who was slurping up her soup greedily, a scone clutched in her other hand.

"Well, I—" he said, but his mother interrupted by laying a hand on his shoulder.

"Go on," she said in a tone of voice that seemed meant to be kindly but that had a subtle edge of menace.

The boy half shrugged, half shivered, as if the weight of her hand were too much for his small body to bear, then he turned and went meekly in the direction of the kitchen.

His mother watched him go, shaking her head. "He's a good boy, really he is," she said, smoothing her flawlessly coiffed hair over her ears.

Claire couldn't for the life of her figure out how—or why—a woman would spend as much time as Paula Wilson evidently did on her grooming. Certainly she was different from most of the women Claire had seen in central Massachusetts and throughout New England; they all had an unstudied look, a refreshing naturalness.

"He's unusually shy," Meredith remarked through a mouthful of scone.

"He's at an awkward age," Paula Wilson replied, sounding irritated at Meredith for pointing it out.

"What is he—eleven?" said Wally.

"Fourteen," his mother replied. "He's small for his age."

"*I'll* say," Meredith exclaimed. "I'm way taller than him and I'm only thirteen."

"But you're tall for your age, Meredith," Claire interjected.

Meredith sighed. "Tell me about it. It sucks being taller than most the boys in my class. 'Course, they're all a bunch of dweebs, anyway."

Paula Wilson's taut body stiffened even more. Claire could see Wally was suppressing a laugh, and trying hard not to meet her eyes. She was afraid Paula would ask her to explain what a dweeb was, but to her relief, the woman made a little "humph" sound under her breath, then went back toward the kitchen. Out in the hall, Shatzy stood waiting for her, his misshapen tail wagging.

"Ha," Meredith said when she had gone. "She's way weird, if you ask me. And her kid is scared to death of her," she added, biting into a scone.

"You're hungry tonight," Wally remarked. Claire wasn't sure if he was changing the subject on purpose or not. It was true, though; Meredith's appetite came and went. Sometimes she ate so much it was hard to imagine all that food in such a thin body; at other times she picked like a bird, eating so little that Claire would fear she was anorexic.

Just as dinner was winding down, the lights flickered briefly and went on. The sudden appearance of electricity was odd after several hours of candlelight.

"Aw," Meredith said in a disappointed voice. "What a drag—just when we were getting used to it."

"Speak for yourself," said Max as he trotted past their table with a tray of salad. "You don't have freezers full of food waiting to spoil."

"Yes, this must be a relief to you," Wally observed.

"You bet," said Max. "God bless Boston Edison."

That night, on her way up to the room, Claire stopped by the bookshelf in the hall; it was stuffed with paperback novels and travel books, complete with outdated maps, she supposed, and quaint regional attitudes about the world. Wally and Meredith had already turned in for the night; instead of getting the girl a second room, Claire had decided to keep her in with them for the time being. She thought it would be safer, and though she didn't say so to Meredith, she and Wally were keeping an eye on her, making sure they knew exactly where she was at all times.

Claire looked at the books tucked so neatly into the shelves, and, putting her face close to them, smelled the musty odor of browning pages. She pulled one out; its pages were brittle as an old person's bones, soft and crumbling under her fingers. Suddenly she thought she heard a sound downstairs, and since everyone else had supposedly gone to bed, she wondered what it could be. She crept down the back stairs and stopped at the bottom, and then realized what she heard was the sound of someone weeping softly. She thought it was coming from the kitchen, so she tiptoed across the thin hallway carpet. A single light glowed in the kitchen, and from where she stood Claire could see the solitary occupant of the room: Frank Wilson. He sat hunched over the counter, head in his hands, weeping quietly. Claire stood still for a moment, then turned and crept back upstairs. She was pretty certain she was the only one who had heard him—as usual, her sensitive hearing picked up things other people missed—and she wasn't sure she wanted to tell anyone else about it. She felt sorry for him; there was something pathetic about seeing such a solid, strong-looking man consumed by grief. And yet the question nagged at her: why was he crying? It seemed to be a missing piece in a puzzle that just kept getting more complicated as time went on.

She went back to find the book she had left on top of the bookcase. She looked at the title—*Girl of the Limberlost*—and sighed. Everything seemed so transitory, ephemeral, and she supposed that Mona's sudden death had brought this grim fact home to everyone in the hotel. Writing was yet another stab at immortality, she thought: every writer hoped that even when he was long gone he would continue to live on in his books.

And a murderer—what does he want? Claire wondered. The thought came to her unbidden, as though a voice inside of her could not leave the subject alone, but kept worrying it like a dog with a bone. Well, good, she thought as she replaced the book, slipping it in between an ancient-looking French cookbook and a collection of nineteenth-century English verse. Good; maybe if I think enough about it, something will come of it. Again the question formed in her mind.

What does a murderer want?

"If you find the motive, opportunity and means are not far behind," Wally had once said. "Everything we do proceeds from our desires—our motives, if you will—and often that will tell you as much as any forensic evidence."

Claire ran a hand through her hair, took a deep breath, and let it out slowly.

What did the murderer want?

Chapter **10**

Unable to sleep that night, Claire lay in bed staring at the maple tree outside her window. Snow clung to the knot in the tree, an uneven white coating nestling in its nooks and crannies, creating an illusion of white eyebrows and beard on the "face" of what Claire had come to think of as the old wood gnome.

As she lay awake in the dark, every sound seemed to be magnified a hundred times; it was as if her senses were suddenly preternaturally sharpened by the lateness of the hour and the stillness of the building around her. She could hear Meredith's gentle snoring, and she thought of all the ways in which life would disappoint the girl, of the pain that lay ahead as she got older. She remembered her mother saying to her once, "You know, there are things I can't protect you from, and that's hard for me." At the time Claire had only a vague idea of what her mother was talking about, but the words always stayed with her. Claire's instinct was to run interference for Meredith, to step between her and all of the harsh realities of the world—and yet. Not only was she unable to, but it would have been wrong to try. To step back and let what must happen just

happen; that was not something that came naturally to
Claire.

Just then a new sound broke into her consciousness. It
was the sound of a door unlatching, followed by the groan
of old hinges as it opened. There was a kind of shuffling
sound, then she heard the door closing again. Slowly, carefully, so as not to wake Wally, she slipped out of bed and
went to the door of their room, stepping quietly across the
braided rug, its knobby surface bumpy under her feet. She
felt for the doorknob and turned it slowly, trying to make
as little noise as possible. There was a metallic *clink* as the
knob turned; she glanced over at Wally, the moonlight silver on his hair, but he did not stir. She opened the door and
slipped out of the room.

The hall was dimly lit by two brass lanterns at either
end; Claire's room being in the middle, she found herself
standing in the deep shadows between the lights. She
looked toward where she heard the door opening and saw
a tall form at the other end of the hall, walking away from
her, toward the front staircase.

Her heart in her throat, Claire followed, trying not to
step on any of the creaky boards that were so abundant in
the old building. She crept along the hall, sticking to the
side, hugging the wall, on the theory that boards creak
louder in the middle, a theory her brother had formulated
when they were children living in the big house on the
lake. Paul had, during the many family occasions and hol-
idays on which their cousins visited, developed a passion
for sneaking up on their cousins and scaring them. Claire
joined him on many of those forays into familial terrorism;
she especially enjoyed scaring the Miller boys, her cousins
from Toledo. Paul's schemes were inventive and endless;
one night he hid under Donny Miller's bed for an hour,
waiting until Donny was almost asleep before he jumped
out, snorting like a possessed animal. Donny's screams
woke up everyone else in the house, and Claire could still
remember her gentle father alternating between anger and

amusement as he tried to come up with a suitable punishment.

Now she crept along, running her fingers lightly along the wall, inhaling the scent of pine and eucalyptus from a large wreath at the top of the stairs. Something else was mixing with the smell, though—a cologne of some kind, she thought, something with a burned edge to it, like sandalwood. Claire reached the front stairs and looked down the shiny wooden steps. The staircase looked long, too long, stretching down, down into—the thought came to her unbidden—hell.

> Tyger! Tyger! burning bright
> In the forests of the night . . .

She descended the staircase slowly, gripping the hard railing tightly with her right hand. It was only when her hand slid a little on the smooth wood that she realized her palms were sweating. The bare wood steps were like ice under her feet. As she reached the bottom step she heard a sound at the top of the stairs, and turned to see Meredith standing above her, her flannel pajamas hanging loosely on her skinny frame.

"What are you doing?" she whispered, but Claire held a finger to her lips.

Meredith started down the stairs. "What's going on?"

"Shh," Claire hissed.

"Looking for someone?" The voice was right next to her, loud in her ear, and it was all Claire could do not to scream. She turned to see Jeffrey, dressed in a white sleeveless undershirt and striped pajama bottoms. The shirt shone unnaturally white; in the moonlight, it was the color of bleached bones. He carried a parka over one arm.

"Oh, God," she said when breath finally returned to her body. "You scared me to death."

"Did you lose someone?" he said. The muscles of his bare shoulders glistened as though they had been polished.

Claire was uncomfortable being this close to him. She knew Jeffrey was gay, but she sensed a vaguely sexual threat, and she had an instinct to back away.

Meredith took a couple more steps down the staircase and sat down on the stairs. "What are you doing up at this hour?" she asked.

Jeffrey looked at her, a little smile on his handsome face. What was discomforting about him, Claire thought, was that he was so *studied;* every gesture, every expression seemed done for effect. He was like an actor who had carefully rehearsed each response, each line reading, so as to leave nothing to chance.

Jeffrey shrugged, a display of nonchalance Claire didn't quite believe. "I was going outside for a cigarette."

Meredith raised her eyebrows. "At *this* hour?"

Jeffrey laughed softly. "Honey, when you gotta have it, you gotta have it. You're too young to know what addiction is."

"No, I'm not," Meredith snapped. "I live with an addict, so I know *exactly* what it's like."

Jeffrey looked genuinely nonplussed. "Really?" he said, with a disapproving look at Claire.

"Oh, not *her*," Meredith snorted. "I mean my stepmother."

"Your stepmother?" he repeated blankly, looking thoroughly confused now. He glanced at Claire for help. "Then who—"

"It's a long story," she said. "Meredith and I aren't related."

"But you look—"

"I know, I know; we look alike, right?" said Meredith. "That's what everyone thinks."

"Well, not *exactly* alike," Jeffrey corrected. "So your stepmom is a smoker?"

Meredith rolled her eyes. "I *wish* that were all. Yeah, she does that, but she goes in for the hard stuff, too— coke."

"Really? That's tough on you." Jeffrey seemed genuinely concerned. There was something softer in his manner when he talked to Meredith; it occurred to Claire that this jaded, world-weary young hustler might be more comfortable around children than adults.

Meredith shrugged. "I'm used to it."

"Well, don't let me stop you from having your cigarette," Claire said to Jeffrey.

"You shouldn't smoke, you know," Meredith admonished.

Jeffrey looked at her in mock astonishment. *"No,"* he said. "Really? I never knew!"

"Hardy-har-har," Meredith responded, then she sighed. "I don't get grown-ups. They do all this disgusting stuff they know is bad for them."

"Welcome to the world, honey," Jeffrey replied dryly. "Well, see you later." He slung the parka over his shoulders and made his way through the darkened building, trailing a faint scent of sandalwood behind him. Claire heard the front door opening; a cold gust of wind blew down the hall, then the door closed again and all was quiet.

"So were you trailing him?" Meredith said, standing up and rubbing her bony knees.

"Well, not exactly."

"You *were*, weren't you? Come on, admit it. You were spying on him!"

"I heard someone moving around and I was curious, that's all."

Meredith picked up one of her feet and held it against her knee, storklike. "Come on, 'fess up. It's not a crime, you know."

"Fine," Claire said. "Let's go back upstairs."

Back in the room, Claire slipped into bed next to Wally with a sigh. She had missed the feel of him next to her, the solid architecture of his shoulders, where she could lay her head, his rough cheek next to hers, the warm vapor of his breath, so mysteriously sweet, as he slept. Her feet, always

cold in the winter, longed to seek out the heat of his body;
his feet, it seemed, were never cold, and were like a fire beside which she could warm her own. She missed the regu-
larity of his breathing, so soft and soothing, his mouth
slightly open when he slept. Sometimes she would lay a
hand upon his chest so she could feel his heart, that faithful, rugged pump the Greeks believed was the seat of the
soul. But most of all she missed his hands, long and beautiful, containing in their touch all that was good in him, all
that was good in life. After their first time together she had
been unable to erase the memory of his hands upon her
body; they expressed so much. She thought with hands like
that he could have been a sculptor or a pianist or a sur-
geon—but instead he was a detective. Very well, she
thought as she lay in the dark beside him, a detective was
what was needed now, and she was glad he was here.

Chapter 11

Claire was slow to rise the next morning, taking a long time to extricate herself from the heavy dreams that clung to her as she dragged herself back into consciousness. Meredith informed her that Wally had already gone down to breakfast.

"Whenever you're ready, I'd appreciate a little privacy for my chanting," she said, folding her extra blanket neatly at the foot of her cot. Meredith regularly asked for extra blankets, but she always ended up tossing off all her bedding during the night.

"Oh, fine," Claire replied. After a quick shower, she pulled on a green cotton turtleneck and joined Wally in the breakfast room, leaving Meredith to her morning chant. The sound of her voice followed Claire down the long hall.

"Nam yo ho reynge kyo, nam yo ho reynge kyo . . ."

Claire wondered how long it would take Meredith to become thoroughly bored with the whole Buddhist thing, but for now she welcomed anything that might exert a calming influence.

The snow shone crisp and white in the flood of yellow

sunlight that fell on the landscape; Claire had to shield her eyes from the glare as she took her seat across from Wally.

"Hello, sleepyhead," he said, smiling. He looked rested, if a bit ungroomed, his grey hair falling in unkempt curls around his face. Claire especially liked his hair; even combed, it tended to be unruly.

"You're the heavy sleeper," she answered as she reached for the coffeepot.

"What do you mean?"

"Didn't Meredith tell you? You slept through all the excitement."

Wally frowned. "What excitement?"

Claire told him about the nocturnal visit with Jeffrey, and he nodded thoughtfully. For some reason, she didn't mention seeing Frank Wilson crying in the kitchen; she felt a little embarrassed about it, as though she had been spying on him.

"Hmm," Wally said after she finished her story. "Jeffrey said he was going outside for a smoke?"

"Yes, and he had the cigarette to prove it."

"Interesting."

Claire looked around the room. It seemed she was the last to come down to breakfast. Paula Wilson was already busy clearing Richard and Jeffrey's table; and Chris and Jack were such early risers that Claire assumed they had already come and gone. She didn't envy Chris; in addition to caring for his aged father, he would now have to make funeral arrangements for his sister. She wondered how long it would take the medical examiner's office to release the body into his custody.

Just then Lyle and Sally entered the room, and Claire saw that she was not the last to come to breakfast after all. Sally looked pale and a little more distracted than she had the previous night, and Lyle's blond hair looked unwashed.

"I did *too* see her," Sally said as they took their places a couple of tables away.

"Look, Sal—" Lyle began, but Sally shook her head.

"I *saw* her, I said!"

Paula Wilson approached their table with a fresh pot of coffee, pouring them each a cup. Sally muttered something and pulled at a strand of hair. Lyle responded by pushing a lock of greasy blond hair off his forehead. Lyle and Sally were always fiddling with their hair; like a lot of couples, they shared certain mannerisms.

"I saw her," Sally mumbled, reaching for the cream pitcher.

"Who did you see?" asked Frank Wilson as he entered carrying a basket of sweet rolls while his wife returned to the coffeemaker to refill her pot. Claire hadn't seen a sign of Philippe or Otis yet that morning, and it had been Mona's job to serve breakfast.

"She thinks she saw the Woman in White," Lyle replied as the innkeeper placed the rolls on their table.

Frank Wilson smiled. "Oh? Then you're very lucky; not that many people have actually seen her, you know."

"Well, I don't know if Sally's the most reliable eyewitness," Lyle began, but Sally cut him off by banging her fist on the table sharply.

"I *did* see her," she protested loudly. "I saw her coming up the—"

But at that moment the coffeepot slipped from Paula Wilson's grasp and fell to the floor with a crash. They all jumped a little at the sound, but Sally appeared especially startled; she practically catapulted from her chair and stood trembling, staring at the jumbled mosaic of jagged pieces of the coffeepot, the black liquid oozing into the cracks between the floorboards. She stared down at the floor, her hand to her head, a frightened expression on her face. She looked up again at the other people in the room, as if she was searching their faces for something—an answer of some kind, perhaps.

"How incredibly clumsy of me," Paula Wilson muttered, bending over to pick up the broken shards of china.

"Don't do that—you'll cut yourself," her husband said, laying a hand on her shoulder.

She looked at him intently for a moment, then straightening up, turned abruptly away. "I'll get Max," she murmured, her heels clicking sharply on the bare wooden floors.

The chef returned a few moments later with a broom and a dustpan and speedily disposed of the broken china. Young Henry Wilson then appeared with a rag and solemnly mopped up the spilled liquid. It was at that moment that Meredith strolled into the room.

"What's going on?" she said, sliding into the vacant chair next to Claire.

"Nothing, just a broken coffeepot," Claire answered.

"It's probably because of that letter you found last night," Lyle added, pushing a strand of hair from Sally's face.

"What letter?" Meredith chirped.

"Oh, it was one of those letters in our bedside table," said Lyle.

"Yeah, I know; we've got 'em, too," said Meredith. "What did yours say?"

"Oh, it was by someone who supposedly saw the ghost—you know, the girl who wanders around here at night."

"Really?" said Meredith. "Can I see it?"

"Yeah, I guess so," Lyle answered with a look at Sally, who was sitting now, staring at Henry as the boy carefully mopped up the last of the coffee. Her eyes looked haunted, and her lower lip trembled as she sat, hands folded in her lap. Lyle laid a hand gently on her arm.

"It's okay, Sal, it's going to be okay," he said softly.

Claire supposed Sally was unnerved by the murder, but there seemed to be something else going on as well, something she had noticed when she first saw the young couple. There was an intensity about them, as there often is with very creative people, that was both intriguing and un-settling.

She watched as Henry carefully picked up the wet rag and carried it back toward the kitchen. The Wilsons' dog Shatzy greeted him in the hall with a couple of furtive licks on his arm, but the boy ignored the dog, intent upon his mission.

"That boy has entirely too much sense of responsibility," Wally commented after he had gone. "No kid his age should be so damn quiet."

"You got that right," Meredith said as she slathered orange marmalade on a sweet roll. Nothing could ever be quite sweet enough for Meredith; she heaped spoons of sugar into her tea, dipped her cookies in maple syrup, and, when Claire wasn't looking, would eat piece after piece of cake, washing it down with chocolate milk.

Even if the hotel residents had been able to pretend to some kind of normalcy, the yellow plastic tape with the warning POLICE LINE—DO NOT CROSS wrapped around the entrance to the basement made it impossible to forget that the inn was the scene of a murder. Claire walked past it on her way back to the room, and as she turned the corner into the front hall, she saw the tall, thin form of Detective Hornblower. He wore a grey parka that looked too short on his long body, and he was engaged in conversation with Frank Wilson. They were speaking very softly, and Claire couldn't make out their words. She pretended not to be overly interested, but Meredith had no such guile.

"Hey, what's up?" she said, gliding over to where the two men stood.

"Meredith, don't interrupt them," Claire said, pulling her back.

"No, it's all right," Frank Wilson said. "We have to get everyone together, and maybe you can help."

"All *right*!" Meredith chirped. "You can count on me!"

When everyone was finally gathered, in the small dining room adjacent to the bar, Detective Hornblower entered the room, his stern face unreadable. At the detective's request, James Pewter, too, was there. Claire had not seen the historian since the previous afternoon, and she thought he looked more rested and less jumpy than everyone else. Without much preamble, Detective Hornblower delivered his news. The medical examiner's office, he said, had determined that Mona Callahan was two months pregnant.

Everyone received the announcement in shocked silence, all except Meredith, who muttered, "I *knew* it!" under her breath.

With a glance at Meredith, the lanky detective cleared his throat and continued. "There was also the presence of sperm in the victim's vagina . . . and we're going to be asking for saliva samples from all the men present for the purposes of DNA testing."

James Pewter crossed his arms and cocked his head to the side. "Can we refuse?"

Detective Hornblower nodded. "Yes, you can. This will be done on a voluntary basis. However, we can get a court order—"

Jeffrey snorted. "Well, hell, I don't mind. I've got nothing to hide!"

No one appeared particularly amused by his comment. Hornblower ignored him and continued.

"Detective Murphy will be collecting the samples in the taproom, so if the men would remain here, the women can go."

Otis Knox stepped over to the detective. "Was she— was there any sign of . . ." He paused and swallowed hard.

Hornblower looked at him. "There was no indication that she was sexually assaulted, if that's what you were going to ask," he answered gently.

Otis nodded, and Claire saw that he was biting his lower lip so hard that it bled.

Meredith begged to be allowed to watch, but Claire assured her that it would just be a bunch of men spitting into sample dishes.

"Oh, all *right!*" Meredith said with a sigh as they stood in the hall outside the dining room. "I never get to do *any-thing* around here!" she whined as they passed Detective Murphy.

"I'll tell you what you can do," Max said, coming up behind her. "After I'm done here, why don't you come help me in the kitchen?"

"Oh, *okay,*" Meredith said, a tragic look on her face. She might have the IQ of a genius, Claire thought, but she had all the self-dramatizing, melodramatic moods of a typical adolescent.

"I have work in the kitchen," Max said to Detective Hornblower. "May I go first?"

"Certainly."

When Max emerged from the taproom, Meredith followed him. Claire poked her head inside the kitchen for a moment.

"Are you sure she won't be in the way?" she asked.

"No, she can help me prepare dinner," Max replied. "That's funny," he said, pointing to a wooden rack of knives hanging on the wall by the stove. "My big carving knife seems to be missing . . ." He rooted around some more, looking through a stack of cutting boards, poking around in drawers filled with utensils.

As he was doing this, Frank Wilson walked into the kitchen. "You didn't miss anything," he said to Meredith. "It was just spitting into jars."

Meredith shrugged. "Whatever."

"Hey, Frank," Max said, "have you seen my carving knife?"

Frank Wilson shook his head, his lips tight, a distracted look on his broad face. "Maybe you misplaced it during the blackout," he commented vaguely, and wandered out again.

"I can't understand it," Max muttered, rifling through

yet another drawer, the kitchen utensils rattling as his big hands pawed through them.

"Maybe you should tell Detective Hornblower," Meredith suggested.

Max stared at her, his blue eyes wide. "Really? You think—do you really think so?"

Meredith shrugged. "Sounds likely to me. If you ask me, it was a pretty big knife that stabbed her."

Max's pink face turned pale. "Oh, *Gott in Himmel* . . . you mean maybe they used the knife—my knife . . ." His face darkened again and he frowned angrily. *"Schweinhund . . . es ist wirklich unglaublich."* He lumbered heavily out of the room, muttering to himself in German.

Meredith turned to Claire. "Well, I don't want to be morbid, but don't you think it's logical?"

"Yes," Claire had to admit. "I do."

Meredith wanted to wait around to see how Max's announcement would be received, but Claire suggested a walk. She felt the girl had been cooped up inside too long, and she herself was feeling a little stir-crazy. She would have suggested they drive into town, but she didn't trust her old diesel Mercedes to start up in this weather without a lot of coaxing, and she didn't have the energy. Wally had taken the train up, so her car was all they had for transportation.

"Where can we *go*?" said Meredith when Claire brought up the idea of a stroll outside.

"Oh, we can just walk around the woods. Or how about the mill; we can go over and look at it in the snow. Wouldn't that be fun? Maybe we can find a sledding hill somewhere. I'll bet there's a sled somewhere in the hotel."

Meredith sighed as she pulled on her red down jacket, a present from her father. Meredith loved wearing red, even though, with her orange hair, Claire thought it made her look like a multicolored lollipop.

"Don't forget your earmuffs," Claire said. Meredith had a tendency to get earaches in cold weather.

"Earmuffs, check," Meredith replied, sliding them on over her grey wool hat.

They pushed open the heavy front door and stepped out into the thin wintry air. A frigid blast hit Claire square in the face, taking her breath away.

"Wow, this is intense," said Meredith as they picked their way across the frozen landscape, their boots crunching against crusty snow. The ground was now so covered in its thick whiteness that Claire could not imagine it any other way. For some reason, she felt curiously alive in this deep freeze of winter.

"Hey," said Meredith, "earth to Claire. Where are we going, anyway?"

Claire stopped walking. She realized that she had become totally lost in her thoughts, just wandering along without thinking where they were going.

"Sorry," she said. "Want to go see the mill?"

"Whatever," Meredith replied. "It's damn cold out here." Claire ignored the girl's attempt to get a rise out of her; "damn" was hardly a word worth getting upset about.

They walked across the road and up the little hillock that led to the mill house. The mill wheel turned on and on, as inexorable as time itself. The heavy wooden paddles groaned and creaked, pushed upward by the rushing water underneath, the stream bubbling and gurgling below. Claire stood staring at the turning wheel, the wind cold against her cheeks, mesmerized by the slow, rhythmic motion.

The wind was bitterly cold, a biting, frigid blast of northerly air that swept across the open field. Claire folded her arms across her chest, pushing her hands into the armpits of her jacket to warm them. She looked across the bare, hard stubbled wheat field, layered with snow blowing off the brown stalks that stuck up through the snow. It came off in wispy white gusts, like sea spray.

Meredith was walking all the way around the building, standing on her tiptoes to peer in the windows.

Claire looked at the mill wheel, and it occurred to her that it appeared to be turning more slowly than it was when she had last seen it. Was it her imagination, she wondered, or was there an unevenness to the motion of the big wheel as it rotated on its thick iron axle? Claire took a step closer, standing at the brink of the stream, and peered across the water at the gears of the wheel.

There was an odd sound, a sort of ker-*chunk,* ker-*chunk,* that didn't seem right to her. She looked closer, and then she saw it: wedged in the gears of the big wheel, its blade twisted and rusting, was a long-bladed kitchen knife.

Chapter 12

"O h, *man*," said Meredith, standing beside Claire, shivering as they were hit by another icy gust of arctic
wind. They stood watching Detective Hornblower and
Wally working to extricate the knife from the gears of the
mill wheel. "This is totally outrageous."

"What is?" said Claire. "Do you mean the weather?"

"No," Meredith replied, wrapping her thin arms around
her body. "I was talking about your discovery—the knife.
It's awesome—talk about an important clue!" She covered
her mouth with a mittened hand, blowing into it, sending a
thick white cloud of breath into the air. Her mittens were
red with white snowflake patterns on them, and Claire was
reminded once again that Meredith was after all just a child.

"Well"—Claire dug the toe of her boot into the snow—
"there aren't likely to be any fingerprints on it at this point.
And even if there were, it couldn't really prove anything."

"Maybe not," said Meredith, "but it's still way cool that
you found the murder weapon."

"If it *is* the murder weapon."

Claire watched as Hornblower, his legs held by Wally
and Detective Murphy, leaned out over the rushing water,

attempting to wrest the knife from the gears of the wheel. She was worried he was going to slip and fall into the stream, but Wally had a firm hold around his waist. Finally he succeeded in untangling the knife and was pulled back to safety.

Detective Hornblower brought the knife over to where they were standing, a solemn expression on his long face.

"Do you think that's it; is that the murder weapon?" Meredith asked. Unable to contain her excitement, she hopped up and down a little as she talked, her breath coming in little frozen gusts.

"Oh, I can't answer that," he replied. "Forensics will have to determine that. It looks to be about the right size," he added, dropping the knife carefully into a clear plastic bag, the kind you might use for storing leftovers. Claire suddenly had an image of the detective's refrigerator, stuffed with plastic bags full of murder weapons and evidence: here a screwdriver, there a hair sample, a bag of blood-stained fabric in the vegetable bin.

That led her to wondering if he had a wife at home, someone to look after him. Not that she was particularly attracted to him, but something in him awakened her maternal instincts, so long dormant, now brought to life again by Meredith's presence in her life. His sad eyes, the distracted, faraway look that he usually disguised with all that New England austerity—all of this pulled at something inside her.

They walked back to the inn, where they were greeted at the door by Max.

Detective Hornblower held up the plastic bag. "Is this your missing knife?"

The chef peered at it. "I think so. It's a little hard to tell now." The knife was badly twisted and the tip had broken off. "Yes, that is it," Max concluded, after studying it. "You can see the manufacturer's name on the label. I order all knives from them; there is no better to be found."

If it was good enough for Max, Claire thought, then perhaps it was good enough for a murderer.

"Well, we'd better get this down to the lab," Detective Hornblower said, handing the plastic bag to Detective Murphy. The state trooper took it gingerly, as though it contained nitroglycerin.

"I can take it to the lab," he said. "I'm going over there now anyway with these DNA samples."

"All right—thank you," Hornblower answered, adjusting his worn fedora on his head.

"Do you think you'll lift any prints from the knife?" Meredith asked as the state trooper left. A big gust of wind blew in as the front door opened and closed, bringing a few stray flakes of snow that swirled about and then settled on the floor.

The lanky detective shook his head and pulled absently at his little beard. "Probably not. That knife's been through a lot. And even if we do," he added with a glance at Max, "they won't necessarily point us in the right direction."

"Oh, I *see*—right," said Meredith. "Because if it's Max's knife it'll be sure to have his prints on it—right?"

"Among other people's, I would think," Wally added. "Lots of people have access to the kitchen."

"Right," Hornblower agreed. "Any prints we find are likely to be inconclusive as evidence. "Still," he sighed, "it's worth a try." He looked around as though he were looking for someone, then pushed his hat back and scratched his head.

Just then Frank Wilson entered the hall and approached the detective. "Have you had lunch yet, Rufus?"

"Well, no, but I don't think . . ." Hornblower replied wistfully.

"There's some chicken soup left over from last night."

"Well, I don't . . ." He licked his lips and shrugged.

"Come on—you look hungry," the innkeeper said, clapping a hand on his shoulder.

Claire thought it was a rather familiar gesture for a potential murder suspect to be making toward the detective in charge of the investigation, but Hornblower didn't seem to mind. He sighed gratefully.

"Thanks, Frank. I am a little hungry, I guess."

"How is it they know each other?" Meredith whispered as the two men went to the kitchen. Max trotted after them, rubbing his big hands together.

Wally shrugged. "Small town, I guess."

Now that the roads were cleared, curiosity seekers began driving by the inn, drawn no doubt by reports of the murder in the local paper. Some of them took pictures or just stopped their cars and stared, though when they saw the police cars parked in the lot they usually moved on. A reporter from the local paper came to the hotel hoping for quotes from the residents, but Frank Wilson turned her away, saying he didn't think it would be appropriate, since any of them might be potential suspects. She was a young, intense-looking woman with horn-rim glasses and serious dark eyes, which widened behind the thick lenses when he said this. She held a small tape recorder in one gloved hand, a yellow legal pad under her arm. Claire stood watching from the hall as the young woman, biting her lip, tried to reason with the innkeeper. He was polite but firm, suggesting she speak to Detective Hornblower instead. Finally the woman pocketed her little tape recorder and left, lifting her feet carefully as she negotiated the icy patches on the concrete path to the parking lot.

Meredith was angry when she heard the woman had been sent away. "Oh, *man*! I would have talked to her; why didn't you come get me?" she said, looking up from the book she was reading, *Zen in the Art of Archery*. She lay on her back on her cot, her shoes in the middle of the floor where she left them, her wool socks hanging loosely on her feet.

"Maybe Frank's right," Claire said. "Maybe it's best none of us talk to her."

"Oh, *man!*" Meredith repeated, kicking at her pillow with her heel. "I never get to have *any* fun!"

Claire sat on the edge of the bed. "Would you rather go back to Connecticut?" It was a low blow, but she wanted the girl to be more appreciative; she needed to shake her out of this adolescent selfishness.

"*No,* I *don't,*" Meredith replied. "You *know* I don't!"

"Then stop complaining."

She wondered if perhaps she should send the girl back to her father; maybe it wasn't safe here, even with Claire and Wally keeping an eye on her. She left Meredith to her book and went back downstairs, where she found Frank Wilson tearing apart a cardboard liquor box to make a sign, which he hung on the front door: CLOSED. He came back into the hotel, stamping the snow off his feet, and sighed heavily.

"I don't want to sound callous or insensitive," he muttered, "but this couldn't have been worse timing for business." He looked at Claire. "Do I sound insensitive?"

"You're just being honest," she answered.

The innkeeper sighed. "Most people who come here have no idea how difficult it can be to keep a place like this going month to month. They don't think about overhead."

"Is yours very high?"

"Salaries, real-estate tax, supplies, repairs. Yeah, pretty high. Repairs alone on an old building like this . . ." He shook his head.

"Oh, right."

"And if I go under, not only do all my employees suffer, but the town will lose a lot of out-of-state tourist dollars. Oh, well . . ." Wilson brushed a few flakes of snow from his shoulder. "Hopefully we'll be able to reopen soon."

"What's stopping you?"

Wilson shook his head. "Nothing, I guess . . . just a sense of propriety. It doesn't seem right until . . . well, at least until Mona's been properly buried." His face suddenly crumpled and there was a catch in his voice as he said these words. He turned away quickly, but Claire could see that he

was on the verge of tears. She remembered seeing him
weeping in the kitchen and it was so obvious that she wondered why she hadn't seen it before: he, too, had cared
deeply about Mona Callahan.

The sun was setting earlier each day now, and a little after
five o'clock Claire sat alone in the bar, working on a cross-
word puzzle. Wally and Meredith had both fallen asleep upstairs, Meredith snoring away on her cot, Wally sprawled
out on the bed, a pillow over his head to drown out the
sound of Meredith's snoring. Claire took a sip from her
mug of Sam Adams. Alcohol loosened something inside
her, making her more responsive to life as it was, not as she
felt it ought to be. Her need to judge things carefully disappeared under its influence and she was content to merely
observe; to watch the world flow by in all its disturbing
sound and color.

She took a sip of the beer, cold and sharp on her tongue.
No wonder Protestants reputedly drank so much, she
thought: it was the only way they could loosen their relentless grip on themselves, letting go for a little while of the
damnable need to do, do, do—this drive for achievement
that Claire had always bought into but which lately made
her a little dizzy . . . she wondered if she would ever be able
to stop tormenting herself for all the things she hadn't
done—or, worse yet, for the things she would probably
never do.

A candle burned on the table in front of her. Claire stared
at the calm, still point of the flame, undisturbed by any
breeze. She gazed into the blue center of the wick, surrounded by the yellow flame, which cast a circular pool of
light all around.

Claire watched as the candle shuddered and flickered
momentarily, blown by an unseen draft. Mona Callahan
had died as a result of someone else's passion—the fire that
destroys, even as her body contained within it the seed of
life. Had that person also been trying to stem the flow of

life from her womb? Meredith could be right—the stabbing in her abdomen would be guaranteed to snuff out not only the mother's life but also the life of her unborn child.

Fire in the belly.

Claire sighed. Poor Mona Callahan had sacrificed her life, perhaps—her candle put out by an unseen hand, just as this one was at the mercy of an invisible wind. The hand was unseen as yet, though sooner or later, she believed, every hand will reveal itself to the right observer. Claire only hoped when it happened, the observer would know what to look for.

As she left the bar, Claire walked past the small dining room adjacent to it and heard the sound of voices inside. It was two men talking, but that wasn't what caught her attention. What made her stop and listen was that they were speaking German.

"Ich bin böse, aber du bist auch böse."

Claire recognized Max's voice. German had been her second major in college, and though she had lost some of it, the words were simple and she was able to translate: "I'm evil, but you're evil, too."

The other man answered, his voice low and urgent. *"Vielleich, aber was noch kann ich tun?"* ("Maybe, but what else can I do?")

Max sighed. *"Es ist gerade schade."* ("It's really too bad.")

There was the sound of a chair scraping against the floor, and Claire sprang away from the door and tiptoed quickly around the corner. She started up the stairs, but halfway up, bent down to peer through the slat in the banister at the two men as they left the room. As she had thought, one was Max von Schlegel. The other was Frank Wilson.

Chapter 13

After dinner Claire and Meredith were lying on the bed playing To Hell and Back with a deck of cards Claire had borrowed from Frank Wilson. The cards were dog-eared, with tattered edges, their surface sticky from years of handling. The jokers lay discarded in a pile, grinning up at them wickedly.

"Ha—gotcha," said Meredith, picking up the pile of cards she had won.

Wally entered the room; he and James Pewter had been out helping Frank Wilson dig his car out from under a snowdrift. "What kind of person would kill a pregnant woman?" he said, shaking his head as he closed the door.

"Well, the question is, did they know she was pregnant?" Claire said.

"Bet they did," Meredith remarked, shuffling the cards. "I mean, look where she was stabbed—verrry Freudian, if you ask me."

Claire tended to agree with Meredith; the placement of the stabbing did not appear to be accidental, but still, the wrong assumption could lead to fingering the wrong suspect.

"What was it that author of yours said about coincidence?" said Wally.

"Oh, you mean Willard?" Claire answered. Willard Hughes was full of little jewels of wisdom about life and art. "He said that coincidence is far more prevalent in real life than in fiction. In fiction, readers will not easily overlook your use of coincidence; in life, no one questions it."

"Right," Wally said, sitting in the green armchair by the window. "And the human brain is always looking for a way to impose order on the chaos that is life."

Meredith shook her head. "Maybe . . . but what if this killer is a case of life imitating art?"

Wally nodded thoughtfully. "I had an instructor once at the academy who said that if you smell a rat, it means there's a rat."

"Hmm," said Meredith. "And how exactly does that apply here, do you think?"

Wally leaned back and crossed his arms. "Let me put it this way: the scent of rodent is strong in the air."

"But we'll know more when the DNA tests come in," Claire pointed out.

Wally shrugged. "Maybe. But they may not be able to draw any useful conclusions from them either—who knows?"

"The Mona Lisa smile," Meredith muttered as she picked up her cards. "Very mysterious and alluring. Someone fell for that smile big time—and then killed for it."

Later, in bed, Claire looked out the window at the maple tree, a dark form in the darkness. She lay awake for some time watching Wally sleeping next to her, captured by the gentle rhythm of his chest rising and falling. She watched his face, so peaceful in repose, the worry lines on his forehead smoothed away by the soft hand of sleep.

She snuggled deeper under the covers and rubbed her toes together under the blankets, feeling the softness of the flannel sheets. Her toes were always cold, little icicles

Wally called them. She wrapped them around his feet, which were always warm. She watched the snow drifting down outside the window, the flakes settling on the branches of the maple tree, soft as cats' paws. Even as a child, she loved the sight of falling snow, and lying awake listening to her parents moving about below her was the most comforting and peaceful feeling she knew. She would lie tucked away tightly in bed, safe under the covers, with her parents downstairs keeping watch over her, going about their business, the floorboards of the Cape Cod house creaking under their feet.

She would hear the soothing sounds of their voices through the pine-paneled walls in her second-floor bedroom, where she lay in bed, still and silent, listening. She would listen for the clink of ice in a tumbler as her father poured himself a drink, or the sound of her mother's laughter as she joined in with the audience watching Johnny do his monologue. Her mother had a boisterous, unfettered way of laughing, and her father always said it was contagious. As a small child Claire used to wonder how laughter could be contagious, like a disease. She imagined little floating spores of contagious laughter infiltrating other people's lungs, causing them to suddenly break out in the same boisterous braying as her mother.

She wondered what Meredith's memories of her mother were. Did she hear her laughter when she lay in bed at night? Was there an unbridgeable gap of sorrow between her and her memories of her mother? Claire's parents had been gone now for ten years, and she was only now beginning to bridge that gap.

Claire remembered Meredith's mother very well from their days at school together. What stuck in her mind even now was her friend's extraordinary magnetism. She could not imagine Katherine without her "acolytes," her faithful little band of followers, all a little jealous of each other, all jockeying for position, for the spot closest to the fire— nearest to her. She did give off a kind of fire, a heat; you felt warmer in her presence. She was so full of purpose, direction, passion, and the force of her personality pulled others along in her wake. Meredith had inherited some of this fire, only in her case she had turned out to be a loner, an odd, ungainly child without her mother's grace.

Wally sighed and turned over in his sleep, his shoulder jutting into the half-light like the silhouette of a mountain. And what of his loss—his wife—how could Claire ever hope to understand what that must feel like? Sometimes she thought that what really united the three of them—her, Meredith, and Wally—was their sense of loss, of being left standing, stunned and dazed, suddenly without the people who mattered to them most.

One of the koans from Meredith's book on Zen Buddhism sprang into her mind: *What is the sound of one hand clapping?*

A koan, Meredith explained to her, is a seemingly insoluble puzzle that can only be deciphered by giving one's self over to the mystical, sometimes obtuse, apparently contradictory tenants of Zen Buddhism. The riddle of the clapping hand was a famous one, and Claire had heard it before. But now another phrase took its place in her mind.

What is the sound of one hand stabbing?

When Claire came down to breakfast the next morning, Chris and Jack Callahan were just finishing up. As usual, they were the first ones up in the morning, it seemed. Meredith was upstairs taking a shower, with Wally in line after her.

"Good morning," Chris said as Claire entered the dining room. He sounded relaxed, even cheerful. She hadn't seen much of him the day before; he spent most of the day in his room talking on his cell phone. After going into town for new batteries in the morning, he had spent the afternoon making funeral arrangements for his sister. It was to be held in Darien in a week's time, and there were relatives and friends he needed to call, as well as booking the church. It seems Mona had been a devout Catholic, and was well known in her local parish for her charitable deeds, or so her brother said.

"Good morning," Claire said, taking a cup of coffee from the sideboard over to her table. Understandably, Frank Wilson had not yet hired anyone to replace Mona, and the guests were doing their best to make things easier on the staff.

Jack Callahan smiled at Claire and gave a little wave. His eyes were cloudy, but he, too, looked cheerful and rested. The more she saw of them, the more Claire thought that the father mirrored the moods of his son. Claire noticed that Jack held something in his hand.

"What have you got there, Jack?" she asked.

"Oh, it's one of those letters from the bedside table; you know, the 'secret drawer,' " Chris answered.

"Really?"

"Papa found it last night and for some reason he's attached to it. I don't even know if he understands any of it, but I figure it can't hurt if he wants to carry it around for a while. Right, Papa?"

Jack swiveled his head toward his son. "She died, you know."

"Yes, Papa," Chris answered softly. "She died."

Claire wasn't sure if he was referring to Mona or someone in the letter. "Can I—can I see it?" she asked.

"Can Claire see the letter, Papa?" Chris said, gently prying the paper from the old man's hand. Jack put up no resistance, but watched as his son handed the letter to Claire.

The handwriting was firm—the pen a ballpoint—and looked to Claire very masculine. It was short and to the point:

I can't help it—I love her. So I am a prisoner like everyone else in this damn place—a prisoner of love. Why we don't all just rise up and leave I don't know; it's as though we're trapped by our own lassitude,

*our failure of courage. And my slavehood is worst of
all, because as long as she's here, I'll never leave—
never. Why hope runs so rampant within me is a mystery to me, but somehow it does. I keep thinking,
imagining, that someday she'll see beyond my appearance to who I really am, and then she'll love me.
Until then, I'm doomed to follow her about like a
poor pathetic dog, waiting for any scrap of affection.*

"Thanks," Claire said, handing the letter back to Jack.
Though she had no way of proving it, the letter made her
think of Otis Knox—especially the reference to his appearance, since she felt instinctively from the first that he
was self-conscious about his harelip.

Henry Wilson appeared at the door to the breakfast
room with a basket of muffins, which he placed on Claire's
table before scurrying from the room just as Meredith
made her entrance. Her hair was still wet from her shower,
and little droplets of water fell on her shoulders as she sat
down. Wet, her hair was the color of a tarnished penny.

"Meredith, you should have dried your hair," said
Claire. "You don't want to get sick."

Meredith rolled her eyes. "You have perhaps heard of
the *germ* theory of disease."

"Yes, but getting cold can lower your resistance," Chris
Callahan pointed out as he dug out a slice of grapefruit for
his father. The old man chewed it slowly, puckering his
lips, his pale eyes watering.

"Whatever," Meredith said with a shrug, diving into the
basket of muffins. "Poppy seed—awesome!" she exclaimed, taking one. "Hey, did you see the *Seinfeld* episode
where Elaine tests positive for opium because she's been
eating poppy-seed muffins?" she asked Chris.

"I don't own a television."

Meredith's eyes widened. "Really? Wow. That's
wild . . . wow."

"Well, Papa, time to go for our morning walk," Chris

said, taking his father by the elbows and lifting him out of his chair.

As the two of them made their way slowly out of the room, Meredith shook her head. "Wow. Imagine—no television."

Just then Lyle and Sally came into the room. Sally did not look good. In fact, Claire thought she looked awful. Her face was strained, and shockingly white next to the blackness of her hair, as though she had been totally drained of blood. With her straight jet-black hair and thin lips, Sally really did look like a vampire.

With a nod to Claire and Meredith, she and Lyle took some coffee from the sideboard and sat down at their table. Sally ran a hand through her disheveled hair. Her hand trembled as she reached for her coffee—then, suddenly, she groaned and pitched forward, as if shoved from behind, over the table, her head hitting it with a clunking sound. Lyle stared at her for a moment as if he couldn't quite register what had just happened, then he leaped to his feet.

"Sally, what's wrong? What is it?" he cried, grabbing her by the shoulders in an attempt to pull her upright. She just groaned, and her eyes were closed.

Lyle looked around the room wildly. "Help!" he shouted, but Claire and Meredith were already on their feet.

"Meredith, go call 911—quickly!" Claire barked as she negotiated the maze of tables between her and Lyle.

"Right!" Meredith replied, her face almost as white as Sally's. She lurched out of the room, rapping her shins against table legs as she went.

When Claire reached Sally, the first thing she did was feel for a pulse. The girl's skin was clammy; in spite of the coolness of the room, droplets of sweat clung to her forehead.

"What's happened?" Lyle whispered as Claire felt for a pulse in Sally's neck.

"Shh," she commanded, locating a faint, ragged pulse. The girl's breathing was rapid and shallow, and when Claire gently lifted her head from the table, she saw that her eyes had rolled up into her head.

Lyle stood by, wringing his hands and moaning softly.

"Oh, Sally, what have you done?" he murmured, rocking back and forth, shaking his head.

"Is this from a drug overdose?" Claire asked.

"I don't know," he wailed. "I thought she was done with that—we both were," he added, seeing Claire's disapproving look.

Meredith came rushing back into the room, followed by Frank Wilson.

"The ambulance is on its way," he said. "What's happened here?"

"She just—collapsed," Lyle moaned. "She felt a little dizzy and nauseous this morning . . . then we were sitting here and—you saw it—she just fell forward all of a sudden."

"Is she alive?" Meredith asked, her eyes gleaming.

"Yes," Claire replied, "but her pulse is very weak."

"Should we do CPR?" Lyle asked.

"I don't think so, unless her heart stops," Claire replied.

They heard the faint wail of a siren in the distance, a sound that grew rapidly louder as the ambulance approached. Claire pulled back the curtain to look out at the red-and-white vehicle barreling down the street and rounding the curve in the road by James Pewter's house. With a loud squeal of brakes it pulled into the driveway and jolted to a stop. One paramedic shot out of the cab as two others emerged from the back carrying a stretcher.

Claire met them at the front door, with Frank Wilson following right behind her. "She's been unconscious for about seven minutes," she said as she followed the paramedics into the dining room. "Her pulse is faint and irregular," she added, suddenly feeling as if she were on an episode of *ER*.

"Any known food allergies?" one of the paramedics asked as the other two lifted Sally onto the stretcher. She was a stern-faced woman of fifty or so, and evidently was in charge. She had a body like a female golf pro: stocky, solid in the hips, with generously proportioned thighs.

Lyle shook his head. "No, I don't think so."

The woman continued her recitation. "Any heart condition, diabetes, history of drug abuse—"

The look on Lyle's face stopped her. She cocked her head to one side and peered at him. "Did she ingest any drugs or alcohol?"

"No! I mean, not anymore," Lyle answered, and then, in response to the look the woman gave him, he added, "We were done with all that. We were both clean when we came here, and I checked her luggage to make sure . . . she was clean, I swear to God."

The chief paramedic couldn't resist a quick roll of her eyes as her colleagues swung Sally's limp body onto the stretcher. The woman's square jaw jutted forward as she continued with her list. "Any history of liver disease, kidney failure, renal disease, tumors, gynecological problems—"

"No, man—look at her!" Lyle cried, his face red. "She's too young to have any of that stuff!"

"No one's too young to have anything," the paramedic replied as her colleagues carried Sally out of the room. "Are you coming to the hospital with us?"

"Yeah—yeah, I wanna stay with her." Lyle was practically in tears now, and Claire felt sorry for him. His lips were swollen, his eyelids were red, and he looked absolutely terrified.

"Do you want me to come with you?" she asked.

Lyle looked at her with a bewildered expression, as though the decision was too much for him, and shook his head.

"No, I'll look after her." He suddenly grabbed Claire's hand and squeezed it so hard that her knuckles crunched.

"Thanks, though, for—everything." Then, with a look at the others who stood around, hands at their sides, he turned and ran out the door, following the paramedics, who were already loading Sally into the back of the ambulance.

Claire watched it drive off as Jack Callahan made his way slowly down the stairs, leaning on his son's arm. They both wore bulky blue snow parkas.

"What's going on?" said Chris, his voice languid as always, even under such circumstances. He guided his father over to a chair in the corner.

"Sally just collapsed," Meredith replied cheerily, hanging on the doorknob and swinging back and forth.

"Stop it, Meredith," Claire told her as Frank Wilson came back into the room.

"Oh, they're gone already?" he said, his big face soft with disappointment.

"Yup," said Meredith. "They were fast."

"I wanted to ask them—"

"What?" said Meredith.

"Oh, never mind . . . it's probably not important."

"What?" said Claire.

"I'll ask Max when he returns," the innkeeper replied.

"Where is he?"

"He went to town to do some shopping," Wilson said, then he turned and went back into the kitchen.

Jack Callahan watched him go, a pensive expression on his face, then he looked at the basket of poppy-seed muffins on Claire's table. "Do you know the muffin man?" he murmured thoughtfully, almost to himself, before letting his head sink onto his chest.

"What's that, Papa?" said Chris Callahan.

Jack raised his head and focused his bleary eyes on his son's face. "He lives in Drury Lane."

"What's *that* supposed to mean?" Meredith whispered to Claire.

"I don't know. It's an old children's song; I remember it from childhood." For the rest of the day she had trouble getting the words out of her head. They ran, over and over again, like a loop, through her mind:

Do you know the muffin man, the muffin man, the
  muffin man?
Do you know the muffin man? He lives in Drury Lane.

Claire had a tendency to trap things in her head—song lyrics, poems, bits of verse, even nursery rhymes or ad slogans—creating for her a kind of internal soundtrack. As she walked down the street, it seemed there was always a phrase of some kind rattling around in her head. Now Jack's words rang in her ears like the voice of Fate itself.

Do you know the muffin man, the muffin man, the
  muffin man?

There was something ominous in this little snatch of nursery rhyme, it seemed to her, some message, if only she could figure out what it was. Out of the mouth of babes, she could remember her mother saying when her younger brother said something particularly cute or astute. Well, there was something in Jack's dry, affectless observations that seemed to lend them the weight of prophecy. Even though she knew it was probably nonsensical, Claire couldn't help feeling there was something to it.

Do you know the muffin man? He lives in Drury Lane.

Chapter 14

Everyone awaited anxiously all morning for word of Sally's condition. Richard and Jeffrey had gone into town after an early breakfast, so they didn't hear that she was ill until they returned a little after one o'clock.

Claire expected Jeffrey to receive the news with a sneer, but to her surprise he shook his head sympathetically.

"Poor kid." He sighed. "Playing with matches . . ."

"How do you know?" said Richard, depositing an armful of packages on the sideboard. "It could have been food poisoning."

Jeffrey shrugged. "I know a junkie when I see one. At least give me that, won't you, dear boy?" he added ironically, with a pat on Richard's cheek.

To Claire's surprise, Richard smiled and blushed. Whatever trouble the two were having, they seemed to have patched things up, at least for the time being.

"Let us know if you hear anything," Richard said as he carried the packages upstairs. "We'll be in our room."

Later, Claire walked past their room and heard the sound of laughter, and underneath Edith Piaf's voice:

> *Non, rien de rien,*
> *Non, je ne regrette rien.*

She smiled and walked on. With so much pain and sadness around, she was glad to see someone carving out a little corner of happiness, tenuous as it might be.

When Claire got to her room, Meredith was lying on her stomach on her cot studying some of the letters from the secret drawer.

"Whatchya up to?" Claire said.

"Studying handwriting," Meredith replied without looking up.

"Yeah? Why?"

"Well, one of the letters may be from the victim—or the murderer."

Claire pulled a thick burgundy sweater from the closet. The inn was chilly, and she had been cold all day. "Well, I guess it's possible."

Meredith sat up and crossed her legs Indian style. "You bet it is! Just *think* what a breakthrough a discovery like that could be!"

"So how do you propose to test your theory?"

Meredith gave her best shot at a mysterious smile. She was hardly a Mona Lisa, though, and Claire tried unsuccessfully to suppress a laugh.

"What's so funny?" Meredith demanded.

"Nothing . . . well, it was the expression on your face."

"What about it?"

"Never mind . . . what's your plan?"

"You'll see," Meredith answered curtly. "When the time is ripe I will reveal all."

"Meredith, it isn't illegal, is it?"

Meredith snorted. "I should hope *not*! Don't insult me—puh-lease!"

She sounded like a New England dowager whose pride had just been injured, a sort of adolescent Margaret Dumont.

"Well, forgive me," said Claire, imitating Meredith's artificial, hoity-toity tone of voice. "I had no idea your moral standards were so high—but I must say I'm relieved."

"Well, they *are*."

"I'm glad to hear it."

Both of them were half kidding now, just playing with each other. Just then Wally came in. "What's going on here?" he said.

"Claire is comparing me to a common criminal," Meredith replied, rolling over onto her back. "Can you *imagine*?"

Wally shared an amused look with Claire. "Outrageous," he said. "She should be horsewhipped."

Meredith's jaw dropped and she sat up. "Really?"

"No, but we'll settle for a spanking." With that, Wally reached for Claire, who screamed and dove across the bed to escape. Laughing, Wally grabbed her wrist and pulled her toward him. Claire was laughing, too, and pretended to bite his hand, just barely touching the skin with her teeth. She could taste the salt on his skin, and a sting of lime aftershave on the tip of her tongue.

By now Meredith was laughing, too, as she helped pull Claire over her side of the bed.

"Come on," said Wally, "take your punishment like a man."

They were making so much noise that they didn't even hear the first knock on the door. The second knock, however, went through them like a gunshot. They all stopped laughing simultaneously, and Claire went to the door and opened it. She knew what the news was as soon as she saw Frank Wilson's face.

"I just got a call from Rufus Hornblower. Sally died at the hospital."

"Oh, God," said Claire. "Oh, my God. What—how?"

Frank Wilson sighed. He looked exhausted, his handsome Irish face puffy and pale. "There'll be an autopsy. It's too early to tell, but it had all the signs of poisoning."

"Oh, God, I'm so sorry," Claire said. "Poor Sally. Where's Lyle?"

"He's downstairs. Hornblower's on his way over here now."

"I *knew* it!" Meredith crowed as Claire closed the door and came back into the room. "Sally knew something, and the killer had to silence her!"

"Oh, Meredith," Claire said, "people die of poisoning all the time. It doesn't necessarily follow that she was murdered, you know."

But even as she said the words, she didn't believe them.

"I'm going downstairs to see if I can help." Wally rose from the edge of the bed. As he passed Claire he reached for her impulsively and gave her a hug.

"E-yew," said Meredith, "no kissing." She herself resisted physical contact of any kind. She called people who hugged all the time "touchy-feelies."

"I'll come with you," said Claire.

"Me, too!" Meredith chirped, following them.

As they entered the hall, Claire caught a glimpse of movement at the other end of the hall. When she turned she saw just the tip of Henry Wilson's head disappearing down the back staircase.

By the time they got downstairs most of the residents and staff were gathered in the small dining room adjacent to the bar. Max was walking back and forth wringing his hands, while most of the others were just sitting in stunned silence. The sun was pouring in through the south window, its fierce brightness only serving to highlight the pain and misery on Lyle's face. He sat by himself in the corner, the yellow sunlight on his blond curls, staring into space.

"I'm glad you're here," Frank Wilson said when Claire and the others arrived. "Detective Hornblower will be here soon and he wants to speak to everyone."

No sooner had he finished than the front door opened and Claire could hear the heavy sound of boots stamping on the mat. Detective Hornblower entered the little room a moment later, his battered fedora in his hand.

" 'Lo, Rufus," Wilson said.

" 'Lo, Frank. Thanks for getting everyone together." He turned to the assembled company and cleared his throat. "Mr. Wilson has told you all of the unfortunate death of Ms. Richmond," he said slowly. *Ms. Richmond.* It hadn't occurred to Claire until that moment that she didn't know Sally's last name.

The detective cleared his throat again and continued. "What I want to impress upon all of you is that there is absolutely no reason to believe at this time that Ms. Richmond was murdered. In fact, as some of you may know, she had a history of drug abuse." As he spoke, Claire watched his Adam's apple bobbing up and down. It was very prominent, and his throat was so long that it was almost impossible not to notice it. "So although Detective Murphy and I may be asking some questions in the next few days, until the completion of an autopsy there is no reason to panic, or feel undue concern." As he spoke, the Adam's apple continued to leap and dance. It reminded Claire of a float at the end of a fishing line. "These things happen," he continued, "and though it's tragic, we have no reason at this time to believe Ms. Richmond was the victim of any foul play."

Detective Hornblower approached Lyle and cleared his throat. "Mr. Lewellyn," he said gently, "when you're feeling up to it, I'd like to ask you a few questions."

Lyle nodded. "Okay. Whatever you want. When?"

The tall detective gave a tiny shrug. "As soon as you're feeling up to it."

"Okay."

"All right." The detective cleared his throat again. It was for him a kind of spoken punctuation, a way to break an awkward silence.

Lyle shook his head. "I know what you're all thinking, but we'd given up that stuff. Sally was clean, man. That's what we were here for—to kind of celebrate our sobriety, you know?" He looked at Claire and the others as if seeking approval. Claire found herself nodding in sympathy.

At that moment Richard and Jeffrey entered the room. Maybe it was coincidence and maybe Lyle didn't really mean to look at Jeffrey when he spoke, but when he continued, it was with a glance at Jeffrey.

"Unless somebody gave her something I didn't know about. But I don't see how," he added. "I was with her— like every second, you know?"

"Every second?" said Hornblower.

"Practically. I mean, we were sticking close together. I don't know . . . maybe she coulda snuck out at night and got somethin', I guess, but I don't think so."

"Then you will have no objections if Detective Murphy searches your room?"

Lyle shook his head. "Whatever. I got nothin' to hide . . . it's ironic, you know, because Sally really loved it here. I mean, it was her idea to come here and everything."

"Oh, really?" said Hornblower.

"Yeah. She found the place and everything."

"How?"

"Through some book, I think . . . she thought it sounded romantic." His voice broke as if he were about to cry, but then he took a deep breath, straightened his shoulders, and stood up.

Claire looked closely at Jeffrey to see how he was reacting to all of this, but his face was impassive; if he had been supplying Sally with drugs, she thought, he was not about to give himself away. He leaned against the door frame, his muscular arms crossed, as if waiting to enter the conversation.

Detective Hornblower coughed delicately. "Do you know of anyone who wished to harm her?"

Again Lyle seemed to be looking vaguely in Jeffrey's direction, but it was hard to tell. "No, man—I mean, nobody here even *knew* her, for Chrissakes." His face crumpled and he hung his head, crying softly.

Jeffrey left his spot in the door frame and approached Lyle. "Hey, I'm really sorry. She was a sweet girl," he said softly.

Lyle nodded, still crying. "Yeah," he said thickly. "Oh, God, what am I going to tell her parents?"

"It's not your fault, man," Jeffrey said. "These things happen."

Detective Hornblower regarded Jeffrey impassively. "Do you know of anyone who might have wanted to harm Ms. Richmond?"

"Nope. Can't imagine why anyone'd want to hurt her," Jeffrey replied smoothly. "But if you have any more questions for me, Detective, I'll be upstairs."

With that, he turned and sauntered out of the room, just as Wally and Frank Wilson came in through the other door.

"Where's Meredith?" said Claire.

"She went to help Max in the kitchen," Wally replied. "Something about a chocolate cake."

"Actually, Frank, I'd like to take a look around the kitchen before he does any more cooking, if you don't mind," Hornblower said.

"Mind? Why should I mind? I'll go tell him," Frank added with a glance at Lyle, who had stopped crying and was sitting with his hands folded on his lap.

"I'll go," said Lyle. "I got nothin' else better to do."

When he had gone, Wally turned to Detective Hornblower. "Do they have any idea what killed her?"

Hornblower shook his head. "Not until the tox screen is back. It was really strange; none of the doctors at the hospital could understand what was going on . . . her organs just gave out."

"Wouldn't that be consistent with a history of drug abuse?" Wally asked.

Hornblower sighed. "Maybe. But, on the other hand, she is young, and the doctors felt that such a sudden meltdown would indicate an acute situation—in other words, a recent overdose."

Wally nodded. "The question then becomes what did she ingest—and where did she get it?"

"Exactly."

At that moment Max came in from the hall, followed by Meredith, whose face was smeared with dabs of flour.

"You need to look at my kitchen?" Max said, standing with his hands on his hips. It was a combative stance, Claire thought, but his tone of voice was not especially challenging.

"Yes, I would," replied the detective. "That is, if you have no objections."

The big chef shrugged. "Just try not to break anything. I run a clean kitchen, you know," he added with a glance at Frank Wilson.

"I'm sure you do," Hornblower answered calmly as Detective Murphy entered the room. He seemed to come from nowhere; Claire hadn't heard the sound of the front door opening. He nodded at Detective Hornblower and stood quietly, hat in his hand, while the detective finished his conversation.

"I'll go have a look upstairs, then?" Murphy suggested when he was done.

Hornblower nodded."Thank you. I'll accompany Mr. von Schlegel to the kitchen."

"Right this way, Detective," Max said, leading him out of the room.

"It's purely procedural, you know," Hornblower remarked, following him.

Max smiled ironically. "In my experience, Detective, nothing is purely procedural."

As Claire listened to the two sets of footsteps receding down the hall, Meredith turned to her. "Does he suspect Max?"

Claire shook her head. "He doesn't even know if it's a murder or not at this point, Meredith."

"But he had to check for clues before the trail gets cold, right?" Meredith said to Wally.

Wally smiled faintly. "Something like that." When he smiled, a faint dimple appeared on the right side of his face. Claire loved that dimple. It was the asymmetries she loved about people, their quirks and oddities, not the qualities that made them just like everyone else.

Meredith was all asymmetry, a sprawling, ungainly child apparently without grace, until you got to know her and found the inner grace beneath her prickly exterior. She was like a porcupine—all bristle and points, but soft underneath, so soft. Claire wondered if the girl realized how much her vulnerability showed through all her fire and lightning. Claire herself was, in a way, her opposite: soft on the outside, but she could harden like molten metal if necessary. Wally, actually, was more like Claire than either of them was like Meredith. But then, no one was quite like Meredith, at least no one Claire had ever met.

Her ruminations were interrupted by the arrival of Chris Callahan and his father, coming in from their afternoon walk. Claire heard them enter the front hall and realized that they probably hadn't heard the news about Sally. She stepped out into the hall as Chris was guiding his father toward the stairs, his hand around the old man's elbow.

"Uh, Chris," she said, stopping in front of the grandfather clock. She was so close she could hear the gears whirring inside it.

When he saw her face, Chris Callahan stopped. "What is it? What's happened? Is it Sally?"

"Yeah," Meredith said, coming up behind Claire. "She's dead."

To some extent, Claire knew, this was all a game to the girl; at her age, she hadn't really grasped her own mortality and therefore the death of others had less impact.

Chris Callahan gave a deep sigh. "What a shame," he said, shaking his head. "It's so tragic. She couldn't have been more than—what? Twenty-five?"

"Yeah," Claire said, but she was thinking that Chris looked very unsurprised by the news, almost as if he were expecting it.

When Philippe and Otis arrived for work later that afternoon, however, they both became extremely upset at the news. They had not been around when Sally took ill at breakfast, so the whole thing came as a shock to them. The innkeeper sat them both down in the main dining room and explained what had happened.

"Jesus," Otis said when Frank told them the news. "That's terrible."

Philippe's response echoed something in Claire's mind she wasn't even aware she was thinking until he said it.

"What next?" he said, shaking his head. "What next?"

As they got up to attend to their chores, Claire thought that at least the staff had something to occupy their minds, whereas all the guests could do was sit around and wonder: what—or who—was next?

Chapter 15

POLICE LABEL SECOND DEATH
AT HISTORIC INN "SUSPICIOUS"

"We are not yet ready to call Ms. Richmond's death a homicide," said Detective Rufus Hornblower, referring to the mysterious and sudden death of one of the guests at Longfellow's Wayside Inn, the centuries-old guest house that is one of Sudbury's main tourist attractions. Detective Hornblower, who is in charge of the investigation into the stabbing death of Mona Callahan, a hotel employee, on the eve of Thanksgiving, admitted that while there were some potentially suspicious circumstances surrounding Ms. Richmond's death, "We have no reason to believe as yet that any foul play was involved."

If it is a coincidence, however, even the detective admits that the situation is "bizarre," to

> *say the least. Ms. Richmond is the second per-
> son to die at the inn in less than a week.*

Claire put down the newspaper and took a sip of tea. The *Town Crier* was the local weekly paper, and Meredith was dying to talk to the reporters who showed up at the Wayside Inn the day before, but Wally and Claire had talked her out of it, convincing her that it would only serve to hamper Detective Hornblower's investigation. It was a good little paper, with well-written articles about local events, but the livid headline splashed across the front page clearly indicated that this was the most exciting thing to happen in South Sudbury for a long time. Claire put the paper down and stretched her muscles. She decided that no matter how cold it was outside, she would go for a jog today. She was alone in the breakfast room, lingering over her tea and muffins while Wally and Detective Hornblower stood out in the hall talking. She had sent Meredith upstairs to put on a sweater; she had complained of a scratchy throat the night before, and Claire wasn't taking any chances.

Wally and Hornblower were talking in low voices, but Claire could hear every word.

"No, they couldn't find anything; the preliminary tox screen came up completely empty," Hornblower was saying.

"Any sign of heart trouble?"

"No; right now it looks like she just dropped dead. There were two strange things in the autopsy, though," said Hornblower. "There was hemorrhaging in the submucus layer of her stomach, which would be consistent with something like phosphorus poisoning. But there was no trace of phosphorus, or any substance they screened for."

"And what was the other thing?" Wally asked.

"Well, her blood wasn't clotting normally—though that's not all that unusual, apparently."

"So they've come up empty-handed?"

Hornblower sighed. "So far. Blood, urine, vitreous fluid—nothing showed up in any of it."

"What's vitreous fluid?" Meredith's voice sang out from down the hall. Claire stood up and went to join Wally and Hornblower at the bottom of the staircase. Meredith stood, a red sweater draped over her arm, at the other end of the hall.

"What's vitreous fluid?" she repeated.

"It's eye fluid," Wally said. "It's one of the first things they check for toxins along with blood and urine."

"Cool!" Meredith stood on tiptoe and touched the top of the door frame. The inn was built at a time when people were shorter, and Claire could easily touch the top of all the door frames. Detective Hornblower had to bend a little to get through some of the lower entryways.

"Don't let me interrupt you," Meredith said hopefully. "Go ahead and talk."

"No, we're just about done," Detective Hornblower answered with a sigh.

"Hey, listen," said Meredith. "About those reporters that have been coming around—"

"Meredith, I thought we agreed," Claire interrupted.

"Well, they just wanted to know—"

"Meredith," said Wally. "I thought we explained how that could damage the investigation."

"But—"

"I'd like to discourage any of you from talking to reporters," Detective Hornblower said. "Of course, I can't stop you, but it would be best for our investigation if you didn't."

"Okay!" Meredith said. "I get the message—no talky, no ticky."

Hornblower stared at her for a moment, then turned back to Wally. "I'll see you later."

"Let me know if there's anything I can do," Wally said as Hornblower replaced his battered fedora on his head.

"Only one thing I can think of," the lanky detective replied. "Think of something that might have killed Sally Richmond."

•   •   •

That afternoon Claire wandered downstairs to get a cup of tea for Meredith, who was still complaining of a scratchy throat. It was after five and already dark when she entered the main dining room. She was filling a cup with hot water when Otis came into the room to light the candles scattered about on the tables. As he was doing this, Henry Wilson wandered into the room and stood watching for a moment, then he picked up a box of matches from the mantel and began to light one of the candles. Otis turned to see him at the same moment Paula Wilson came charging into the room. She swooped down on her son like a bird of prey and snatched the matches from his hand.

"Henry, you know better than that!" she cried, jerking him away from the table. The boy recoiled from her touch, making himself as small as possible. Claire couldn't blame him; Paula Wilson was frightening. "How could you let him?" she hissed at Otis, who shrugged.

"I didn't see him," he answered, his face blank. He stood leaning against the wall, his body in a defensive position, his arms crossed protectively.

"Well, you have to keep an eye out—we *all* do," she scolded, her thin face red, her features sharpened by anger. It was at that moment she noticed Claire, who was standing quietly by the coffee machine at the far end of the room. Her thin mouth hardened into an unconvincing smile.

"Hello," she said. "I beg your pardon. I didn't see you."

"That's all right," Claire replied, anxious to escape the woman's stare but curious about what she had just witnessed. What was the meaning of it all? she wondered. She wanted to stay and ask Otis, but Paula Wilson stood her ground, smiling her rigid smile. It was clear that she was not going to leave until Claire did.

"Can I get you anything?" she said helpfully, her voice as false as a three-dollar bill.

"No, thanks. I was just getting some tea," Claire replied, holding up the teacup as if to prove it. She felt the woman's eyes on her as she turned and went back upstairs, her feet tapping evenly against the uncarpeted steps.

She gave Meredith her tea, then, after waiting a few minutes, went back down to the bar. Otis was behind the counter slicing lemons. Claire ordered a hot cider and sat down in front of the fire.

"What was that all about today with the matches?" she asked, trying to sound casual.

Otis glanced at her and then looked back at the lemon he was slicing. "All what?" he said, his voice measured and deliberately bland. It was so obvious he was lying that it was almost embarrassing.

"All that with Henry and Mrs. Wilson." Claire was on a first-name basis with everyone at the inn, including Frank Wilson, but she couldn't imagine calling Paula Wilson anything but "Mrs. Wilson."

"Oh," said Otis, still avoiding her gaze. "She just didn't want him getting in my way."

Claire took a deep breath. "Otis," she said, "that's a lie. You know it and I know it. Henry's been helping out around this place all week. So if you don't want to tell me, just say so."

Otis finally lifted his head and met her eyes. "Okay," he said. "I don't want to tell you. Mostly because I could get in trouble if I do. I mean, you write mysteries, right?"

"I edit them. It's not exactly the same thing."

"Well, it's just somethin' I can't talk about, okay?"

"I'll tell you what," Claire said slowly. "I'll guess, and if I guess right, you turn a beer mug upside down." She had a vague memory of seeing a variation on this technique used by a detective in a movie.

Otis didn't reply. "I'll take that as a yes," she said, a little thrilled at her own boldness. Maybe Meredith's personality was beginning to rub off on her.

"It was something to do with what Henry was doing," she said. "Let's see . . . I know! He was lighting candles."

To her surprise, Otis reached up to the shelf and quietly turned a beer mug upside down.

"Okay," she continued. "It might have something to do with the candles . . . something about them."

Otis continued slicing lemons.

"Or maybe he was supposed to be doing something else."

Otis finished the lemons and moved on to the limes.

"I've got it!" Claire said. "It's the matches, isn't it? It's something to do with Henry and matches."

Otis reached up and turned over another mug.

Meredith would like this game, Claire thought. At that moment her gaze fell upon the logs smoldering in the fireplace. "My God," she said as it hit her all at once. "That fire two years ago! They think Henry may have started it, don't they? Or maybe they *know* he did," she added, almost to herself.

Otis looked at her, his eyes pained. "Look," he said, "nobody ever knew who started that fire, or if anyone did. It could have been a spark from the fireplace, a candle—anything."

"But Henry is a firebug, isn't he?" Claire said. "That's why his mother was so anxious to get him away from those matches."

"Look," Otis said, "I have to get some more stuff for the bar."

After he had gone, Claire thought about the Wilson family. It all fit together, she thought: a cold, controlling mother in a troubled marriage, her disturbed adolescent son, attracted to the power and destructive potential of fire . . . burning . . . passion. But where was the passion? Paula Wilson was so constricted, so tightly wound, always so in control that it was hard imagining her in the throes of heated passion . . . maybe it was the father? She thought about Frank Wilson and his bluff, hearty manner. Friendly, yes, but hardly passionate. Maybe it was the boy himself . . . at the age of fourteen, his body was just beginning to produce the hormones that could lead to passion or destruction—or both.

Claire shivered and drew her sweater closer around her body. Adolescence was a hazardous time, but she had trouble thinking of timid young Henry as being behind the death of two women.

Otis returned to the bar, carrying a plastic tray full of ice. When he saw that Claire was still there, he looked disturbed. She suspected his trip to get the ice was just an excuse to end their conversation, and that he hoped she would leave before he returned. Now, as he dumped the ice into one side of the sink behind him, she stood up and went over to him. She put an elbow on the counter and leaned forward.

"Do the police know?"

He stopped what he was doing and looked at her. "Look, I told you, I can't really talk about this with you. If you want to know more, why don't you ask the Wilsons?"

She was pretty sure the Wilsons wouldn't tell her a thing about it, wanting to protect their son, and she was certain Otis knew this, too—but she just nodded.

"Okay. I'm sorry if I caused you any distress. It's just that with everything else that's going on, it looked a little strange, that's all."

That was an understatement; it was *very* strange, but then Claire was beginning to think everything at the Wayside Inn was a little strange.

As she passed the small dining room on her way out of the bar, she saw Lyle sitting by himself at a table. She hesitated, then took a step into the room. Lyle sat limply in the chair, his hands folded in his lap. He looked empty, drained of all impulse, all desire. At that moment Claire realized that he must have loved Sally, loved her so much that he was willing to stay with her through what must have been a difficult time—waiting for her body to clear itself of the harmful substances she had filled it with—only to have her poisoned in the end after all. What a bitter irony, she thought, one that a poet like Lyle could appreciate but not one she would wish on anyone.

He looked up at Claire as she passed, his face wan. His lips were pale, almost the color of the rest of his face. He gave a little nod in response to her greeting, and Claire couldn't help thinking that he looked sad, so very sad.

"You okay?" she said impulsively, although his manner didn't especially invite conversation.

He sighed deeply and ran a finger over his upper lip. "I guess . . . it's hard to know what 'okay' is at a time like this, you know?"

Claire sat down on one of the chairs scattered around the room, not too close to him, she hoped. "Yeah, actually, I do know."

He brightened. "You do? You . . . have you—" He stopped and looked away. "I'm sorry; it's none of my business."

"No, that's okay. I think I know something of what you're going through. I lost my parents some years back, and there were times I didn't . . . well, not to be too dramatic, but it was hard to imagine living through it."

Lyle shook his head. "I never lost anybody before. I mean, an aunt once, but she was really old and we weren't that close. I never . . . oh, God," he said, letting his head fall into his hands. "I never knew it could hurt so much." He lifted his head to look at Claire. His eyes were very blue, like New York Harbor on a clear day. "How long does it last?"

She shook her head. "It depends, I guess. When it's sudden like this it can take a while."

"Did your parents die—suddenly?"

"Yes. Yes, they did."

He let his head fall again. "Oh, God. Oh, God." As he spoke, a piece of paper fluttered down off the table. Claire leaned over to pick it up.

"Is this yours?"

Lyle looked at it through tear-streaked eyes. "Yeah, it's a poem I wrote today."

"May I read it?"

He shrugged. "Sure. I don't know if it's any good."

Claire read the poem, written on plain white paper in a shaky hand.

The snow falls white upon the ground,
the flakes settling all around
My heart lies frozen at the break of day
Cold and hard as the soil lying stiffly
beneath this winter garden of weeds
You were here once, your body beside me,
soft and white as a snowdrift
I wait for the spring thaw, but the sun has left with you,
all warmth faded, swept away
People come and people go,
but always there is the falling snow.

Claire sat listening to the tick of the grandfather clock in the hall. In the stillness between them, the tick sounded loud, too loud, like something out of a Bergman film. She could hear the low murmur of voices from down the hall—just like in *Cries and Whispers,* she thought.

"I like your poem," she said. "It's sad and full of feeling."

"You know, it's funny," he said with a bitter laugh, "here I thought of myself as a poet all those years, who wrote about human suffering, but now I find I didn't know jackshit about suffering." He shook his head. "All those poems, all that emotion on the page, and it turns out I didn't know squat."

"Oh, I don't know," said Claire. "There's pain and then there's pain. Children suffer—you suffered as a child. You just forgot."

"Oh, you mean like women are supposed to forget the pain of childbirth?" He snorted again. "No, I'd remember it if I'd felt anything this bad before—I swear to God I would."

"Well, maybe, but time has a way of erasing or at least smoothing over rough times."

He looked at her with tragic eyes. "She wanted to study

anthropology. She was going to go to college and become an anthropologist."

Claire decided that either Lyle had nothing to do with Sally's death, or he had missed his calling and should have been an actor.

When Claire returned to the room she found Meredith and Wally lying on the bed playing Hangman. Claire sat on the edge of the bed. "I've been wondering what poison has a delayed effect . . . since it seems Sally didn't ingest anything that morning."

"That's if you believe Lyle," Wally replied.

"What's not to believe? The guy is heartbroken. He clearly loved her."

"Claire . . ." Wally laid a hand on her shoulder. "Believe it or not, I've seen some of the most convincing displays of grief you can possibly imagine from cold-blooded murderers."

"How can that be?" said Meredith.

"Well, some criminals are just good actors . . . they might actually feel remorse for their crimes, and others can cry just out of the tension and fear of being caught; they turn their fear into a pretty good approximation of grief."

"Wow," said Meredith. "Cheeky buggers."

"And," Wally continued, "perfectly innocent people have been convicted for a crime because they didn't show enough remorse at the death of a loved one. Maybe they were in shock or denial, or didn't know how to grieve. My point is really that you can't tell that much from a person's reaction."

"Well, *I* believe Lyle," said Claire, getting up and taking off her sweater. The radiators were on full blast, and the room was warm, the window glass frosted up on the inside.

Meredith rolled over onto her side and began humming softly while she shuffled the cards. "Do you know the mushroom man, the mushroom man, the mushroom man?"

Claire stared at her. "What are you singing?"

Meredith stopped what she was doing. "Do you know—the mushroom man," she repeated slowly.

"That's not how it goes," Claire said.

"Sorry."

"No, don't be sorry," Claire said, as a tingle of excitement began to thread its way through her stomach.

"How does it really go?" Wally asked.

"Never mind . . . I have an idea."

"Oh? What's that?"

"It's just a hunch . . ." Claire left the room and started down the stairs.

Meredith came flying after her. "Hey, wait for me! Where are you going?" she said as she followed Claire through the hotel toward the kitchen.

"You'll see," Claire replied. "I just want to follow this hunch."

They found Max in the kitchen chopping vegetables. The shiny blade of his knife sliced cleanly through the stalk of celery he held pinned down to the heavy butcher-block counter.

"Hello," he said, looking up as they entered. He was immaculate as ever in his white shirt and apron, the fleshy folds of his neck protruding from his starched white collar.

"Can I ask you something?" Claire began as he tossed chopped celery into a large soup tureen.

"Of course." He reached for a bunch of carrots and proceeded to dice them with the quick assurance only years of practice can give. There was something mesmerizing about his actions; Claire found it hard not to watch as his plump fingers wrapped around the carrots, holding them gently, almost delicately, as the knife fell swiftly and cleanly on the cutting board. There was a pleasure in watching someone do something well, she thought, even if it was only chopping vegetables.

"What did you want to ask me?"

She could hear the drift of the Danube in his speech, his

Austrian origin thickening his consonants like cornstarch in a sauce.

"What did Sally have to eat for dinner yesterday?"

Max stopped and looked at her. "Why do you want to know?"

"She has a hunch!" Meredith declared.

"Really? A hunch?" said Max.

Claire shrugged. "Yeah, I guess."

Max pursed his thick lips. "Let me see . . . she had the chicken marsala . . . no, that's what her boyfriend had. She's a vegetarian. She had . . . the wild mushroom crêpes."

Claire felt the tingle in her stomach grow. "Are you sure?"

Max nodded. "Yes; I remember she was the only one who ordered it. Why do you ask?" His pale blue eyes widened, and with his smooth pink skin and bald head, he suddenly reminded Claire of an oversized baby.

Claire shook her head and looked out the kitchen window at the old church, which looked lonely and deserted in the snow.

"Wow," Meredith said softly. "The mushroom man."

Max frowned. "Who's that?"

"No one," said Meredith. It's just this nursery rhyme I was singing, only I got the words wrong, and Claire got this idea—"

"Well, it's a long shot, I'll admit." Claire sighed. "But something killed that girl, and if it wasn't drugs, then someone's got to track it down. Where do you get your wild mushrooms?"

"Mostly from the market. But sometimes from James."

"James Pewter?"

"Yes, he's a mushroom collector. He knows quite a lot about them."

"Really?"

"Oh, yes—he keeps jars of dried mushrooms in his cellar. You should go have a look."

"We might just do that," Meredith answered, with a look at Claire.

"And last night?" said Claire. "What did you use last night?"

Max thought for a moment. "I used some from this jar." Opening the lid of the dishwasher, he displayed a rack of clean glasses.

"You already washed it," Claire said, disappointed.

"Yes, last night."

"Where did the mushrooms come from?"

"From . . . I guess they were some of James's." Max ran a hand over his plump chin. "This is one of his jars."

Claire left the kitchen and headed back down the hall, where she found Wally waiting for her.

"Well?" he said.

"Claire thinks it's the mushrooms," Meredith said as she came around the corner, chewing on a stub of carrot.

"Mushrooms? What mushrooms?" Wally ran a hand through his thick grey hair, a gesture that always made Claire's heart jump a little. She loved his hair, loved the way it curled at the nape of his neck or fell in rumpled locks over his forehead.

"The mushrooms in the *food*!" Meredith called out excitedly.

"It's just a theory," Claire said.

Meredith hopped up and down. "See, Sally had mushrooms for dinner, and Claire thinks—"

Wally frowned. "But she didn't show any symptoms until the next day."

"Right," said Claire. "Excuse me—I have a phone call to make."

She went up to the room and dug her little blue address book out of her suitcase. She had thrown it in at the last minute as she was packing, just in case. She leafed through the book's dog-eared pages, looking for the number of the man she hoped could help her: Willard Hughes.

It was not a conversation she was looking forward to. Willard Hughes was an enormously successful writer, but as a human being, he was a disaster. Never very at home around people, he was a man of jerks and starts, his body like a badly tuned engine. His personality had jagged edges you could cut yourself on if you weren't careful. With his restless, twitching body and his whiny voice, he made most people uncomfortable. But now that Blanche DuBois was dead, Willard was Claire's star author. Mysteries just seemed to come pouring out of the fiction machine that was Willard Hughes.

When he first came to her office, Willard was living in a fifth-floor walk-up on the Lower East Side, but *Death Pays a House Call* had taken off quickly, and now he owned a penthouse on the Upper East Side, just off Fifth Avenue, not far from where Jackie Kennedy lived in the last years of her life.

She located his number and went down to the phone at the front desk. She dialed his number, and he picked up after the second ring.

"Willard Hughes here." He always answered the phone this way.

"Hello, Willard, it's Claire."

"Oh, hello. What can I do for you?"

She took a deep breath. "I wanted to ask you about something in one of your books."

"Sure, go ahead." She prayed he would not ask her any questions, such as why she wanted this information. She didn't want Willard prying into her affairs, and she didn't feel like explaining to him the events of the past few days. She just wanted to get her answer and get off the phone.

"You remember in your first book you had a mushroom poisoning?"

"Vaguely . . . that was quite a few books ago, you know." Willard liked to boast about how prolific he was.

"Yes, I know, but I know how thorough your research is. I wonder if you'd remember the name of that particular mushroom?"

"No, I really don't." He sounded irritated.

"Well, if I were at home or at work I'd have a copy of it, of course, but I wonder if you'd mind looking it up for me."

Willard sighed. "Just a minute," he said, putting the phone down. Claire could hear his footsteps as he went into the other room. After a few moments he returned.

"It was *Amanita virosa.*"

"Oh, thank you," Claire said, jotting it down.

Sure enough, then, the inevitable question came: "Want to have lunch when you're back?"

"Sure, that would be nice."

"Okay, give me a call."

Claire hung up the phone and looked at what she had written: *Amanita virosa.* She remembered her dear late friend Amelia Moore had mentioned once that most of the truly deadly mushrooms were members of the amanita family. Well, poor Amelia was gone, but Claire knew just who to call to get the rest of the information she needed. She picked up the phone again and dialed Sarah DuBois. She knew the number by heart; since her sister Blanche's death, Sarah had become one of Claire's closest friends.

The ringing of the phone on the other end was tinny and faint.

"Hello?" The voice sounded far away, as if Sarah were underwater.

"Sarah?"

"Yes. Claire?"

"Yes, it's me."

"Are you still in Massachusetts? You sound so far away." There was the familiar edge to Sarah's voice, austerity in every syllable.

"I know. We've only just got the phone lines back up and some of the connections aren't so good."

"How many inches did you get up there? We got about twenty-two inches here in New York."

"Over thirty. Listen, Sarah—"

"Good Lord—you were *buried* up there!"

"Yes. Uh, Sarah, can I ask you a favor?"

"Certainly. What is it?"

"Well, there's been a murder in South Sudbury . . ."

There was a short pause on the other end, then a crackling sound on the line, and Claire thought for a moment she had lost Sarah. Then her voice came through, louder and stronger than before.

"Sudbury! Good Lord, Claire; do you mean the poor girl in the inn? Is *that* where you are?"

"I'm afraid so."

"It's been in the news down here. Not a front-page story, but I read about it. Are you all right?"

"Yes, I'm fine. I need to ask you to do something for me."

"Of course—anything. Is the child with you?" Sarah always referred to Meredith as "the child."

"Yes, she's fine, too. Wally's here."

"Oh, thank God for that. Is he—"

"Listen, Sarah, I hate to rush you, but there's only one phone here, and—"

"I'm sorry. What can I do for you?"

"Do you still have Amelia's books on mushrooms?"

"Well, yes, actually. I think they're in one of the bookshelves downstairs."

"Would you look up *Amanita virosa* for me?"

"Yes. You'll have to give me a few minutes to find the book. Hold on; I'll be right back."

Sarah put the phone down and Claire could hear her footsteps on the creaky floorboards of her nineteenth-century town house. After a few minutes she returned.

"I've got it!" she said, a little breathless, perhaps from excitement. The eagerness in her voice surprised Claire, who thought of Sarah as the epitome of restraint.

"Here it is—*Amanita virosa*. The common name for it is Destroying Angel."

Destroying Angel. How bizarrely appropriate, Claire thought.

"Can you read to me the symptoms of poisoning?"

"Why? Was someone poisoned?"

"That's what I'm trying to find out."

"Claire, what's going on up there?"

"I'm really sorry, Sarah, but I don't have time to explain everything right now."

"All right, all right." Sarah sounded irritated. "Just a minute, I have to look in the back for the symptoms. All right, here it is: 'Symptoms of poisoning . . . include dizziness, nausea and vomiting, diarrhea, cramps, auditory and visual hallucinations. Kidney and/or liver dysfunction follow and can result in death.' "

"Thanks. One more thing: does it say anything about how soon the symptoms occur?"

"Yes," said Sarah. "In the back here it says that symptoms can occur six to twelve hours after eating, typically ten to fourteen hours later."

"Wow." Claire shivered, and thought of poor Sally, and how she had suffered, everyone all the while thinking it was a drug overdose. "Thank you so much for your help," she said into the phone.

"Can I do anything else?"

"No . . . wait, yes. Would you call Peter Schwartz at Ardor House and tell him I'm all right and that I'll call him as soon as I have a chance?"

"Of course."

"Thanks."

"Not at all. Claire?"

"Yes?"

"Be careful, will you?"

"I will. Thanks again, Sarah."

Claire hung up the phone. *Destroying Angel.* She looked down the long dark corridor of the front hall and shuddered. *Visual and auditory hallucinations* . . . the thought occurred to her that a Destroying Angel would look very much like a ghostly Woman in White . . . and might very well prove to be even more deadly.

Chapter 16

"Well?" said Wally when Claire returned to the room. "Any luck?" He and Meredith were lying on the bed playing another game of Hangman. Wally was great at keeping Meredith occupied and out of trouble.

"Amanita virosa," Claire said softly.

"What?" said Meredith. "What's that?"

"Destroying Angel."

"Destroying Angel," Meredith repeated reverently. "Awesome."

"That's a mushroom?" said Wally.

Claire explained her conversations with Willard and Sarah, and described the poison's delayed effects.

"Well, it sounds a little farfetched to me," Wally remarked. "But I guess it's worth a try. I've never come across a case of mushroom poisoning in New York, but . . . I guess you never know. I'll call Detective Hornblower about it and see if he wants to run another tox screen."

He paused and cocked his head to one side. "What made you think of mushrooms as the murder weapon?"

"I don't know exactly," Claire answered. "Call it a

hunch, I guess. I'll tell you something else, by the way. Some people think Henry Wilson set that fire two years ago. What do you think about that?"

"What?" said Meredith. "Where did you hear *that*?"

"Oh, I have my sources," Claire answered, glad to have the drop on Meredith for a change.

"What fire?" said Wally.

"Oh, that's right; you weren't here when they talked about it," Claire said. "Well, there was a terrible fire two years ago that nearly burned the place down."

"Really. And who thinks young Henry is behind it?"

"Well, his mother, for one . . . and Otis Knox," Claire answered, feeling a little smug.

"Oh, *man*!" Meredith moaned. "Where was I when all this went down?"

Claire shrugged. "Snooping around somewhere else, sleeping, whatever. But don't breathe a word of this to anyone. I practically had to wring it out of Otis, and if anyone finds out I got it from him, he's in big trouble."

She went on to tell them about the candle-lighting scene with Paula Wilson, followed as it was by her odd conversation at the bar.

When she was finished, Wally shook his head. "This is not a happy family."

"And they're unhappy in their own individual ways," Claire agreed.

"Oh, *man*!" Meredith muttered. She was evidently upset at having missed some of the "action," as she liked to call it. Actually, Claire was planning to send her back to Connecticut, but she was not looking forward to breaking the news to her. Even with Wally and herself taking turns keeping an eye on Meredith, she was worried about the girl's safety. After all, there was a murderer most likely close by—maybe very close by—and Meredith had a propensity to stick her nose in places where she wasn't welcome.

She looked at Meredith, sprawled out on the bed, her

bony feet dangling over the edge of the blanket, toes twitching. Claire sighed. Tomorrow . . . tomorrow she would talk to her about returning to safe, boring Hartford.

"I feel sorry for the kid," Meredith said suddenly.

"What kid?" asked Wally.

"You know, the boy—what's his name?"

"Henry," said Claire.

"Yeah, Henry. Poor kid." She sighed. "Living with screwed-up grown-ups is the pits, let me tell you."

"Yeah," said Claire, "I know."

Wally left a message for Detective Hansom at the precinct, then the three of them went downstairs for a mug of cider. The only other person in the bar was the inn historian, James Pewter.

"Ah, just the man I wanted to see," Wally began in a friendly voice, but Claire knew him well enough to hear the edge behind his tone.

Pewter looked up at them. "Oh?" he said. "What about?"

"I understand you collect mushrooms," Wally remarked, sitting down across from him in a chair nearer to the fire. At that moment Philippe came into the room and took his place behind the bar. Not wanting to miss the conversation, Claire sent Meredith over to get their drinks.

"I'm an amateur mycologist, yes," Pewter replied calmly.

"Does anyone have access to your collection other than you?" Wally said.

The historian looked from him to Claire and back, his handsome face showing concern. His thick eyebrows were drawn upward in an expression of bewilderment.

"The Wilsons have a copy of the key to my house—and I have a copy of theirs. But sometimes I don't bother to lock my door," he added, shrugging.

"Really?" said Wally. "You leave your house unlocked?"

"Sometimes. This isn't New York City, you know," he remarked dryly.

"Yes, I'm aware of that," Wally answered. "Maybe if someone had told the killer that, we wouldn't have this mess on our hands."

Claire looked at Pewter to see his reaction to this. It occurred to her that the testiness between the two men was only partly about the murders, and that the challenging tone they took with each other might have something to do with her. She looked at Wally; his grey eyes were calm, but narrowed in a way she recognized. There was certain stiffness to his shoulders, a tightness in his voice . . . yes, she concluded: he was jealous! She bit her lower lip to keep from smiling, out of amusement and—she had to admit it to herself—triumph. There was a certain satisfaction in seeing two handsome men square off over her. She shocked herself a little, but there was no denying the thrill: it was some ancient mechanism—the same one, perhaps, that made the two men bristle at each other. Claire suddenly had the image of two charging rhinos, and that made her want to smile even more, so she turned her head away.

"Unfortunately, Detective, murder doesn't confine itself to urban areas. If it did, we'd all be better off," Pewter remarked, sitting back in his chair and crossing his legs. Had Pewter noticed her admiring his legs, she wondered, and was this a deliberately provocative gesture? Claire tried to not look at the muscles of his thighs, so thick and firm under his corduroys. Wally looked good in corduroy, too; he had a brown corduroy jacket with leather elbow patches that made him look like the teacher he had once been.

"Do you know that the crime rate in New York City is lower than in eighteen other major cities—among them Gary, Indiana?" Wally pointed out.

James Pewter snorted. "Gary! It's just a suburb of Chicago."

Wally chose not to reply to this observation and got straight to the point. "So you're saying that just about any-

one could have broken into your house and taken mushrooms from your collection?"

Pewter shrugged. "Why would anybody want to do that,
Detective?"

"To *kill* someone, of course!" Meredith's voice came
from across the room, piercing the air. The historian
looked at her and smiled. He liked Meredith, Claire
thought; she also suspected he saw her as a welcome di-
version from Wally's questioning.

"Well?" Meredith put three glasses of cider on the table
and slid into the nearest chair. "Well?" she repeated. "Do
you think Claire is right? *Was* it the mushrooms?"

"We can't know until we speak to the toxicologist,"
Wally replied. He turned back to James Pewter. "Did you
notice anything missing from your mushroom collection,
anything that had been tampered with?"

The historian shook his head. "No, not that I noticed. It
wouldn't take much, though, to do the job—to kill someone—if you used *Amanita phalloides* or *virosa*."

"The Destroying Angel," Meredith whispered.

"Oh?" Wally replied casually. "How much, do you
think?"

The historian shrugged. "Oh, a couple of grams would
do it. They're both very deadly, you know," he added,
looking Wally straight in the eye, as though he were issu-
ing a challenge of some kind.

"Really?" Wally replied tersely. Again Claire had a wild
impulse to laugh, not because she found anything funny,
but because the tension in the air was so palpable. It hung
over them, heavy as the thick white blanket of snow that
lay over the Massachusetts landscape.

She looked at Meredith, who was watching the two men
expectantly, as if she were at a boxing match. "Claire said
the toxins in it destroy your liver and kidneys and can lead
to massive organ failure," she said, plucking the cinnamon
stick from Claire's cider and sucking on it.

"Why do you keep samples of such a deadly mushroom?" Wally asked, fixing the historian with a steady gaze.

But Pewter just shrugged, and ran his finger around the lip of his mug. His hands were thick and strong, Claire noticed, though not as beautiful as Wally's. "The jar is clearly labeled 'poison,' Detective. I would be willing to bet you that half the household items under your kitchen sink are chemical poisons."

"That may be, but as you know, there are uses for those chemicals, such as cleaning. What use do you have for a deadly mushroom?"

"I am a mycologist, Detective—an amateur, it is true, but dedicated nonetheless. In fact, there are probably only a dozen or so professional mycologists in the country."

"What's a—mycologist?" Meredith asked, swinging her legs back and forth under her chair.

"Someone who studies mushrooms," Claire replied.

"Cool."

"And I do study them," James Pewter said, "even if I don't make a living from it."

"So you keep those samples around to study them?" Wally asked, not even attempting to disguise the distrust in his voice.

"Yes, I do. Have you ever seen a mushroom spore under a microscope, Detective? It's a beautiful sight, really. It looks sort of like a snowflake."

"And no two are alike?" Meredith asked.

"No two are alike," Pewter replied, "just like people."

"*Duh,*" said Meredith.

"It may interest you to know that certain toxins are being used now for medicinal purposes. For instance, curare, which is a poison that paralyzes nerves and muscles, is being injected into people's skin for cosmetic reasons—and a form of botulism is being used to treat a rare disorder that affects the vocal cords."

"I see. So you keep these poisons around in order to serve science?"

Pewter smiled. Claire couldn't help notice how his face was even more attractive when he smiled. The right side of his mouth lifted just slightly higher than the other, and the effect was striking. She looked away, afraid Wally would somehow read her thoughts.

"So if the jars were labeled poison, then presumably anyone could have come in, seen it, and taken some out of the jar?" Wally continued.

Pewter took a sip of cider. "Presumably."

"Why do they call it Destroying Angel?" said Meredith, taking a gulp of cider. A plate of scones sat on the table in front of them, and she reached for one.

"Well, it's a beautiful mushroom, tall and snowy white, with a veil on the cap," the historian replied. "I can see where they got the name."

"Beautiful but deadly, eh?" Meredith mumbled through a mouthful of scone, crumbs flying from her lips as she spoke.

Pewter rose and stretched himself, displaying his long, muscular back. "Well, Detective, if you'll excuse me, I've got some work to do." He emphasized the word "detective" just enough to communicate his disdain. He smiled at Claire and laid a hand on her shoulder. "I'll see you later, I hope." The gesture was deliberate, she thought—and his hand lingered for a moment longer than necessary.

"See ya," said Meredith.

"So long," he answered, and left the bar.

Claire glanced at Wally, who was frowning, his lips tightly pursed.

"I don't like him," he muttered.

"I do!" said Meredith. "And Claire thinks he's cute."

"Meredith!" Claire said, but she felt her face burning.

"Well, we all know how trustworthy her taste in men is," he snapped.

Even Meredith gasped at this remark. It was so uncalled for, and so hurtful, that it stunned all three of them for a moment.

"Oh, God, I'm so sorry," Wally said before Claire could catch her breath and reply. "That was a horrible thing to say."

Claire just looked at him; she couldn't think of anything to say.

"Man," Meredith muttered, "are *you* in the doghouse!"

"I'm sorry, really," Wally repeated. "I don't know what came over me. I just—I just don't know how you could . . . well, I've never understood why—"

"Why I fell for Robert?" Claire said frostily. She could feel the icy chill in her voice, feel it spread all the way down to her heart. "I don't know. Maybe you're right; maybe my taste in men isn't so good." She put her mug down and stood up. "Excuse me; I've got some work to do."

"Oh, come on, Claire," Wally protested, but she left the room without looking back.

She could hear Meredith's voice as she closed the door behind her.

"Oh, *man,* are you in trouble!"

Claire was hurt and angry, but most of all she was confused. What Wally didn't know was that his words echoed a question she had asked herself, one she had wrestled with ever since Robert tried to kill her: What if Wally was right? What if she couldn't trust her feelings? If she could fall for a killer, then maybe—just maybe—she could be fooled again.

She went upstairs to the little sitting room at the top of the stairs, with its eighteenth-century reproductions. She sat down in one of the straight-backed chairs and looked out the window. It was a clear night, and the moon hung high in the sky, hard and round and unreachable, a shiny yellow eye looking down impassively at the earth, bright and cold, removed from the struggles of humanity.

"Poor sods," Robert used to call unfortunate people. Claire thought about Mona and Sally. Poor sods, she thought, poor sods.

Chapter 17

That night Claire went to bed feeling a heaviness in her head and an ache in the back of her neck. She awoke in the night shivering, her body filled with fever. Not wanting to disturb Wally, she slipped out of bed and put on her wool turtleneck sweater, sweatpants and socks over her pajamas, then crawled back into bed and pulled the quilt up to her chin. She lay in the dark staring at the pattern of shadows the moonlight caused the maple tree to cast on the ceiling.

The dark outline of branches reminded Claire of long scraggly fingers, reaching across the ceiling toward where she lay in the bed. Robert's fingers were long, she remembered, long and tapered like a painter's. He had the hands of an artist, a pianist, a murderer—

She suddenly was seized with a fit of shaking, so violent that she woke up Wally. He sat upright in bed, and said in a clear, completely alert voice, "What's wrong?"

Startled, she shook her head. "I'm all right. I'm just shivering for some reason."

He put a hand on her forehead. "My God, you're burning up."

As he said it she realized he was right. Relieved, she sank back into the covers. It wasn't fear that made her shake after all; it was only the fever. Somehow, that seemed so much easier to deal with—physical, concrete, a fever had biological causes. It wasn't her inability to let go of old ghosts after all; it was just a touch of the flu.

But Wally seemed concerned. He rose and went into the bathroom, turning on the light, which fell in a pale yellow rectangle on the polished hardwood floor. The light hurt Claire's eyes, and she turned her head toward the window, looking out at the bare branches of the maple tree shivering in the wind. She was shaken by another wave of chills, her jaw shuddering so hard that her teeth rattled.

Wally emerged from the bathroom holding a thermometer. "Here," he said, shaking it, "let me take your temperature."

"Why? What difference will it make?" Claire had trouble focusing on him; with the light from the bathroom behind him, she couldn't make out his face.

"Because," he said, "if it's too high I'm going to take you to a hospital."

"No, no hospital," she moaned, suddenly aware that her joints ached from head to toe.

"Open up," he said, and she obeyed, feeling the thin cold glass clank against her teeth as he slid it into her mouth.

"Under the tongue," he said in a commanding voice. "Keep your lips together."

She nodded obediently, glad he was there to take charge of things. What she wanted more than anything was to let go, to have no demands made upon her. She felt weak and woozy and fuzzy-headed. The fever seemed to block out her peripheral vision, and she felt capable of concentrating only on a limited field of sight. She looked up at Wally and saw the concern on his face. His forehead was furrowed, his lips pressed tightly together. It occurred to her that having been through such loss in his life already, any illness of hers might be especially difficult for him. He looked so tense, so worried, that she wanted to reassure him.

He stood up and returned to the bathroom, and she heard the sound of water running. She sank back into the pillow and closed her eyes. The sound of water running . . . she thought of the mill house, and of the heavy wooden wheel turning endlessly on its axle . . . she looked over at Meredith, sound asleep on her cot, a pillow over her head. Meredith could sleep through anything. She closed her eyes again.

"A hundred and three."

Claire opened her eyes, cloudy with fever. The thermometer was gone from her mouth and Wally was standing over her again.

"Hmm?" She felt sleepy, but the ache in her limbs nagged at her.

Wally sat on the edge of the bed. His thick grey hair stood out in unkempt clumps, silver in the moonlight. She lifted a hand to smooth it down, but she couldn't reach him.

"Your hair," she murmured, trying to sit up. He intercepted her hand in midair.

"Never mind about that," he said, placing her hand firmly on the blanket. "You've got a very high fever. A hundred and three."

"Oh?" Claire said groggily, feeling rather pleased. "That high? That's high, isn't it?"

"Yes, it is. Here, take these." He pressed two aspirins into her palm. She placed the pills on her tongue, tasting their chalky bitterness, and drank eagerly from the glass of water Wally offered.

"More," she said, suddenly very thirsty. "More water, please."

He went back into the bathroom and once again she heard the sound of water running. Water, giver of life . . . and death. Once again she thought of the mill wheel, turning, turning, the relentless flow of water running over the rocks, tumbling downstream . . .

"You know the human body is over seventy-five percent water?" she said when he came back. "Isn't that amazing?"

He shook his head. "I see Meredith's beginning to rub off on you."

"Whaddyou mean?" she said, aware that she was slurring her words but not caring.

The rest of the night and all the next day, Claire drifted in and out of consciousness, her body stiffened with joint aches, her head fuzzy, as though a swarm of insects were buzzing around it. At times the fever made her shiver uncontrollably, no matter how many blankets were piled on top of her; at times she felt like she was burning up, and, flinging all the blankets onto the floor, lay panting on top of the sheets. She was only dimly aware of the coming and going of people in the room: Wally, Meredith, Henry bringing clean towels.

She lay wrapped in the blanket of Wally's concern for her, warm and snug as a cocoon. His hand on her forehead reminded Claire of her mother's hand, so cool and comforting to her when she had fevers as a child. She had never known a man who could be so nurturing, and yet so essentially masculine. All her doubts of the previous evening vanished, and it struck her as something of a miracle, a blessing even, that she had met him. Neither of them mentioned their fight of the day before, and she thought they were both relieved to put it behind them.

She drifted in and out of fever dreams, swaddled in the sheets like a chrysalis in a cocoon. Swathed in her own sweat, Claire felt at times like she was underwater, caught in her subconscious; cradled in its thick dark imagery, at times she hardly knew whether she was waking or dreaming . . .

Images of early spring, the smell of onion grass on a dandelion-spotted lawn, green with yellow polka dots. She dozed off dreaming of her tawny collie Laddie, grinning and wagging his feathery tail, waiting for a game of tag on the beach. She dug her heels into the coarse, sun-warmed sand, grinding the tiny grains between her toes as she ran, until fi-

nally, glistening with perspiration, she dove into the waiting
waves, Laddie beside her, to swim deeply down into the
dark blue water, surrounded by it on all sides, pressing in on
her, cutting off her air—

"Claire, wake up!"

She opened her eyes to see Wally leaning over her. In
the dusky half-light, for a brief moment she could not
make out the features of his face and saw another face
bending over her, a face she had tried for many months to
forget. Her hands shot up in self-defense as a scream gathered in her throat, but the sound of Wally's voice broke
through her panic.

"Claire, it's me."

She fell back on the pillow, exhausted. Wally sat on the
edge of the bed. "You were having a bad dream."

She wanted to tell him that he was wrong, that it wasn't
a bad dream at all—at least not until the end—but she didn't
have the energy. She looked at the window, where frost
etched the corners of the glass in delicate crystalline patterns.

"What time is it?"

"Nearly six. You've been sleeping all afternoon," Wally
answered, laying a hand on her forehead. His palm was soft
and cool and soothing, and Claire closed her eyes.

"Your fever seems to have gone down a little," he said.
The two vertical lines in the middle of his forehead were
showing; Claire called them his "worry lines."

"It's just the flu, you know," she said. "I'll be fine."

He nodded, but the lines didn't go away. "I know. It's
just . . ."

He looked out the window, and Claire knew what he didn't
want to say: he'd been through it all before, and it frightened
him. She knew he didn't want to talk about *her*, about his
dead wife, with Claire, but she thought sometimes he
needed to do this more than he knew. Still, she was reluctant
to invade his privacy; he would talk when he was ready.

Claire closed her eyes. The notes of a Bach cantata

drifted up through the floorboards, serene and orderly, lucid musical symmetry.

> *Tyger! Tyger! burning bright*
> *In the forests of the night . . .*

She opened her eyes. The room looked foggy and surreal, as though she were viewing the world through a thin layer of gauze.

> *Tyger! Tyger! burning bright*

The candle on the dresser flickered, the flame dancing unevenly as little currents of air struck it—gusts too faint for Claire to feel, but which caught the candle flame and pushed it about. She stared at it, dazed, mesmerized by its tiny erratic movements. *Burning bright . . . flame . . . passion . . .*

There was passion in this murder, and in the murderer, she thought. There was something else, something at the back of her mind, but she couldn't pull it forward into the light.

She could hear the clatter of plates and silverware in the dining room below, the click of heels on ancient rustic floorboards. The murmur of voices mixed with the silky sound of strings . . . was it one of the Brandenburgs? She recognized the piece as Bach, but wasn't sure . . . she thought she heard Meredith's cackling laugh over the forest of sounds in the dining room.

> *In what distant deeps or skies*
> *Burnt the fire of thine eyes?*

Her head felt light, and her limbs were heavy. She could smell wine sauce and roasted garlic . . . she sighed and snuggled deeper into the blankets. Good old Max . . . Claire wished she had the appetite to enjoy the delicacies he continued to produce in his kitchen, but the thought of food left

her totally indifferent. She felt curiously detached from her
body, and from the world. She wondered if death was like
this—a gradual dimming of desire until nothing was left but
the memory of it. There was something peaceful and comforting about this semidream state, with its lack of striving,
the experience of surrendering, finally letting go. Blake's
poem continued to rattle around in her head.

> *On what wings dare he aspire?*
> *What the hand dare seize the fire?*

There was something else about the poem, though, a
thought lurking around in the back of her mind . . . she remembered something about Otis Knox telling Frank Wilson
that the basement light was burned out, but there was something else.

> *Did he that made the Lamb make thee?*

Was it something to do with Max? No, that wasn't it.
Claire struggled to think. Her head ached, swollen with
fever. Her mind wandered to Henry Wilson. The son of un-
likely people, there was something mysterious about
him . . . *What the hand dare seize the fire?* Henry's obsession with fire was the sign of a troubled mind, certainly, but
had he set the fire two years ago, or was he—the phrase
jumped into her mind—a sort of sacrificial lamb? *Did he
that made the Lamb make thee?* Poor Henry; who had as-
signed him the role he now played? Was he literally taking
the heat for someone else, and if so, who was it? Claire
thought about Frank Wilson, his big friendly face filling her
mind; she tried to picture that face contorted by rage, tried
to imagine him as a murderer.

She heard the sound of voices in the hall outside her
room.

"Look, it's none of your business. It's between me and
Mona!"

Claire thought she recognized Philippe's voice, but she wasn't sure.

"Yeah, well, she's dead now, isn't she?"

The second person was definitely Otis; there was a slight lisp to his *s*'s, probably because of his harelip.

"Look," Philippe said. "All I'm saying is that I didn't get her pregnant! We used protection. We were very careful!"

"Well, if it wasn't you, then who was it?"

"That's what I'd like to know."

They were interrupted by the sound of footsteps coming down the hall. Claire heard them make a quick exit down the back stairs. The door opened and Meredith appeared at the doorway. She wore a red flannel shirt several sizes too big for her. In her hand was what looked like a chocolate chip cookie.

"You look better," she said.

"Did you get a look at who was in the hallway just now?"

"Naw—I heard 'em scurrying down the back stairs, though, in a big hurry." She sat down on the edge of the bed. "Want a cookie? Max made them, and I helped."

"Not right now, thanks."

Meredith stood in the doorway, her head cocked to one side. Backlit by the light from the hall, her hair surrounded her head like a frizzy orange halo. She frowned. "You really should eat more, you know. It'll help you get well."

Claire shook her head. "What's the saying? Stuff a cold and starve a fever."

Meredith sighed. "Whatever. You're always telling me to eat, and now the shoe's on the other foot."

Claire smiled. "I don't remember ever encouraging you to eat more chocolate chip cookies."

Meredith rolled her eyes. "Well, maybe you should. Reverse psychology and all that."

"That's overrated—and besides, would it work if you knew it was being used?"

"I don't know . . . maybe."

"Hey, listen, speaking of psychology, what do you think of Henry Wilson?"

"Now that's one screwed-up kid. I know I'm weird, but that kid is on another plane. I mean, what's *with* him?"

"That's what I'm trying to figure out. I've got a feeling he's the key to this whole thing."

"Yeah? Well, let me know if you come up with anything, Sherlock. Meanwhile I'm pursuing my own line of investigation."

"Really? What?"

Meredith smiled and took a bite of cookie. "All in good time, my dear, all in good time," she said through a spray of crumbs.

"Let me guess," said Claire. "Margaret Hamilton in *The Wizard of Oz*?"

Meredith rolled her eyes. "*Duh*. It's only like the most famous movie ever *made*!"

After Meredith had gone back downstairs, Claire stared out the window. What would it take to murder someone? she wondered; how desperate or angry would someone have to be to commit the ultimate sin against his or her fellowman? She tried to imagine the moment: the adrenaline building up, the heart racing, muscles tensed for action, until the final moment when knife met flesh, and then it was all over in a matter of seconds and there was no going back.

It was so irrevocable, so final, she thought . . . a life had once existed and did no longer; suddenly the world was a little thinner. What a terrible burden to place upon your soul; how unbearable it must be to live with. She tried to imagine the feeling but her mind fell short, unable to wrap itself around a horror of such magnitude.

> *In what distant deeps or skies*
> *Burnt the fire of thine eyes?*

Chapter 18

Her fever broke during the night, and Claire woke up feeling much better. She could smell the coffee brewing in the dining room, and to her surprise, it smelled good. The voices downstairs sounded louder than usual, the clatter of footsteps seemed to be made by more than the usual number of feet, and Claire had an impression of a general hubbub. She sat up in bed, and just as she was reaching for her robe, the door opened and Wally appeared with a tray.

"I thought you might like some breakfast."

"Yes, actually, I would," Claire replied, suddenly ravenous. The aroma of eggs and toast, which yesterday left her indifferent, now smelled good.

Wally set the tray on the bedside table. "I just talked to Detective Hornblower, and I thought you might like to know they're going to screen for amanita toxins."

Meredith appeared at the door holding a manila folder. "Yeah—they have to look at the stomach contents. Gross!"

"Right." Wally handed Claire a glass of orange juice. "Apparently that's the only place it would show up."

"Cool, huh?" Meredith said, plopping down on the armchair in the corner of the room. She wore one of Claire's

sweaters, a grey mohair, over black leggings. Claire
thought she looked unusually stylish.

"They've put a rush order on the test," Wally remarked,
pouring himself a cup of coffee from the stainless-steel
coffeepot.

"So they found my argument convincing?" Claire said,
taking a big gulp of orange juice. It tasted great, and she
realized she was very thirsty.

"Well, to be honest, it's more like they were at loose
ends; their questioning hadn't led anywhere, and . . . well,
Rufus confessed that there weren't any promising leads."

"They were desperate." Meredith kicked off her shoes.
"Poor buggers," she added with a glance at Claire. Meredith had recently taken to using vulgar British expressions.
It was a subtle way of testing Claire's authority, Claire figured; she would have to protest if they were American
swear words, but these English vulgarities fell into a
grey area. The best way to eliminate this kind of behavior,
she reasoned, was to ignore it. She wondered if Meredith
used these words at home, and if so, how her stepmother
reacted.

"Well," said Wally, "hopefully, they should know something by tomorrow."

Claire looked down at the plate of fried eggs, which reminded her of two large yellow eyes, staring up at her. She
broke off a piece of toast and jabbed it at the thick lemony
yolk, which broke and bled over the egg white. She stuffed
the toast into her mouth, savoring the creamy taste of egg
yolk. "And what if it isn't the mushrooms?"

Wally shook his head. "You've got me there. Poor
Rufus—the DA is breathing down his neck, the local reporters are hounding him, and now the national press has
got wind of the story. I wouldn't want to be in his shoes. I
don't know what his strategy is; he's not sharing everything with me."

"Well, I know what *my* strategy is!" Meredith said from
her chair.

"Oh?" Claire said. "What is it?"

"Oh, you'll see," Meredith replied with a mysterious smile. At that moment Claire remembered that she had been planning to send Meredith back to Connecticut, but the onset of her illness had prevented her from bringing up the subject. She sighed and took another bite of toast. She would deal with it later, when she was feeling up to it. She did not look forward to the inevitable scene that would come when she told Meredith she had to leave.

"Oh, that reminds me," Claire said to Wally. "I overheard an interesting conversation the other day, and I meant to tell you about it."

Meredith leaned forward. "Yeah? What?" she said eagerly.

Claire went on to describe the day she had stood outside the little dining room listening to a conversation between Frank and Max.

"At least I think it was Frank and Max," she said. "They were speaking German, but I was able to understand most of it. Max said something like 'All right, I'm evil, but you're evil too.' And then Frank said, 'I know, but what can I do?' "

"Wow," Meredith commented. "That's *wild*."

"What do you think they were talking about?" Wally asked.

"I don't know; I came by in the middle of it. Strange choice of words, though, don't you think?"

"Yes, and why were they speaking German, of all things? I thought for some reason that Wilson's people were Irish. I mean, he *looks* so Irish."

"I know." Claire shook her head. "It just doesn't add up."

"Or maybe it does," Meredith suggested, "but we don't have all the information yet."

"It's hardly the kind of thing we could tell Detective Hornblower," Claire remarked. "I mean, how stupid would that sound? Excuse me, but I couldn't help eavesdropping on a conversation in German—something about being evil. Thought you might like to know."

Wally shook his head. "I don't know . . . you'd be surprised what's useful in an investigation. I remember once I was working this case down at the Fulton Fish Market . . . everybody figures it was a mob hit, but I kept looking for something else because it just didn't feel right to me. It felt like a copycat mob hit—someone trying to make it look like a mob hit. But something just wasn't right . . . I mean, the victim was part Italian but he didn't run with wise guys."

"Mobsters," Meredith whispered to Claire.

"I know what they are," she answered. "So what did you do?"

"Well, the case finally broke on a pair of Gucci shoes."

"Gucci shoes?"

"It turns out the killer saw that he had to walk through a muddy lot to get away, so he traded shoes with the victim so he couldn't be traced from his shoes."

"Wow," said Meredith.

"Except that the victim was cheaply dressed, and his body turns up with eight-hundred-dollar shoes on his feet. So when this fish-market guy shows up with expensive shoes that don't match the rest of his clothes, all we had to do to narrow the list of suspects was to find out who liked fancy clothes. Turns out the killer, idiot that he was, always wore Guccis. Nothing else, only Guccis."

"Wow," said Meredith, her eyes shining. "Why did Mr. Gucci kill the guy?"

Wally shrugged. "Oldest motive in the world. Jealous husband. He thought of everything—gloves, untraceable gun, so there were no prints, but he forgot about the shoes. So, you see, the strangest things can give people away."

"Guess so," Meredith said. "That's pretty strange, all right."

"Want some more juice?" Wally asked, seeing that Claire had finished hers.

"Yes, please," she replied, handing him the glass.

"Be right back," he said, and left the room.

"He's cool"—Meredith sighed when he had gone—"even if he is old."

"How old do you think he is?" said Claire.

Meredith shrugged. "Oh, I dunno—at least forty." She bent down and retrieved the manila folder from the floor where she had placed it.

"What have you got there?" said Claire.

"Ah . . . papers," Meredith answered.

"What kind of papers?"

"Restaurant checks," she replied, holding them aloft.

"Who gave you those?"

"Nobody. I took them."

"Meredith, that's stealing!"

Meredith shrugged. "I just *borrowed* them. I'm going to put them back."

"That's not the kind of thing you do without permission from the hotel staff."

Meredith rolled her eyes and sighed her most exasperated sigh. "Must I remind you that one of the hotel staff could very well be the murderer?"

"That may be, but still, you shouldn't have taken them."

"And how else am I going to find out if the handwriting on the letters is a match for anyone on the staff?"

"Meredith, why don't you leave that to the police?"

Meredith snorted. "Look who's talking—little Miss I-Just-Couldn't-Help-Overhearing-the-Conversation! You've been snooping around eavesdropping on people."

Claire had to admit the girl had her there. She had the unpleasant thought that the situation had become a competition between her and Meredith, each of them trying to outdo the other.

"Besides," Meredith continued, "Detective Hornblower doesn't see the letters as 'a worthwhile lead at this time.' I think that's how he put it. Boy, am I going to put *him* straight!" She threw herself down on Claire's bed with such force that the whole bed shuddered and the bed-springs groaned in protest.

"All right," Claire conceded, taking a bite of home fries. "Where did you find them, anyway?"

"In the front-hall desk. You know, where we checked in. There's a stack of used checks in the cabinet." She began leafing through the checks. "Let's see . . . what I want first is to see if any of those are a match to Mona Callahan's handwriting."

Claire looked over her shoulder. The server's initials appeared on the top right-hand corner of every check— "PH" must be Philippe, "OK" for Otis Knox, and "MC" for Mona Callahan.

"There's one of Mona's," she said, pointing to it.

"I can *see* that. Now all I have to do is see if it fits one of these letters . . . 'lamb chop, spring salad, tarte aux pommes,' " she read. "Well, we know this diner had lamb chops and . . . isn't that a fancy word for apple pie?" she asked, squinting at the page.

"Not exactly," Claire replied. "A tarte is—"

"Whatever," Meredith said impatiently. "So, what can you pick up that's unusual about her handwriting?" She examined the check, holding it close to her face.

"Meredith, why don't you wear your glasses?" Claire said, wiping the last of the egg yolk from her plate with a piece of toast.

Meredith shuddered. "*Ugh.* One of these days I'll just have that laser surgery," she said. "My dad can afford it. If he can afford my stepmother's coke habit, he can afford that."

"I thought she had given it up."

Meredith shrugged. "Once an addict, always an addict . . . you know how it is."

Claire studied the check. "I don't know if this is unusual, but it does seem to be idiosyncratic," she remarked, pointing. "See how she makes her *l*'s with a single, detached loop at the beginning of words, as in 'lamb chop,' but in the middle of the word she connects it to the other letters. See—there in 'spring salad'?"

Meredith peered at the paper. "Yeah, you're right! Let's see if we can match this to any of the handwriting in these letters."

She went eagerly to the bedside table and fished out a stack of letters from the drawer. Spreading them out on the bed, she pulled up a chair and began going through them one by one. "Hmm, let's see . . . nope, none of these," she concluded, laying aside a small pile. She looked at Claire. "You want to help?"

"Sure. Give me a few."

When Wally returned to the room with Claire's orange juice, he found the two of them surrounded by stacks of letters, deeply engaged in studying the handwriting on each one. He stopped in the doorway and shook his head. "I leave you two alone for a few minutes and look what happens."

"Shh—we're working," Meredith answered without looking up.

"What's this all about?" Wally put the glass of juice down on the bedside table.

"Handwriting analysis," Claire answered, holding up a handful of letters. They were written on anything and everything: postcards, notebook paper, doilies, even the backs of coasters.

"No, you go on ahead." Wally flicked a stray piece of paper from the bed so he could sit down. "Well, I'm glad to see you did so well with your breakfast," he commented, setting aside the breakfast tray.

"Mmm," Claire replied, not really listening. She was studying the letter in front of her. It was on plain notebook paper, a letter she remembered reading before, but now she was struck by how similar the handwriting was to Mona Callahan's.

*What would he do if I broke it off with him? What
would he do? I don't know, and that frightens me. Do
you ever really know someone, know what they are
capable of when they feel they have run out of options?*

"Look at this," she said, handing it to Meredith. "Doesn't
this look like Mona's handwriting?"

Meredith seized the paper and peered at it, her nose
close to the page. "Yes!" she cried after a moment. "Look
at the two ways she makes her *l*'s." She handed the letter
to Wally. "Look—I think we've found a clue!"

Wally studied it and then handed it back. "I wonder who
she's talking about?"

"It's too bad there's no date on it." Meredith sighed,
then perked up immediately. "I know! I'll start by finding
out how long Mona had been working here."

"About two years," said Claire.

Meredith stared at her. "How do *you* know?"

"Her brother told me. We were just talking at breakfast
one day and he mentioned it had been about two years."

"Geez," said Meredith. "I'll have to start getting up earlier." She looked at Wally. "Are you going to show this to
Detective Hornblower?"

Wally nodded. "I think I should. He'll probably want to
go through the rest of the letters. Are there letters in the
other rooms, too?"

Meredith shrugged. "Far as we know."

"Look, here's another one in the same handwriting!"
Claire said, pulling a letter from the pile.

*Again and again I ask myself why I am doing this,
and I arrive at the conclusion that I seem to be powerless to resist . . . why this is I don't know; there is
a dark pull in the man which keeps me coming back,
like a hopeless charmed rabbit frozen in front of the
swaying snake who is about to devour it.*

"Yeah," Meredith said. "He sounds scary. Wonder who it is?"

"Well, she and Philippe had something going, apparently," Wally pointed out.

"Yeah, but that doesn't sound much like Philippe, does it?" said Meredith.

"Not really," said Claire, "but maybe there's a side to him only she saw."

No one said anything for a few moments; they were all thinking about Robert, Claire supposed. No one had seen that side of Robert until it was almost too late—including, most disastrously, herself.

"So that means she was involved with someone else," Wally mused.

"Or it could even be about her brother," Claire pointed out.

"*E-yew,*" said Meredith. "That's *gross*!"

"No, I didn't mean anything sexual, but we're just assuming that it's about a boyfriend. What if she had a sort of dark, neurotic relationship with Chris?"

"I don't know," Wally observed. "It sounds pretty sexual to me."

"Well, the point is, we shouldn't rule anything out," said Claire.

"True," said Meredith. "Remember, once you have eliminated the impossible—"

"Then whatever remains, however improbable, must be the truth," Claire and Wally finished for her in unison.

Meredith frowned. "Boy, are you two getting annoying."

Claire laughed. "Meredith, how often have I heard you say that?"

Meredith crossed her arms and plunked herself down in the brocade armchair. "Well, that's no excuse to be *rude*!"

Wally smiled. "If that's your idea of rude, my girl, you have a rude awakening coming!"

Wally's occasional attempts at wordplay were sometimes closer to the mark than that one, but Claire smiled anyway. Meredith grimaced. "Oh, *man!* Did someone fart?"

"Meredith!" said Claire. "That's unnecessary vulgarity."

Meredith rolled her eyes. "Oh, *sorry;* next time I'll make sure it's *necessary* vulgarity!"

"All right, all right," Wally interjected. "I'm going to take these letters down to Detective Hornblower."

"He's *downstairs?*" Meredith cried, jumping up from her chair.

"Yes, he's down there with Ms. White from the district attorney's office. They're interviewing people again."

"Don't they want to interview *me?*" Meredith said. "I might have something useful to tell them!"

"Well, I guess they'll let you know if they do," Claire said, reaching for her robe.

"Where do you think you're going?" said Wally.

"To take a shower. I feel much better today, only after all that sweating I could use a long, hot shower."

He picked up the breakfast tray. "Okay; I'll take this downstairs and leave you to your shower. Come on," he said to Meredith. "Let's go see what's happening downstairs."

"O*kay!*" she answered, hopping up and down a little as she followed him out.

When they had gone, Claire smiled and breathed a little sigh of relief. She wished scientists could invent a method of channeling human energy; she was certain Meredith's energy, if properly harnessed, was capable of running the Hoover Dam.

Chapter 19

In the shower, as she let the hot water slide over her body, enveloped in steam and warmth, Claire thought about the letter and what it might mean. The more she thought about it, the more it seemed that it really could be about anyone—not just a boyfriend or lover, but someone Mona worked with—even, say, Max, for example.

She squeezed a generous amount of Lily of the Valley shampoo into the palm of her hand and rubbed it into her hair, massaging the skin of her scalp. Well, human nature was unpredictable; maybe even big, friendly Max had his dark side.

After her shower, she dried her hair carefully, then pulled on some black leggings and a light blue cashmere sweater. Claire loved sweaters, and always welcomed cold weather as an opportunity to wear her collection of wool pullovers and cardigans. She still felt a little dizzy from her illness—giddy almost—but she was anxious to see what was going on downstairs.

She arrived at the bottom of the staircase to find a general feeling of expectation in the air. She headed toward the sound of voices coming from the small dining room just the other side of the bar. The first person she saw in the hall was Richard, who inquired courteously how she was feeling.

"Much better, thank you," she answered. "What's going on in there?" She indicated the dining room.

He rolled his blue eyes. "Oh, nothing good, I'm sure, dear girl," he answered, giving her arm a little squeeze. "You take care of yourself now. You still look a little pale, you know."

"Thanks," she said as he went off toward the back stairs. She liked Richard. He always struck her as a little sad, a little bit lonely; even his immaculate grooming and expensive clothes seemed like an effort to disguise loneliness she found touching, perhaps because it reminded her of her father.

The voices coming from the dining room grew louder. Claire took a few more steps toward the door. She recognized Rebecca White's smooth cultivated voice.

"Look, you're not giving us much to go on, and my people in Cambridge are getting nervous. It's an election year, you know, and—"

"Don't give me that election-year crap, Becky!" Detective Hornblower broke in, as agitated as Claire had ever heard him, his voice low but angry. "You know as well as I do that we can't make an arrest without more evidence! Even with the rush order, you can't get any conclusive results from DNA testing for at least two weeks. The guys at the crime lab have been working their tails off over this—"

"Then give us something else," she answered. "*Anything*. We're not asking for a conviction; all we want is an arrest, for God's sake!"

"But what's the sense in an arrest if we can't get the charges to stick?" He sounded exasperated, at the end of his rope.

"Well, so far this whole thing is making us look like a bunch of clowns. I mean, South Sudbury is to Boston as

Podunk, Iowa, is to—Chicago, or something. But you wouldn't know it for all the press this thing is getting. And now with this second death—"

"Which we don't know is a murder," he pointed out. "The girl had a history of drug abuse."

"Yeah, right," she muttered, "and *I'm* Tinker Bell. Give us something we can work with, Rufus, before the political vultures swoop down and destroy us all!"

There was the sound of a chair scraping across the floor, and Claire jumped back from the door and quickly ducked around the corner, where she bumped into Max. It was sort of like bumping into a marshmallow wearing an apron.

"Hey, where are you going so fast?" he said, grabbing her by the shoulders.

"Uh, nowhere." She glanced over her shoulder to see who was coming out of the dining room. The door opened and Rebecca White emerged, as cool and crisp as ever, as though she had just emerged from a relaxing spa instead of a heated argument. She was followed by Detective Hornblower, who had not fared quite so well: his tie was loosened, his jacket rumpled, and he looked as though he could use a drink.

Ms. White nodded curtly to Claire and Max and marched right out of the hotel. Detective Hornblower stood where he was and watched her go, shaking his head. "That young woman is going to do very well for herself in Boston," he commented. "She has the soul of a prosecutor—or a shark, which is pretty much the same thing." He turned to Claire. "I understand you have some letters of interest up in your room."

She nodded. "I—I mean, we—think so."

"Good. Would now be a good time to go get them?"

"Sure. You need the key?"

"I have a master key to all the rooms in the building," said Frank Wilson, coming up behind Max. "What is it you need a key for?"

Detective Hornblower explained about the letters, and

the innkeeper frowned. "The staff isn't supposed to be leaving letters in the drawers; it's for the guests. Are you sure it's Mona's handwriting?"

"Pretty sure," said Claire, then she realized that the obvious question to follow was how she knew, which could lead to the revelation of Meredith's theft of the restaurant checks. Fortunately, though, she was saved by Meredith herself, who came running down the hall, all out of breath, followed by Jeffrey. He wore a grey parka, a pack of cigarettes stuffed into the top pocket. It appeared that he was on his way outside for a smoke.

"Have you heard?" Meredith said excitedly. "Detective Hornblower is offering to pay for anyone to stay at the inn until he's finished with his investigation! Cool, huh?"

"Sort of tidy, keeping all the suspects together under the same roof, huh?" Jeffrey said smoothly, sliding an unlit cigarette into the corner of his mouth.

"It was Ms. White's idea," the detective said. "The DA's office in Boston doesn't want to lose potential leads."

"Or potential murderers. Well, sounds good to me," Jeffrey said. "I'm glad Richard convinced me not to order the crêpes," he added as he sauntered down the hall toward the front door.

"When will the tests for the mushrooms be done?" Meredith said.

"Probably tomorrow . . . maybe even later today. I'm on my way to the crime lab as soon as I finish upstairs," Hornblower answered, placing his bedraggled fedora on his head.

"Well, then, let's go," Frank Wilson said, holding up a thick set of keys attached to a chain that was itself attached to his belt. Claire had not noticed the key chain before, and she wondered if he always wore it.

When the innkeeper and the detective had gone upstairs, Max turned to Meredith. "I have something I was working on in the kitchen, but I'm not sure if it's quite right. Do you want to come taste it for me?"

"What is it?" she said, her expression half-expectant, half-suspicious.

Max cocked his head to one side. "Well, it's got a lot of chocolate in it . . . let's see, what else does it have?"

"*Okay!*" Meredith said. "That's good enough for me!"

She followed Max into the kitchen, skipping. Claire kept thinking about what Jeffrey had said so casually: *I'm glad Richard convinced me not to order the crêpes.* Was he trying deliberately to implicate his friend, she wondered, and if so, what else did he know? She remembered seeing Sally in Richard's room that day, listening to his Piaf recordings—or so he said.

Claire spent the afternoon in front of the fire in the tavern reading one of the paperback mysteries she'd found in the bookshelf upstairs. Surrounded by real death, she had a sudden, sharp craving for fiction, for the safety of make-believe murders and fictional killers. The inn was quiet: Jeffrey and Richard had gone into town for the afternoon, and Chris had taken his father out for a drive to the police station to talk about when Mona's body would be released to the family. Detective Hornblower had made it clear that the body would remain in police custody until all the forensic evidence was gathered, but the yellow plastic tape cordoning off the basement—or "crime scene," as Meredith liked to call it—had been removed early that morning, and Chris expressed hope that his sister's remains would be released soon. Poor Lyle was in his room, which he'd apparently hardly left since Sally's death.

Wally and Meredith were also out, in Wally's car, to get some Theraflu for Claire and—no doubt—cookies for Meredith. Claire was enjoying her time to herself, and the gentle crackle of the logs in the fireplace was the only sound in the room. She was reading a noirish crime thriller entitled *Lucky Stiff* and had just gotten to the part where the detective, a hard-drinking ex-boxer, was about to make love to the dame—who was probably crooked, but he didn't care because she was so alluring, with "lips that just kept coming at you, like ripe strawberries, only sweeter" when she suddenly heard the door to the bar opening slowly, tentatively, its hinges creaking softly. She looked up to see young Henry Wilson, half hiding behind the door, leaning only his head and shoulders into the room.

"Hello," said Claire.

" 'Lo," he replied softly.

"Is there something you'd like?" she said.

He shook his head, then his soft brown eyes widened. "Do you need more wood on the fire?"

Claire looked at the logs in the grate; admittedly, the fire could use some more wood. "Oh, that's okay," she said. "I can do it."

He sighed deeply, then swallowed. "Please," he said in an even softer voice. "Please let me do it."

Claire half expected Paula Wilson to come swooping into the room, but out in the hall all was silent. She looked at the neat pile of logs stacked to one side of the hearth.

"All right," she said. "Just one or two—okay?"

"Okay," Henry agreed, stepping into the room. He wore a flannel shirt a size or two too big for him, jeans, and snow boots. Claire didn't think it could hurt to let him put a log or two on the fire . . . after all, she was there to watch. As the boy walked quietly over to the kindling, Claire was filled with pity for him. Physically, he took after his mother; small for his age, he was thin and fragile, and had her quick, nervous hands and unhappy eyes.

As the boy bent to load the wood on the fire, Otis Knox entered the bar carrying a case of beer. When he saw Henry, he put the case down and approached Claire.

"What are you doing?" he whispered.

"There's nothing wrong with letting a boy put a few logs on the fire," Claire replied, watching Henry stack the wood expertly on the rear of the andirons. Doing this task, his painful awkwardness vanished, and he became graceful and efficient; his movements had the economy of practice. He seemed unaware that they were talking about him; in fact, he didn't appear to be aware of their presence at all.

Otis moaned and ran a hand through his curly hair. "Oh, man, what if Mrs. Wilson comes in and sees this?"

Claire turned to him. "Does she have you all so frightened as that?"

Otis frowned. "What do you mean? I'm not frightened, I just don't want any trouble!"

"Well, then, you can blame it all on me," Claire said smugly, and turned back to Henry, who had picked up the poker and was giving the fire an expert jab to move the logs closer together. A little flurry of sparks flew as the heavy iron poker struck the wood, shimmering briefly and then dying back. Henry leaned the poker back up against the stone hearth, brushed off his hands, and returned to Claire's chair.

"Thank you," he said in a small voice. There was hunger in his deep-set brown eyes—but hunger for what? Claire wondered. Attention, companionship, understanding, love? He was such a pathetic, fragile thing that she longed to wrap him in her arms and soothe away all the cold frost that had built up in his heart.

Otis turned back to the bar with a shrug. He picked up his case of beer and heaved it up onto the counter, then went behind the bar to put the bottles away. Henry stood hesitantly by Claire's chair, his weight on one thin leg.

"Would you like some cider?" Claire asked.

He opened his mouth and was about to answer when the sound of his mother's voice came from down the hall.

"Henry! Where are you? I'm looking for you!"

The boy froze, his whole body rigid. Then he sprang to the door, flung it open, and called out, "Coming, Mother!" With a final longing look at Claire, he disappeared from the room, closing the door behind him.

Claire watched Otis unload bottles from the case of beer, his muscular arms thick as the oak logs on the fire. She was about to say something to him about Henry when she heard the sound of a car engine outside. She went to the window and peered out at the back parking lot to see Wally Jackson's car pull up. The door opened and Wally got out, hatless, hunched up against the cold. A bitter wind was blowing in from the north, and it whipped across the barren landscape, rattling the shutters and shaking the whole house like a living thing. Meredith got out of the passenger side holding a plastic bag. The wind almost ripped the bag from her hand.

Claire met them at the front door. Wally stamped the snow from his boots and rubbed his bare hands together; he had apparently gone out without gloves. Claire shook her head.

"It's cold out there," she said. "Shouldn't you be—"

"I know," he interrupted, "but there are more important things."

"Oh? Like what?"

Meredith squeezed in from behind him. Her face was flushed, and she was out of breath.

"You were right!" she exclaimed. "It *was* the mushrooms!"

"What?" Claire said. "How do you know?"

"The guy from the crime lab is down at the police station talking to Detective Hornblower about it right now!"

Claire turned to Wally. "Is that true?"

He nodded. "Yes. We stopped by just as Detective Murphy was talking to Hornblower about it. He said that they found—"

"Alpha and beta amantadines!" Meredith cried. "Right? Isn't that what they called them?"

"Right. Anyway, it's a very specific toxin, and they wouldn't have caught it unless they knew exactly what to look for."

"How about that?" Claire murmured.

Wally shook his head. "You know, in all my years in New York, I never even heard of a mushroom poisoning . . . not in my precinct, or in any other. And here we are in the middle of Massachusetts . . . I don't know; it's pretty strange."

"*I'll* say!" Meredith exclaimed. "It's downright *creepy*!" Her tone of voice, though, said that it was absolutely thrilling.

"How about that?" Claire repeated. She couldn't help the sensation of pleasure she was feeling. Yes, it was a horrible thing that had happened, but . . . if it weren't for her, there was no telling how much longer it would have taken to determine the mysterious cause of death—if they ever did.

But her next thought was not pleasant at all: someone had deliberately poisoned poor Sally.

"It's interesting," Meredith observed. "The first murder was so disorganized, passionate—and phallic."

"Meredith!" Claire frowned and shook her head.

Meredith rolled her eyes. "Well, it *was*! It reeked of grand opera—Carmen and Don José and all that. And yet the second killing is so different . . . so well planned, and tidy. And not only that," she added, "but poisoning is a traditionally 'feminine' way of killing."

"But not used exclusively by women," Wally interjected.

"No, but by the second murder the killer had changed character entirely . . . I wonder if we're dealing here with a schizoid personality disorder, someone with a confused gender identity—or even multiple personalities."

"Or multiple killers," Claire suggested.

"That hardly seems likely, unless the two of them are in cahoots somehow," Wally observed. "Two murders in the same place, in the same week; that would be too much of a coincidence."

"Coincidence is more prevalent in real life than in fiction," Claire mused.

"Sure, but come *on*!" said Meredith. "That's farfetched, don't you think?"

"I do," Wally replied. "However, as you pointed out yesterday, 'Once the impossible has been eliminated . . .' "

Meredith cocked her head to one side. "I guess we'd better start eliminating some possibilities."

By late afternoon Claire's head had begun to pound again, so she went upstairs to lie down. She lay on the bed sipping from a mug of Nighttime Theraflu, watching the pale pink light of the setting sun reflecting off the frozen white landscape. The lemon-flavored steam soothed her aching head, and before long she slid into a thick, medicine-induced slumber. Her limbs leaden with sleep, Claire dreamed that she was running across a snow-covered field, pursued by a woman wearing a long white dress. The more she tried to run, the more her feet sank down into the deep snowdrifts covering the field. Everything in the dream was white: the snow stretching in all directions, as far as her eyes could see, the woman's dress, billowing out behind like wings; even the sky was an opaque greyish white, a thick cloud cover hanging low over the field.

The clouds reminded her of the mosquito netting that had hung over her bed when she was a child and her family vacationed one summer on the Riviera. Ever since that summer Claire had suffered from claustrophobia. Those nets, thick and white and impenetrable, and her terror at waking in the middle of the night, disoriented, and having to fight her way through what seemed like endless layers of material—this had stayed with her over the years, developing into a fear of entrapment.

Turning to look over her shoulder at the Woman in White, who was gaining on her, Claire failed to see the deep soft bank in front of her, and her foot sank deeply into the drift and she fell. As the woman hovered over her, her long white dress billowing like the mosquito nets, Claire was seized with the same primal terror she had felt as a child. She opened her mouth to scream—but was choked by the layers of white fabric streaming like waves over her.

She raised her hands in an attempt to claw through the material, but it was closing in on her, cutting off her air . . .

She awoke abruptly, in a heightened state of awareness, conscious of everything around her: the stillness of the room, a single shaft of silver moonlight streaming in through the window. She looked up at the moon, so white and cold, high in the winter sky, a dispassionate eye looking down on her, on them all, utterly indifferent to their pathetic lives.

She sighed and dug her feet deeper under the covers, wriggling her toes between the flannel sheets. She missed the warmth of Wally's body, the rhythm of his breathing, so steady and peaceful. She looked out the window at the field behind the inn. As she watched, a solitary fox emerged from the woods and trotted across the snow, its feet skimming lightly over the surface. Halfway across, it stopped, sniffed at the air, one paw lifted, like a bird dog on a scent. Then, evidently satisfied, the fox continued on its way, trotting gracefully across the glistening snow, the only thing moving in the moonlit meadow.

She shivered as she thought about the woman in her dream, her white dress billowing around her. For many Native Americans, Claire remembered, white was the color of death—not black, as in European cultures. She shivered again as she thought of the woman hovering over her, floating above her like . . . like a Destroying Angel.

Chapter **20**

Claire awoke a second time to the aroma of bread baking. She lay there for a few minutes, enjoying the smell, listening to the rattling of pots and pans in the kitchen below, then she threw off the covers, pulled on a cardigan, and went downstairs.

Downtairs, Claire heard loud voices coming from the other end of the hall.

"This is ridiculous!"

She recognized James Pewter's voice. He sounded extremely agitated. Claire walked down the hall toward the front door, where she saw the historian being handcuffed by a uniformed officer as Detective Hornblower watched. Rebecca White was there, too, evidently unruffled by Pewter's rage. Wally stood in the corner watching, and Claire slipped in beside him.

"What's going on?" she whispered, but he just squeezed her hand in response.

"You have the right to remain silent," Hornblower was saying as the officer fastened the cuffs behind Pewter's back.

"This is absurd; *anyone* could have sprinkled mushroom powder on her food!" Pewter bellowed.

Rebecca White regarded him coolly. "Perhaps, but who else would have known the deadly effects of the poison?"

"It was right there in the *book,* for Chrissakes!" Pewter exploded. "*Any* book on mushrooms will tell you the same thing!"

Ms. White shrugged. "But you were the one with a motive."

The historian's brown eyes widened in disbelief. "*What?* What motive?"

"You were afraid Sally Richmond was about to expose your affair with Mona Callahan."

"*What?* Who told you *that?*"

In response, the assistant DA merely shrugged again. Pewter's face, already red, deepened to scarlet. At that moment Frank Wilson came hurrying around the corner; it was clear he had just heard the news. Right behind him was Otis Knox, who had his white bartending apron tied around his waist.

"Frank!" Pewter cried. "Tell them they're making a mistake; you *know* it couldn't be me! I wasn't the one having an aff—"

"Come along, Mr. Pewter," Hornblower interrupted. "You'll have plenty of time to tell your side of the story down at the station."

"My side of the story?" Pewter sputtered. He looked around at the others, who stood watching. "Will somebody *please* say something?" he pleaded, but Frank Wilson just looked at him, arms folded, a deep frown on his big face. Otis Knox averted his eyes, and Claire didn't know what to say.

Rebecca White followed Detective Hornblower as he led Pewter away, a satisfied look on her patrician face. The heavy front door slammed with a loud thud, and there was a long, uncomfortable silence, which was broken by the sound of Jack Callahan's slow, rusty voice.

"Somebody knows something, but nobody's talking."

Claire turned to see Chris and Jack at the top of the stairs. "All right, Papa," Chris said gently, guiding his father by the elbow down the steps. "Let's go for a little walk, shall we?"

"I'm walking, but nobody's talking," the old man declared, louder than before, as Chris led him down. He stopped just in front of Wally.

"Do you think James Pewter killed my sister?" he said.

Wally studied his face for a moment, then shook his head slowly. "No, I don't."

"Then why . . . ?" Otis asked.

Wally shrugged. "They must have needed to make an arrest."

"So they arrest just *any*one?" Frank Wilson said.

"Well, he wasn't just anyone," Wally remarked. "After all, he did have a basement full of jars of mushrooms, some of them poison."

At that moment Meredith came running down the hall from the kitchen.

"What did I miss?" she said breathlessly, wiping her hands on a white cotton apron tied around her waist. She was covered in flour; in addition to a light dusting of it all over her green sweater, there were smudges all over her face, and the fingers of both hands were white. "What happened?"

"They just arrested Mr. Pewter," Claire answered, still unable to believe it herself. Everything seemed surreal; still groggy from her nap, Claire had that sense of unreality you sometimes get after a long nap in the afternoon. When she went to sleep it had been light, and now it was dark outside; although the grandfather clock in the hall said it was only five forty-five, it felt like midnight.

"Oh, *man!*" Meredith said in her most disgusted voice, slapping a thin thigh in frustration. A cloud of white billowed up from her apron, and she coughed as she turned to Wally, who stood, hands in his pockets, studying Otis

Knox. Wally wore a rumpled light brown corduroy jacket, the suede-padded elbows slightly soiled. Wally was not a snappy dresser; but then, his lack of vanity was one of the things that had attracted Claire to him.

"Was it the mushrooms?" Meredith said.

Wally nodded, but the look on his face was bemused. "They seem to think he was having an affair with Mona Callahan." He looked at Otis as he said this, and the bartender's face reddened.

"Well, I have to get back to work," he muttered, and, slipping away, disappeared into the tavern. Frank Wilson followed after him; it looked to Claire like he wanted to talk to Otis.

Meredith's jaw dropped, just like a cartoon character, Claire thought. There was something about the girl that evoked a Warner Brothers character; she was so exaggerated, so much larger than life. "No *way*!" she exclaimed. "Out of the question!"

"Really?" said Wally. "Why do you think so?"

Meredith shook her head. "Just couldn't be . . . it's hard to say."

"Is it because he's older?"

Meredith shook her head, and a few flakes of flour floated down from her hair. "Nope, it just isn't right." She turned to Claire. "You know what I mean?"

Claire nodded slowly. "Yes, I do . . . they just don't match. It's hard to explain." She smiled at Wally. "Call it woman's intuition."

"I *knew* you were going to say that!" he groaned, rolling his eyes. Though Wally was by nature restrained, Claire thought that being around Meredith had made him more expressive. When they first met, he would never have resorted to such a theatrical gesture as rolling his eyes, but now it seemed perfectly natural. Well, she thought, people become more like each other as they grow closer; Claire had caught herself adopting little gestures or phrases Wally used, quite unconsciously, just as she had imitated the laugh of a cousin she admired when she was a child. It was almost totemic, this absorption of another person's traits, like Native Americans who dress up in the skin of an animal in order to assimilate its courage, grace, and strength.

"So why did they get him?" said Meredith.

"They showed up with a search warrant for his house and found jars of amanitas in the basement," said Wally.

Meredith shrugged. "Big deal. He's a mycologist. Besides, if he were guilty, don't you think he'd destroy the evidence?"

"Apparently they found a book on mushrooms with the page on amanitas marked."

"Oh, jee*zus!*" Meredith snorted. "I mean, setup city! *Duh.* Do they think he's an *idiot?*"

"I think Wally's right," Claire observed. "They were desperate for an arrest." She went on to tell them about the conversation she had overheard between Detective Hornblower and Rebecca White. When she was finished, Wally frowned.

"Nothing good can come of an arrest made out of desperation; it only leads to more trouble." He shook his head. "Ms. White is obviously an intelligent and ambitious young woman, but both youth and ambition can work against you if you're not careful."

Meredith narrowed her eyes. "Hey, is that meant for *me?*"

Wally smiled. "Not really. Interesting that you thought it was, though."

Meredith rolled her eyes. "What*ever*. You can cut the psychoanalysis crap. My dad keeps trying to get me to a shrink, and I keep telling him I'd be fine if he weren't married to the Saran Wrap queen of Connecticut."

Claire frowned. "Saran Wrap?"

"Yeah. She's so paranoid about germs she has to wrap everything in plastic all the time. Food, I mean."

"Like leftovers?" said Wally.

Meredith shook her head. "Oh, God *forbid* we should

ever eat leftovers—no, no, no—that would surely lead to botulism and death! No, I mean as soon as anything is bought she has to wrap it up—celery, crackers, whatever. It's downright creepy, if you ask me."

"It may be creepy, Meredith, but you need to watch your language and your manners," Claire remarked.

Meredith sighed. "Sorry," she said to Wally.

"Just because you're smarter than a lot of people is no excuse to be rude to them."

Meredith's eyes widened as she looked at Wally. "I never said I was smarter than *him*!"

Wally laughed. "It's all right; maybe you are."

"Saran Wrap, huh?" Claire mused. "That reminds me of something, but I can't think what . . ."

Meredith smirked. "Having an Alzheimer's moment?"

"Very funny. Just for that, I think I won't tell you what it is."

"You mean you remember?"

"Maybe."

"Oh, come on; tell me, please! I promise I won't make any more cracks about your age."

"She's not that old, you know," Wally pointed out.

Meredith sighed heavily. "I *know*. I was only kidding. Now, what was it you remembered?"

"Well, it reminded me of when I used to wait on tables, and how the chef there was crazy about using Saran Wrap for everything."

Meredith's eyes opened wide. "You used to be a *waitress*? No way!"

Claire smiled. "There's a lot you don't know about me."

"Where?"

"A little French restaurant in New York, when I first arrived just after college. But that's not important. What I was thinking was how he would make up the menu each day, and I was wondering if Max did the menu planning himself, or if the Wilsons helped him."

"Well, there's one way to find out," Wally remarked. "Let's just ask him."

Max was in the kitchen putting the finishing touches on his pastries before baking them in the large confectioner's oven nestled against the kitchen's far wall.

"What happened to you?" he said to Meredith as the three of them walked into the kitchen. "I had to finish the pastries all by myself."

"Sorry—I got sidetracked," Meredith replied, hopping up onto a tall stool next to one of the counters. Max kept the stool there to sit on from time to time while he worked, he had told Claire; his back had a tendency to spasm if he stood for long periods of time, and he had heel spurs in both feet.

"How's your back?" Claire asked.

"I've had better days. Ah, well, every job has its occupational hazards," the chef answered with a good-natured shrug. "At least it's better than skydiving."

"We were wondering," Wally began slowly, "who set the menus each day?" Wally had a way of asking questions so they sounded less like a police interrogation and more a matter of genuine curiosity and interest—a useful trait for a homicide detective, Claire thought.

Max slid a tray of puff pastry into the oven, and a wave of heat enveloped the room, making the skin on Claire's face tighten and flush. Max straightened up and wiped the sweat from his pink cheeks. "Sometimes I do them myself, and sometimes Mrs. Wilson gives me suggestions. Why?"

"Who set the menu the night before Sally died?" said Meredith.

Max leaned against the counter, his stomach in its white apron puffing out in front of him like rising pastry dough. "Well, let me see . . . we did it together, as I recall . . . this is right; she had some things she wanted me to cook that night."

"Do you remember what exactly?" said Claire.

"Whose idea were the mushroom crêpes?" Meredith added.

"Well, you know we always have to have a vegetarian entrée, for the poor Miss Sally, who was a vegetarian, you know."

"Yes," Wally remarked. "I wonder who else knew that?"

Max shrugged and ran a hand over his forehead, which was perspiring thickly. "It was no secret, this. I seem to remember Mr. Jeffrey making a remark upon it once, about how some people couldn't stand to eat another animal, and how it might do her some good to have some red meat once in a while."

Claire nodded. "That sounds like Jeffrey. But whose idea were the mushroom crêpes? Can you remember?"

Max cocked his head to one side. "Let me see . . . ah, yes, it was Mrs. Wilson. She wanted me to try a new kind of flour—something with semolina in it, I believe." He made a distasteful face. "I told her it was not good for the cooking, this flour—too grainy—but she insisted I try. I was right, of course," he added with a little smile. "The crêpes were not very good."

"Where is this flour now?" said Wally.

Max frowned and crossed his arms. "I threw it out. One really cannot work with materials like this. It is like trying to paint an oil painting using the finger paints."

"So the crêpes were her idea," Meredith mused.

"Yes, but this is really nothing unusual," Max replied. "She suggested several other things on the menu as well, and as I say, it is not at all uncommon."

"Philippe and Otis were both waiting on tables that night, as I recall," said Claire. "Who besides them would have known which table was getting the mushroom crêpes?"

Max shrugged. "Oh, anyone. All they had to do was look at the order slip; the table number is clearly written upon each one."

"And were you in the kitchen during the whole time?" said Meredith.

"I had to leave several times—once to use the toilet, and another to help Frank carry in some wood from outside. The boys were both busy with their tables, and the fires needed more wood, so I took a few minutes to help."

"I see," said Wally. "So the kitchen was left unattended?"

Max nodded. "And now, if you will excuse me, I must attend to my little friends in the oven. I can smell they are almost ready, and once a pastry is overcooked, it is *ganz schrecklich*—really terrible."

They left Max puttering among his pastries and wire whisks, the picture of contentment.

"So James Pewter was right," Meredith remarked as they crossed the bare wooden floor to the back staircase. "Anyone at all could have slipped poison mushrooms into Sally's crêpes."

"You know," said Claire as Meredith started up the stairs, "the murderer must have thought Sally's being a drug addict provided the perfect cover. He or she must have figured that everyone would just assume it was a drug overdose . . . and in any case, why would they look for a poison as specific as amanita?"

"But the murderer didn't count on you," Wally added, laying his hand on her shoulder and giving it a squeeze.

As she put her hand on the railing, Claire thought she heard something—a kind of yelping sound. It wasn't coming from inside the house, but from somewhere outside, she thought.

"Wait a minute," she said to Wally.

Meredith, who was halfway up the stairs, turned around. "What? What is it?"

Claire shook her head. "Hold on a second. I think I heard something . . . there! There it is again."

It was a kind of wailing, like a cry for help, only it

didn't sound quite human. Claire put her hand in the air. "There! Did you hear that?"

Meredith came clomping loudly back down the stairs. "Hear what?"

"There—there it is again. It sounds like someone's in trouble. I'm going to find out what it is."

"Wow, you *do* have good ears," Meredith marveled as she followed Claire down the hall toward the back entrance, which opened out onto the parking lot.

"You can't go outside without your coats," Wally said. "It's too cold."

"I'll get them!" Meredith cried, sprinting up the stairs two at a time. Moments later she returned laden with parkas, hats, and gloves. The sound had died down while she was gone but returned as they were putting on their coats. This time Meredith and Wally heard it, too.

"I hear it now!" Meredith cried as she pulled on her red mittens. "It does sound like someone's in trouble!"

They charged out the back door and into the icy parking lot, where they stood listening, but the air was still, silent. "It's stopped," Meredith said, her breath a puff of white mist.

They looked around, but there was no sign of movement. Not even a wisp of breeze stirred the barren tree branches, black and stiff as sentinels in the frigid air.

Then it came again—clear and chilling, a yell of pain.

"This way!" Claire called, pushing through the snow in the direction of the sound. Several hundred yards behind the inn, where field met woods, a little wooden shack was nestled among a pile of tall yellow weeds. Claire had noticed it before and supposed it was a toolshed of some kind. As she charged toward it, her legs plowing through knee-high snowdrifts, she could hear plainly that the sound was indeed coming from inside the shack.

"This way!" she shouted over her shoulder to Wally, who had Meredith by the hand and was dragging her along behind him. The girl's long spindly legs were not built for this kind of work, and she was struggling to keep up, her breath coming in frozen gasps, her red scarf dangling down to her knees as she plunged from one drift to the next.

As she neared the shed Claire noticed two sets of tracks in the snow, coming from another direction: one was a person, and the other looked like the prints of a medium-sized dog. The prints led right up to the door of the shack.

By the time Claire reached the shed, the sounds had stopped. The door was closed tightly; she reached for the handle and pulled hard. The snow provided less resistance than she expected, and to her surprise the door flung open.

There, standing hunched over, with a stick in one hand, was Henry Wilson. The other hand was clasped firmly around the collar of his family's dog, Shatzy. Claire realized instantly what was happening in the toolshed, and a sickening sensation crawled up her legs, leaving her weak-kneed: the boy had been beating the dog with the stick. Suddenly everything turned white, like a movie screen fading out, and Claire heard someone screaming. The next thing she knew Wally was holding her, pulling her away from Henry Wilson, who stood cowering in the corner, terror on his sallow face.

"No, Claire!" Wally was saying, and then Claire realized the person she had heard yelling was herself. She looked down at her right hand, which Wally was restraining, and saw that she held the stick formerly held by Henry Wilson. "It's all right now," Wally whispered, and Claire looked around for Meredith. The girl stood in the doorway to the shed, looking at her with an expression Claire had never seen before: a combination of horror and awe. Claire looked down at the stick in her hand, and at that moment she was even a little afraid of herself.

Chapter 21

"Please don't tell my mother!" were the ⟨...⟩ Henry Wilson spoke as Wally took the ⟨...⟩ him. Poor Shatzy cringed as Wally reached down ⟨...⟩ his head.

"It's all right now," he murmured as he petted the dog, who was still shivering in fear, the hair on his misshapen body standing up in all directions. "No one's going to hurt you anymore," Wally said as Meredith, recovered from her shock at Claire's behavior, rushed to the dog, hugging it tightly in her arms.

"You poor thing!" she cried. "What did that terrible boy do to you?"

"Not so tightly, Meredith," Wally said, and then he turned to Henry Wilson, who stood trembling in the corner. "Why did you do this, Henry?"

The boy just shook his head, his eyes wild with fear. "Please don't tell my mother," he rasped. Furious as she still was, Claire couldn't help noticing that the boy was so terrified that he could hardly speak. The words stuck in his throat, clogging his windpipe, and his pale face was even more ashen than usual.

Still, her heart hardened against him when she saw the poor dog shivering in Meredith's arms. "Why shouldn't we tell her, Henry?" she said coldly. "Tell me that."

Henry lowered his head as though he couldn't bear to look at her. Indeed, Claire felt a bit like Medusa. "Why shouldn't we tell her, Henry?" she repeated, and she felt as if it was her heart that had turned to stone.

The boy still refused to look at her. He cringed against the wall, shaking his head, then he covered his face in his hands and exploded into loud sobs. Startled, Claire looked at Wally, who shook his head.

"Come on, Henry, let's go back inside where it's warm," he said.

"Don't—tell—my—mother," Henry gasped through his sobs as Wally gently raised him to his feet.

Meredith scooped the dog up in her arms and followed *t*em as they trudged through the snow back to the inn. The *ligh*ts in the windows were beckoning, inviting them back *to t*he land of warmth, but still Claire felt a creeping chill in her heart as they made their way across the frozen landscape.

It was difficult for Wally and Claire to know what was the right thing to do, under the circumstances. Henry Wilson was clearly a deeply disturbed child, but given the recent events at the Wayside Inn, they could hardly blame him. They were worried about the dog, however, and were determined to protect Shatzy from any further harm. In the end they decided that they would keep the dog in their room until Wally had a chance to speak with Frank Wilson. Claire wasn't sure, but she thought Wally was as afraid of Paula Wilson as everyone else—including herself— seemed to be.

Wally attempted to talk gently to Henry about the incident, but the boy appeared to be traumatized, and just kept repeating, "Don't tell my mother—please!" over and over. Finally Wally gave up and sent him back home until they could speak with his father, who was in town running errands.

"That kid is in bad shape," Meredith remarked as they closed the bedroom door.

"What a strange family," Claire said as she stroked Shatzy's ears. Fortunately, the dog had no visible marks, but looked traumatized after his ordeal. He trembled from time to time, and when anyone petted him he licked their hand obsessively, as if doing so would prevent them from hurting him. "Poor Shatzy," she said. "Don't worry; we'll protect you."

Meredith lay down on the rug next to the dog. "Maybe we could keep him. He needs a new home."

"We?" said Claire. "What is this 'we'?"

"Well, I mean, you could keep him in New York, and I could come visit him."

"Right. Ralph would really go for that!" Claire couldn't imagine her fat white cat sharing the apartment with any other animal, let alone a scraggly mixed-breed terrier.

Just then there was a commotion downstairs; Claire heard the sound of loud voices and the slamming of several doors.

"Hey, something's going on down there!" Meredith cried, and was out the door before Claire could stop her. Claire and Wally followed, and when they arrived downstairs, they saw Detective Hornblower in the front hall. With him was Philippe. The door to the bar was open, and it looked to Claire as if both of them had just emerged from the room.

"There is no mistake in the DNA, Mr. Houis," Hornblower was saying. "The match is precise. Now, if you'll just step back inside with me—that is, unless you'd rather come down to the station to answer questions."

As he spoke, Otis Knox emerged from the main dining room, followed by Frank Wilson.

"*Okay,*" said Philippe, "I had sex with her that night, but I *didn't* kill her. I swear it!" He looked around at the others as though trying to find someone who would believe him. Claire looked at the faces of the others: Otis Knox stood staring at the floor, biting his lower lip, as though he didn't trust himself to look at Philippe. Detective Hornblower looked at Philippe calmly, with his usual impassive stare, and Max averted his gaze—out of a sense of modesty and decorum, Claire felt. What surprised her was the look on Frank Wilson's face. The innkeeper stared at the waiter with an expression of raw fury; he didn't just stare, he glowered, as if Philippe had just confessed to the murder. Claire glanced at Detective Hornblower to see if he noticed how upset Wilson was, but the detective was hard to read; his face did not betray what he was thinking or feeling.

"No one's saying you did, Mr. Houis," he said evenly. "But if you were with her that night, there's a chance you may have seen or heard something."

"She *was* seeing someone else, you know," Philippe blurted out. "And I can tell you one thing: it wasn't Jim Pewter!"

"Don't look at me!" Otis said as eyes turned upon him. "Why don't you talk to her brother? She told me she was thinking of suing him over the power of attorney for their father."

Hornblower sighed. "Mr. Callahan has already told us that." He turned back to Philippe. "So the last time you saw her was when she was in your room?"

"Yeah. We made love on the spur of the moment, and then I fell asleep. When I woke up she was gone. I just assumed she'd gone back to her room, and I didn't think anything of it until . . ." He stopped and lowered his head. Everyone knew the words he had left unsaid: *until she was found dead.*

Detective Hornblower picked up his battered fedora. "If any of you would like to amend your statements, please feel free to do so. Whatever you say will be held in confidence." He rose in one smooth motion and, replacing his hat on his head, stretched himself. "Well, thank you for your time."

Before he left, Wally inquired about the DNA testing on the fetus Mona had carried in her womb, but the big detective shook his head. "Not finished yet. We had to put in a rush order just to get what we got. Usually this kind of thing takes weeks, if not months. A complete DNA profile is complicated and time-consuming. I'll tell you something in confidence, though," he said, leaning closer. "The DNA sketch of the fetus so far is real different than the sperm in her body—so it looks as though she was buttering both sides of her bread."

"Wow," Meredith said later over tea and dessert. "Someone knows something they ain't telling." She reached across the table for the plate of orange scones.

"Meredith," Claire cautioned, "watch your boarding-house reach."

"Sorry," said Meredith. "Please pass the scones."

"It makes you wonder, doesn't it, who told the detective that James Pewter was the 'other man'?" Wally mused as he spread blackberry jam on a scone.

"Yes, it does," Claire agreed. "And that is probably the key to the whole thing."

Meredith and Wally decided to take Shatzy for a walk after dinner, and Claire went upstairs to lie down. Alone up in their room, Claire saw Meredith's book on Zen training lying on the bedside table. Curious, she opened it to the chapter on koans.

> *The Sound of Firewood Tumbling Down.* A certain monk suddenly realized his Original Self when he heard the sound of a heap of firewood tumbling down. In that sound he heard all things collapse—delusive thoughts, the habitual way of consciousness—leaving pure existence exposed.

Claire put the book down and looked at the maple tree outside the window; its bare branches seemed to reach toward her. *Pure existence* . . . it sounded so inviting, a life of contemplation and peace, the serenity of Zen enlightenment. She sighed. How different that was from this jumbled, messy existence she knew, full of ungoverned passions and human frailty. *The sound of firewood tumbling down* . . . she thought of young Henry Wilson, of his beating of poor Shatzy with a stick, and his obsession with fire.

> *Tyger! Tyger! burning bright*
> *In the forests of the night.*

"Oh, my God," she whispered to herself. "Oh my God." A thought formed in her mind, a tiny seed of suspicion, but once it began to take root she could feel it growing rapidly. Without bothering to put her shoes on, she left the room abruptly and went downstairs.

Detective Hornblower seemed surprised to hear her voice when she reached him at the police station. He seemed even more surprised when she told him that Henry Wilson held the key to the murders.

"Are you accusing him of murder, Ms. Rawlings?" he said, his voice wary.

"No, of course not!" Claire answered impatiently. "But you need to talk to him!"

"Would you like to explain your reasoning?"

"Believe me, it would take longer to hear than you would want. It all involves Zen koans and firewood."

"Firewood?"

"Just talk to him!"

She waited impatiently for Hornblower to arrive, and finally saw his car pull up in front of the Wilsons' house. Before long he appeared at the front door of the inn to tell Claire that Paula Wilson had said she wasn't feeling well and Henry was in bed with a fever.

"And she is dressed in her nightgown, but she doesn't look all that sick," he added, stomping the snow from his boots.

"All right," said Claire. "Then you should arrest Paula Wilson."

Detective Hornblower frowned. "Are you going to explain to me what this is all about?"

"It's very difficult, I'm afraid," she replied, "because it involves more intuition than logic. But I'll try."

They went into the bar to talk, but within minutes their conversation was interrupted by the arrival of Meredith, who burst breathlessly into the room.

"There's a fire over at the Wilsons'!"

After grabbing a coat from the front-hall rack, Claire and Detective Hornblower followed her outside. Sure enough, a blaze had blossomed in the Wilsons' attic, and the flames were shooting up into the night sky. As Hornblower pulled out his cell phone to call the fire department, Claire noticed someone in white running away from the Wilsons' across the snow in the direction of the mill house.

"Look!" she said to Wally, who was already on his way to the Wilsons' house. "Who's that?"

"Looks like Paula Wilson," he called over his shoulder. "I'm going over to see if everyone's okay." Released from his leash, Shatzy followed after him, barking.

Just then the front door to the Wilsons' house opened and Henry Wilson came running out. "Where did my mom go?" he wailed, loud enough for Claire to hear him across the road.

She followed Wally across the street to where Henry stood, looking around.

"Is anyone else in there?" Wally pointed to the house.

Henry shook his head. "No. Where did my mom go?"

"The mill house," said Wally. "I think I saw her running toward the mill house."

Within minutes Claire heard the sound of fire-engine sirens, and shortly thereafter two bright red trucks came careening around the corner. By this time people were coming out of the Wayside Inn, and they stood, arms folded, watching the firemen pour out of the trucks; with their black rubber coats and bright yellow stripes, they reminded Claire of large honeybees, swarming around the coils of hose wrapped around the fire trucks. Standing in the driveway, Claire could make out Richard and Jeffrey, as well as Chris Callahan and his father. There was no sign of Lyle. Frank Wilson and Max were still in town, she supposed.

But Henry Wilson wasn't interested in the fire; he sprinted off toward the mill house, and Claire and Wally followed him. Indeed, the fire did not look very big, and the firemen appeared confident that they would soon have it under control. Meredith managed to grab Shatzy's leash and loped along after Claire. He ran beside her, barking, looking rather pleased by all the excitement. It was about the length of two football fields to the mill house, and they covered the distance quickly in spite of the snow.

When they arrived, they stopped abruptly. There, in the moonlight, perched precariously on a narrow ledge directly over the churning wheel, dressed only in a white nightgown and slippers, was Paula Wilson. She stared at the rushing water below her, but when she saw Claire and Wally she called out.

"Don't come a step nearer or I'll jump!"

Claire turned to Meredith. "Go get Detective Hornblower—quickly!"

Chapter 22

Paula Wilson stood, poised above the mill wheel, her hands outstretched as if in surrender, spread out from her body in the attitude of a crucified Christ. Her long white nightdress billowed out behind her like a sail and Claire was struck by how much she resembled the Woman in White from her dream. Her usually tightly coiffed hair flew loose in the wind, her long white gown flapping behind her like wings, and she looked as if she might indeed take off into the sky at any minute.

Detective Hornblower came rushing up to where Claire and Wally stood at the same moment as Frank Wilson drove up in his car. He climbed out of the driver's side as Max emerged from the passenger seat. They both hurried over to Hornblower.

"What's going on?" Wilson demanded.

Paula Wilson looked down at her husband. "Why couldn't you love me?" she wailed, decades of bitterness welling up in her voice. "Why was that so hard?"

Frank Wilson stood, hands at his sides, a tortured expression on his face. He shouted into the wind but the sound flew back into his face and Claire couldn't make out the words. The gale was gathering in force, and it took Claire's breath away. Some of the other hotel residents had come across the road and now stood close by, arms wrapped around their bodies, a small band of people standing on the hard, windswept plain of frozen snow.

Frank Wilson yelled again, and this time Claire heard clearly what he said.

"Paula—no!"

Wally stepped forward. "Mrs. Wilson, come down! Please let us help you!"

She shook her head. "The time for help is past! No one can help me now."

"Paula, please come down!" her husband shouted.

She stared at him as if he were the one who had lost his mind.

"Why? Why does it matter to you?" Her thin face hardened, her eyes cold as flint, deep dark pieces of black coal. "Why was it so hard to love me?" she repeated.

Claire looked at Paula's son, who stood next to Max, his thin little body pressed against the comforting bulk of the big chef. Max had his hands on the boy's shoulders, and Claire couldn't tell whether or not he was holding him where he was, keeping him from running to his mother.

Max stepped forward. "Please, Mrs. Wilson, come down! This isn't going to solve anything. Think of your son!"

Her face softened as she looked at Henry, pressed up against Max. "Oh, Henry, forgive me," she said. A gust of wind caught at her and she wavered and almost tumbled from her perch.

Suddenly the boy broke free of Max and rushed toward her. "Mother! Don't jump—please!" he wailed. After a few steps, however, his legs failed him and he stumbled and fell to his knees in the snow. He struggled to rise but then collapsed weeping in a heap.

Frank Wilson stepped forward and lifted his son from

the ground. "Paula, we need you!" he called. "Please come down!"

His wife's face regained its hardened look. "*You* don't need me!" she said bitterly. "You've *never* needed me!"

"Mrs. Wilson, come down and we'll talk," said Detective Hornblower, stepping in front of the innkeeper.

"There's nothing to talk about," she called back.

Meredith, who had been standing quietly next to Claire all this time, stepped forward. Her usually pale face was red, either from the cold and wind or from emotion.

"Look at him!" she shouted, pointing to Henry, who stood staring at his mother, terror etched on his thin features. "Don't do this to him—don't take away his mother! It's a terrible thing to live without your mother; believe me!" She spoke with such conviction that everyone looked at her. The force of her emotion surprised even Claire, who had never heard Meredith speak so passionately in all the time she had known her. It was as if a dam had burst inside her and all the sorrow and anger at her own mother's death was rushing out.

Detective Hornblower made a brief movement, as if to stop Meredith, but then he stopped and just looked at her, hands at his sides. He looked like he had reached the end of his rope, run out of alternatives, and now Meredith represented a last-ditch chance to rescue the situation.

Meredith struggled to be heard over the wind whipping across the flat white surface of snow. Her eyes watered and her nose was running as she cupped her hands around her mouth and yelled at Paula Wilson with all her might.

"Please!" she cried, the physical effort shaking her thin body. "Please don't leave your child!"

There was a pause that seemed to last forever, and Claire felt as though everyone was holding their breath. She could feel her own heart pumping away underneath her jacket, pressing heavily against her chest. Her throat was so tight she could hardly breathe; it felt as if the muscles were so constricted that the thin, icy air could hardly make it through the narrow passageway. She straightened her shoulders and took a big gulp of frosty air into her lungs.

At that moment Paula Wilson, who had been poised still as a statue upon her precarious perch, let out a heartrending wail, too loud for her thin body, Claire thought—it was the scream of an animal in pain, the release of years of bottled-up agony. For a moment no one moved and everything was still. Even the wind itself seemed to die down.

Claire looked around at the others; they were all watching Paula Wilson, who stood poised on her ledge. For a second Claire thought Paula leaned forward, toward the churning mill wheel, and she closed her eyes and held her breath, afraid to watch. But instead of jumping, Paula Wilson's whole body seemed to deflate, and she sank to her knees, burying her head in her hands. The sound of her sobs could be heard over the whistling wind, which had picked up once again, slicing through Claire's clothing, sharp as a knife.

All at once everyone seemed to explode into action. Detective Hornblower leaped forward with an agility Claire would not have imagined him capable of. In an instant he had covered the ground between himself and Paula Wilson and grabbed her securely by the shoulders. She didn't appear even to notice him; she remained on her knees, her body collapsed in on itself. Her son ran to her, throwing himself in her arms sobbing as Hornblower lifted her gently to her feet.

Wally followed after him, and helped Hornblower support Mrs. Wilson, who was still sobbing. She squeezed her son in her arms, her tears falling upon his upturned face. Then Detective Hornblower pulled him gently from his mother, and the boy ran to his father, who embraced him awkwardly. Claire looked at Meredith, who was watching mother and son, standing as still as Claire had ever seen her. There was a look on her face—hunger, loss, envy—that Claire had never seen before. It was a sad expression, but it was more than that; it seemed to Claire that as she watched, Meredith's expression changed from grief to understanding to acceptance. Though she couldn't be sure, she thought she was watching the girl beginning to process her mother's death for the first time. After bottling her grief inside her, afraid no doubt of its power and fury, she was finally allowing it to manifest itself in, for her, that most foreign of all places, her body.

Claire had an impulse to hug her, but something told her Meredith wasn't quite ready for that. Instead, she laid a hand lightly on her shoulder as Wally and Detective Hornblower brought Paula Wilson over to them. Frank Wilson took a few steps toward his wife, but she gave him a look of such hatred and anger that he took a step back and let them pass. Max put a hand on his arm and the innkeeper looked at him gratefully.

The little group broke into two columns to let Detective Hornblower and his prisoner pass. Everyone looked sober and chastened; even Jeffrey's face was devoid of its usual smirk. Paula Wilson walked with her eyes focused straight ahead, a detective on either side of her, a calm expression on her face. Claire thought she actually looked relieved. It was as if now, with everything behind her, her guilt at last discovered, she could finally relax and surrender herself to her fate.

The fire chief chose that moment to come strolling across the snow. He was a big, ruddy-faced man with a day's growth of beard. "Got the fire under control. Need some help here?"

"No, we're fine," Hornblower replied.

As Paula marched by them, flanked by her captors, Claire heard Detective Hornblower's dutiful recitation of those words that were as familiar to her as the Pledge of Allegiance: ". . . under arrest for the murders of Mona Callahan and Sally Richmond. You have the right to remain silent . . ."

The right to remain silent. Well, her victims had been

silenced forever, but Claire wondered whether Paula Wilson would take advantage of her right. Somehow, she didn't think so. She was a woman who for too long had sat in stony silence, bearing her grief stoically, watching her husband's infidelities through clenched teeth even as she bore his child. After years of such silence, Claire had a feeling that Paula Wilson was ready to talk, to explain what dark, buried passions had led her to kill, first in the heat of the moment, and then later on in cold blood. It occurred to her that on some level Paula Wilson's dark deeds were her subconscious making a cry for help—a twisted, terrible way out of her situation, but it was an escape.

Everyone stood there for a few moments after Paula Wilson passed. Then, leaving a respectful distance between themselves and the accused, they filed silently after, their boots crunching the crust of frozen snow as the moon rose higher in the frosty sky.

Back at the hotel, the police cruisers were lined up in a crooked row, their bumpers pointing in all directions, their lights flashing. Claire counted four of them, plus Detective Hornblower's plain sedan. Evidently more than just the local Sudbury police had responded to his call for backup; everyone seemed to want in on the action. They looked like they were having a grand time, scurrying around, radios blaring. One of the fire trucks had already left, and a few of the remaining firemen had come over to talk to the policemen. Claire had a glimpse into a society she had seen mostly only on television—these big, athletic men with their heavy rubber boots and strong hands, their bodies expressing the easy confidence of men who spend their days facing down danger.

Claire watched as Hornblower put Paula Wilson into the back of one of the cruisers, placing his hand on her head just as she slid into the seat.

"Wow," said Meredith as she watched him close the car door. "It's just like on TV."

"Yeah," said Claire, "it is." But then it occurred to her

how odd it was that we perceive life as imitating television, when in reality it was the other way around.

The patrol cars began to pull away one by one as Wally came over to stand next to Claire and Meredith. Max and Frank Wilson stood a few yards away, forming a loose group with Richard and Jeffrey, who was talking to Chris Callahan. Jack gazed vacantly around, not really focusing on anything in particular, muttering to himself. There was still no sign of Lyle.

When the last of the patrol cars had pulled away, Detective Hornblower came over to where Claire and Meredith stood with Wally.

"Thanks," he said hoarsely, tugging at his little beard. This was evidently hard for him, and Claire saw he was doing his best to be gracious.

"Anytime," Meredith answered breezily, her breath a little puff of white steam.

Just then another patrol car pulled up and James Pewter got out of the backseat.

"Well, well," he said, sauntering over to Detective Hornblower, "I see you finally got your man—or woman, as the case may be."

Hornblower coughed once and looked down at his boots. "My apologies, Mr. Pewter; I know this was difficult for you." He cleared his throat. "There was considerable pressure to make an arrest, and while I disagreed—"

"I know, I know," Pewter broke in. "The policy wonks in Boston needed someone's head on a platter. So it was all political. But then, what isn't?" he added, smiling. Claire thought he was enjoying Hornblower's discomfort.

Hornblower frowned. "Again, you have my sincerest apologies—"

"Duly noted, I'm sure," Pewter remarked, then turned and went into the inn. Hornblower watched him go, then shook his head and sighed.

"In some ways it's the hardest part of the job, isn't it?" Wally commented.

In response, Hornblower just sighed again.

"You mean dealing with people you've screwed?" said Meredith.

"Meredith!" Claire snapped.

"What?" Meredith said innocently.

"The problem with a crime like murder is that it touches so many more people than just the victim," Wally observed.

"Yes," Claire agreed. "It's like ripples on a pond that just keep spreading."

Hornblower cleared his throat again and stamped his boots on the sidewalk, stirring up little flurries of snow. "Well," he said, "I have a report to write up. I may as well get started." He shook Wally's hand, then Claire's.

"Until we meet again," Meredith said, thrusting her hand out. For the first time Claire saw amusement on the detective's long face. It was the closest thing to a smile she had seen on a face not made for smiling.

"Yes," he replied, "until we meet again."

As they watched the taillights of his plain black sedan disappear around a bend in the road, Claire turned to Wally. "Well," she said, "shall we go inside?"

The others had long since drifted into the building, and only the three of them were left in front of the inn. Wally looked up at the cold, bright moon, which hung just over the mill house.

"Yes," he said, "let's go inside."

Chapter 23

As Claire expected, Paula Wilson made a full confession to the police: she killed Mona Callahan in a sudden fit of jealousy. Having found out that the girl was pregnant, she assumed—rightly, it turned out—that the child was her husband's, and this insult was too much to bear. She lured the girl into the wine cellar and then stabbed her with a knife she took from the kitchen. Paula had been wearing her long white nightgown on the night of the murder, and Sally's blathering about the "Woman in White" sounded to her as though Sally had seen her kill Mona, so she set her sights on eliminating poor Sally.

Apparently young Henry had seen his mother dispose of the knife, which was one of the reasons why the boy had been acting of late even more disturbed than usual. Claire took very little satisfaction in the fact that she had correctly put together the elements and guessed the motives in Paula's disturbed mind; now two people were dead and a little boy had lost his mother.

The next night, though, in spite of everything, Claire felt relief in the air, thick as the aroma of roast lamb with rosemary that poured out of the kitchen. It was their last dinner at the inn, and in addition to the lamb, there was duck liver pâté, butternut-squash soup with caramelized onions, and cherries jubilee. If anyone thought it a little odd that Max was making such a feast, nobody said anything.

Max went around from table to table, checking on each customer. Meredith was off using the bathroom; she was in a particularly restless mood and had twice wandered away from the table. Claire still had an urge to keep an eye on her, but she stifled the impulse to tell the girl to keep her seat. After all, there was no more danger now, and she wanted to give Meredith as much freedom as possible.

"You are enjoying?" said Max, patting his stomach.

"Oh, yes," Wally answered. "We are enjoying very much."

Claire looked around the room and saw Richard and Jeffrey, alone at their corner table. Even Jeffrey looked less sullen than usual, as though the capture of the real murderer had relieved him of the burden of playing the villain. Richard, too, looked more relaxed, and the red wool sweater he wore made him look ten years younger. It was an early Christmas present from Jeffrey, who had shown it to Claire the day before after buying it in town.

Chris Callahan had gone down to the police station for the release of his sister's body, and had still not returned. His table sat empty in the corner.

At that moment Lyle entered the dining room. Claire had not seen him since the day before, when he read her his poem. For once his curly blond hair looked combed, and he wore a clean white shirt over black pants. There was a stiffness in his movements, as though he were still in some kind of shock, and he walked with a slow, almost hypnotized stride, like someone recently back from the land of the dead. He nodded almost imperceptibly to Claire as he passed her and took a table in the far corner of the room. Max watched him and shook his head.

"You know," he said, "maybe I should have known when Mrs. Wilson asked me to make the crêpes with the wild mushrooms . . . I keep thinking what I could have done different so that the poor young girl would not have to die." His expression changed from cheerful to mournful. There was an innocence about Max, with his ability to switch rapidly from one emotional extreme to another. Looking up at him, a worry line on his usually smooth forehead, his blue eyes misty with tears, Claire couldn't help feeling sorry for him.

"Can I give you some advice?" she said.

Max tilted his head and crossed his muscular forearms. "What?"

"Don't think that way. It won't do you any good."

"But—"

"She's right," said Wally. "It won't, you know. What's happened is over, and blaming yourself doesn't do anyone any good."

Max sighed. "Perhaps not, but that young man looks so sad that I feel very sorry for him."

Wally glanced at Lyle, who was studying the menu. "Yes," he admitted, "but, as they say, time is the great healer. It may sound like a callous thing to say, but, you know, we all get over it."

Claire looked at him, a little surprised by his words. If that was true for him, and the suffering he had endured after losing his wife, then maybe, she thought . . . maybe what? She wasn't sure; the thought remained half-formed in her mind.

"This may be the best lamb I've ever had," she declared suddenly, eager to change the subject.

Max's placid face spread out in a broad smile. "Really? You really think so?"

"No question about it," Wally agreed as Meredith came bouncing over to the table.

"No question about what?" she said, sliding into her seat.

"That Max is a culinary genius," said Claire.

"Oh, abso*lute*ly!" Meredith agreed loudly. "A gen-i-us. Best muffins I ever had," she added, reaching for one.

"Meredith, how about eating some of your lamb?" said Claire.

"Americans eat too much meat," Meredith answered through a mouthful of muffin, stuffing it in before Claire could stop her.

"That may be, but you eat too much sugar," said Claire, "and it's going to have to stop."

"Brain food," Meredith replied.

"No," Max corrected her. "Fish is brain food."

"I *know*," she said. "I was just kidding."

Max looked confused.

"Can I ask you something?" said Claire.

"Sure."

"Well, this is a little embarrassing, but during the investigation I happened to overhear you and Frank Wilson talking in German—something about being evil. Do you remember what you were talking about at the time?"

Max's face reddened. "*Ach . . . es ist ganz*—how do you say?—unimportant. *Etwas mit die Gesellschaft.*"

"It was about business," Claire translated.

"Yes, taxes. Frank has a—well, a creative way to do his taxes."

Wally nodded. "I see. I don't think you should tell us any more."

"No," Claire agreed. "I think we've heard enough."

Max excused himself with a little bow and went on to chat with other customers. As he moved away, Lyle came over to their table. "Excuse me," he said to Claire, "but I wrote another poem. I don't want to bring you down or anything, but I thought you might like to see it."

Claire put down her fork. "Thank you, Lyle. I'd love to see it."

He fished a crumpled piece of paper out of his shirt pocket. "I mean, seeing as how you're a professional and everything." He handed Claire the paper.

"Lyle," said Wally, "do you mind if I ask you something?"

"Sure."

"What exactly was Sally on?"

Lyle studied his hands, head low, his blond hair almost covering his face. "Mostly it was horse," he said in a low voice. "That's heroin," he added with a sigh.

"I *know* what that is," Meredith snorted. "After all, I live with a—"

"That's enough, Meredith," Claire interrupted.

"Could she have been having delusions from withdrawal?" said Wally.

Lyle shrugged. "I don't know. Yeah, I guess so. It happens. Why?"

"Just wondering."

Lyle rubbed his hands together and pushed some hair out of his face. "Well, I'll let you get back to your dinner. Thanks for looking at that," he said to Claire.

"Thank you for showing it to me."

As Lyle wandered back to his table, Claire looked at the poem. Meredith studied it over her shoulder.

The folding of the day, the sinking of the sun,
Reminding me of what's behind and things already done
A secret darkness in my soul slips in between the sheets
I lie in sinking silence as I try in vain to sleep
It could have been with you I waked and with you gone to
*   bed*
Your arm casually tossed over a blanket
On the pillow a tousled head
But I awake to secret grief
And silence, only silence, instead.

"Not bad," said Meredith. "Not great, but not bad."

"And now I want to ask you something," Wally said to Claire. "How did you know that it was Paula Wilson?"

"At first I didn't. I just knew that Henry was the key. His setting of the fires, the beating of the dog—he was expressing his terrible unhappiness, and I knew he was a soul in torment."

"Fair enough," said Wally, "but I still don't understand."

"Well, it's kind of hard to explain, actually. I was reading this koan in Meredith's book about firewood tumbling down, and I suddenly had this moment of enlightenment."

"Satori," said Meredith.

"Whatever. I saw Henry as just a conduit, a vessel—like a sponge, if you will—for some kind of evil his parents had done. His passion for fires, his need to punish the dog; it all added up to something, only I wasn't sure what. But then it occurred to me that if the man in Mona's letter was Frank Wilson, then it all fell into place. Paula killed Mona out of jealousy, and her son somehow knew she was involved. Except that he was caught; he couldn't betray his mother—he loved her but was also afraid of her—so he took his anger and frustration out on the dog."

"Poor Shatzy," said Meredith. "What's going to happen to him?"

"I heard James Pewter's going to take him," said Wally.

"What I'd like to know is whether Sally actually saw Paula Wilson the night Paula killed Mona Callahan," Claire remarked.

Wally shook his head. "I guess we'll never know. She may have been having delusions caused by her heroin withdrawal."

"*Or* she may have actually seen a ghost!" Meredith declared, squirming in her seat. "The Woman in White," she said reverently.

Claire shivered. Once again Blake's poem ran through her head.

> *Tyger! Tyger! burning bright*
> *In the forests of the night*

She looked out across the field at the trees at the edge of the woods, their branches silver and grey in the moonlight. The landscape was as frozen as ever, but not all the ice and snow in the world, she thought, was enough to quench the fire of human passion. She looked across the table at Wally, at the reflection of candlelight on his hair, soft grey curls with their blond highlights. Her passion for him simmered within her, a quiet cauldron, deep and steady. She thought about the woman whose passion for her husband was so intense that she had murdered not once but twice. Claire wondered if she was capable of such violence. A few years ago she wouldn't have thought so, but she was beginning to think that anyone was capable of anything, given the right circumstances.

She turned to Wally and raised her glass. "I'd like to drink to something, but I can't think of anything appropriate."

He smiled, and she remembered how much she liked the creases around his eyes when he did. "Why not drink to our future?"

Meredith grabbed her glass of cranberry juice and raised it high. "To the future!"

Claire clinked glasses and smiled. "To *our* future."

"Right," said Meredith. "That's what I meant."

For some reason, this struck Wally and Claire as funny. They were still laughing when Max came over to refill their wine glasses.